RAGE OF THE ANCIENT GODS

RISE OF THE ANCIENT GODS SERIES: BOOK 2

CRAIG ROBERTSON

RAGE OF THE ANCIENT GODS

RISE OF THE ANCIENT GODS SERIES: BOOK 2

by Craig Robertson

There's nothing as bad as a bad god comin' back.

Imagine-It Publishing
El Dorado Hills, CA

ALSO BY CRAIG ROBERTSON:

* Podium Entertainment has produced audiobooks for all the below titles except the older standalone books.

For specifics as to the correct order for reading the Ryanverse, click here.

BOOKS IN THE RYANVERSE:

THE FOREVER SERIES (2016)

THE FOREVER LIFE, Book 1

THE FOREVER ENEMY, Book 2

THE FOREVER FIGHT, Book 3

THE FOREVER QUEST, Book 4

THE FOREVER ALLIANCE, Book 5

THE FOREVER PEACE, Book 6

THE FOREVER BOXSET, Part 1, Books 1 & 2

THE FOREVER BOXSET, Part 2, Book 3 & 4

THE FOREVER BOXSET, Part 3, Book 5 & 6

GALAXY ON FIRE SERIES (2017)

EMBERS, Book 1

FLAMES, Book 2

FIRESTORM, Book 3

FIRES OF HELL, Book 4

DRAGON FIRE, Book 5

ASHES, Book 6

GALAXY ON FIRE BOXSET, Part 1, Books 1 & 2

GALAXY ON FIRE BOXSET, Part 2, Books 3 & 4

GALAXY ON FIRE BOXSET, Part 3, Books 5 & 6

RISE OF ANCIENT GODS SERIES (2018):

RETURN OF THE ANCIENT GODS, Book 1

RAGE OF THE ANCIENT GODS, Book 2

TORMENT OF THE ANCIENT GODS, Book 3

WRATH OF THE ANCIENT GODS, Book 4

FURY OF THE ANCIENT GODS, Book 5

FALL OF THE ANCIENT GODS, Book 6

TIME WARS LAST FOREVER SERIES (2019)

RYAN TIME, Book 1

LOST TIME, Book 2

FRAGMENTED TIME, Book 3

SHATTERED TIME, Book 4

FINDING TIME, Book 5

HEALING TIME, Book 6

THE TIMELESS VOID (2021)

RYAN'S GAMBIT, Book 1

RYAN'S PHANTOMS, Book 2

RYAN'S ENIGMA, Book 3

RYAN'S UNDOING, Book 4

RYAN'S REBOOT, Book 5

RYAN'S RESOLUTION, Book 6

THE WHALES OF TIME (2023)

Ryan In UnWonderland, Book 1

How Ryan Saves Time, Book 2

Saving Alice Ryan, Book 3

NON-RYANVERSE BOOKS:

A Teenager's Guide to Saving The Earth (2025)

An Apocalypse and Then Some, Book 1

How to Survive Surviving the Apocalypse, Book 2

Is This Apocalypse Over Yet?, Book 3

TIME DIVING (2024)

Letters From Hell, Book 1

Purgatory's Best Shot, Book 2

Heaven Says Wait, Book 3

Into the Nexus, Book 4

ROAD TRIPS IN SPACE SERIES (2019):

THE GALAXY ACCORDING TO GIDEON, Book 1

THE EARTH ACCORDING TO GIDEON, Book 2

OLDER, STANDALONE WORKS:

THE CORPORATE VIRUS (2016)

THE INNERgLOW EFFECT (2010)

WRITE NOW! THE PRISONER OF NaNoWRiMo (2009)

ANON TIME (2009)

For more information about Craig, his books, various series, or to see images and videos for some of his wild alien characters, please visit his website. You'll be glad you did: https://craigarobertson.com/

To sign up for Craig's newsletter to get announcements, updates, and his

recommendations for other great Sci-Fi reads go to: https://preview.
mailerlite.io/forms/2369493/188634426375144501/share

ISBN: 978-1-7328724-1-7 (E-Book)
978-1-7328724-2-4 (Paperback)
979-8-7754130-5-7 (Hardcover)

Cover design by Jessica Bell
https://www.jessicabelldesign.com/

Formatting services by Drew Avera
drewavera@gmail.com

Editors: Michael R. Blanche
Neil Farr
Forest Olivier

First Edition 2019
Second Edition 2019
Third Edition 2020

To my blessed children, Chris and Kim.

PROLOGUE

Zarathus relaxed after the climax of his realization. Truth was *not* universal. Throughout all of endless time he had pondered that question. Over the expanse of the ages, he had posed and answered most any question that could be framed. Now few queries escaped his keen mind's solutions. This both pleased and worried Zarathus. Yes, questions were left, to be certain. Was one truly responsible for their own actions? Did the entropy of a closed system always have to increase? Why was π, the circumference of a circle divided by its radius squared, an irrational number? Where was the best pizza to be found? He still had to labor to crack those tough eggs. But in resolving each elusive question, the number of intellectual quests remaining became fewer and fewer. What would he do when the last conundrum was laid to rest? He almost laughed. *What would he do* would always be unanswered, so hopefully he would never need fear rest.

Before Zarathus began to focus on his next philosophic sortie, he begrudgingly admitted he must take a break to review the nearby universe. It was not his *responsibility,* so much as it was his *obligation* to be aware of the goings-on. In some cases he even had to intercede. If events warranted or a situation was particularly dire, he could remediate matters. He always had and always would. Zarathus had long ago decided it was his duty to act as a morally positive force if his intervention was the only guarantor of a good outcome.

There had been the time a wayward rogue star was on a course to impact a populated system. Zarathus diverted that star because the system under threat was home to a number of valuable species. And when a thermonuclear war erupted on a far-off planet, he went there personally to reverse the explosions and broker a peace, albeit a bit forced on the combatants. For their part, they seemed to lust for horrific deaths. But he could not allow that. And he had lost count of the number of stars he'd prevented from going nova and destroying that which deserved to survive.

Having the ability to do whatever he wanted mandated that Zarathus be the parent figure to the children that were all his neighbors, both the animate and the inanimate. To those who lived or would ever live, for he knew them, too. He liked to say he was *modestly* omniscient. Having complete command of science, engineering, and technology, he could always right the wrongs he could not help knowing about. But such was not a burden. No, he realized it was the highest ...

Zarathus angled his head. There was something moving in the sector he called Billie. Well, many things *moved* in Billie, but what he knew was there now had not even existed seconds before. Quantum mechanics allowed for the appearance and disappearance of particles spontaneously, but what moved was large. And it headed along one vector for the briefest period before it altered course. The unimaginable was coming straight at Zarathus. And it was coming fast. The object had accelerated from a few miles a second to nearly nine times the speed of light in the breadth of a thought.

So be it, reflected Zarathus. Any new creation doing the impossible and heading right for him was undoubtably a negative contributor to the universe. It was saving him the trouble of hunting it down in order to terminate it. On its present course it would arrive in a few days. Time enough to have a meal and return to the questions that still needed to be ...

Zarathus looked up with a start. Before him stood a figure. It was reptilian, seven feet tall, standing on two feet and resting back on a massive tail that was studded with spikes. He knew this, because he knew nearly everything, to be Marropex. But what Marropex was and why he was present were empty spaces in Zarathus's mind.

"I am Zarath—"

"No, you are not," taunted Marropex. He spoke with hisses and pops. His words were ladened with antipathy, disgust, and most of all they were one with rage.

"I do not wish—" began Zarathus.

"Nor should you, for you are not." After that challenge, he reared his head back and howled at the sky. His cry was of triumph, of hatred, and of the lust of death.

Zarathus had never heard such a hellish wail, but he knew its essence at once. Into his mind crept a completely novel emotion. He began to know fear. Zarathus also conceived for the first time of his own mortality. "You threaten me. You cut me off when I wish to say I am Zarath—"

"I *never* threaten. To issue a threat involves the issuance of words and implies there is more than one possible outcome. And I stop you from saying that you *are* anything. You are *not*. You do not *exist*."

"I clearly do." With that Zarathus directed a machine of his creation to form ten black holes in Marropex's chest.

Marropex bent backwards, nearly touching his head to the ground. He laughed the most insane, the most xenophobic, and the most contemptuous laugh ever to exist in our universe. The Cleinoid god of atrocities cackled and spat for hours, for days, and for what remained of Zarathus's life. Then without warning he straightened and was silent. He slapped his hands together in Zarathus's direction. The kind, responsible, and the loving Zarathus was crushed by invisible forces into a sheet of single atoms extending in all directions for miles. Marropex separated his hands, and the atoms that were Zarathus for so very long scattered in the breeze as dust and were forgotten.

ONE

"Oh come on," I taunted my stick-in-the-mud purported friends, "we got nothing else to do. I'll start. I'm bigger than a breadbox."

"I don't want to play, but what the *heck* is a breadbox?" questioned an irritated Sapale.

"Oh, sorry, you guys didn't have them on Kaljax, did you?"

"Well, for starters, we didn't have *bread*, so no, it's unlikely we had a box for it."

"Back in the day you stored a loaf of bread in a metal box on the counter. A breadbox."

"It needed its own storage compartment? Was it toxic back then? Explosive?" my alien wife asked.

"No, it ... you have to store it somewhere. Where would you put it?" I replied feebly.

"You don't want me to answer that, do you?"

"Anyway," I changed the subject, "a breadbox is like so." I pantomimed a rectangular box to show the size.

"I said I'm not playing," she insisted.

"Me, neither. It's a stupid game and now's the least appropriate time conceivable," added Toño.

Couple a spoilsports. "We have little else to do," I reminded them. "Why not have some fun?"

"Fun? Jon, you're more insane than even *I* suspected," Sapale replied. "We're hanging over lava by one ankle waiting for some awful death. Where does 'fun,' or the need for it therein, arise?"

"So what would you like to do?"

"I don't know. Oh, wait, I do. I'd *like* to escape," she responded sarcastically.

"Okay, going with your thought, let me work through this. We've been here three days. No one has come to free us or kill us or feed us, taunt us or even spit in our faces. We have come up with zero plans to extricate ourselves from this predicament. If we think longer and harder about how to escape when it is not possible we will accomplish nothing. I say twenty questions beats the hell out of just hanging around waiting for badness."

"Twenty questions most definitely does *not*," replied a bitter-sounding Toño. "Boredom is preferable. Now, if you two will be quiet, I will continue to try to reason a way out."

"Please allow me to help, Professor," I snarked. "If we cut our ropes, we crash into lava. That would be bad. We could extend our probes and hold on to the ceiling and then cut the ropes. That would allow us to swing to the ledge surrounding the lava, except there *is* no ledge. There's just lava as far as the eye can see. We could sprout wings and fly. I mean, there has to be an edge somewhere. But try as I might, the damn wings won't sprout."

"What if that's not lava?" responded Toño. "They have used illusions in a detention setting before."

"Yes, they have. But my sensors indicate the area below us is hot to around two thousand Celsius. If it's not lava, it'd still ruin our shiny skin."

"Can't *that* be part of the illusion?" asked Sapale.

"Unlikely," Toño responded thoughtfully. "Optical sensors can be tricked. But our temperature sensors and probes could not be simultaneously fooled. It's hot below us."

"So since we just proved we can't escape, can we play twenty qu—"

"I'd rather take my chances with the lava," snapped Toño.

"It *would* be more pleasant," agreed my unhelpful life partner.

Our bickering was interrupted by the sudden appearance of a catwalk. It began in the heat-obscured distance and ended right in front of us. Damn godly magic. It was most annoying. The walkway was not, like us, upside down.

Vorc stepped toward us at a brisk pace. Bethniak was conspicuously, at least to me, absent. A long flowing, pencil thin centipedeish critter walked alongside the boss. Behind him followed a most peculiar sight. A cloudy memory. Who needed one of those in tow? Vorc and the oversized bug chatted perfunctorily until they came to the end of the road. Vorc made a show of pulling up a ledger and scanning it with a finger. Then he passed the book to the cloud.

"I was told the leader of your band awoke," Vorc began. "Damn inconvenient of you taking so long."

"Sorry to be so vulnerable. That little bitch packs quite a wallop. Plus, I needed my beauty rest." I patted my cheeks.

"Amen to that," growled Sapale.

"I am not in the mood for disrespect or games. I believe I will convince you quickly that flippancy and cute responses will lead to dire consequences."

"If we piss you off, what? You're going to do something worse to us than you already are?" I asked coolly.

"Yes. Do not tempt fate."

"I *am* fate," I replied confidently.

That actually made him a tad nervous. Funny. "Come come," Vorc replied anxiously. "Of course you're not. Fate is an independent force of nature, not a being."

"I meant to say I'm *your* fate. Treat me well, and you might just have a future."

Vorc was back to looking mad. "Such ill-advised bravado. Now, I will ask you a series of questions. I will ask once. You will answer directly. Failure to respond acceptably will result in one of your deaths. It will be swift and certain. Who are—"

I made the sound of a buzzer going off. "*Wrong.* I seem to need to point out a very stark weakness in your threat *and* your approach. To me, it looks like you intend to do us all in. Of course, that's not even remotely possible, but it seems to be your intent. So wherein lies any of our motivations to comply? If you kill us separately or together, won't we all be just as dead?"

He turned to the centipede. Without words he gestured from buggie to me. An arc of liquid sprang from the creature's butt, which it had swung around to point at me.

The stream was heading straight for my face. I felt safe in

assuming what was intended was not pleasant. I threw up a partial membrane. The fluid dribbled to the lava below.

Vorc flared in anger. "How *dare* you."

"Vorc, I don't know you all that well, so I'll just ask. Are you mentally challenged? I stop you from harming me and you're *insulted?*"

"Do not attempt self-defense. I forbid it. Such actions will only delay the unavoidable and worsen the consequences. It is very foolish to anger a god, little one."

"My thoughts exactly, little dicked. I am Ryanmax, god of warriors. I'm a totally pissy god, too, so lighten up."

"You are *not* a god. If I had more time I'd have you dissected and learn your true nature, but I don't have that luxury. Because of you, the long-planned egress has been altered. Hopefully you caused no more than a delay. I'd worry if I were you if it turns out you corrupted the entire incursion."

"If you were me? You should be that lucky, Rumple Foreskin. If I'm not a Cleinoid god, how is it I know of our plans to invade Prime? How is it I know this is our fifth Transheaval? I'm pals with Gorpedder, the big rock head. I spent my life avoiding impotent pukes like you, so maybe you don't know me. But I know *you*, Vorc, son of Hurvetova. I also see the future. I see you entombed at Beal's Point. If you don't release my friends and me immediately, I might put you there personally."

"I believe this—" Vorc stopped when the cloud inched up and nudged him. He turned to the floating assistant and they spoke quietly. Vorc seemed to grow more and more agitated as the conversation progressed.

Because I was always me, I cleared my throat loudly.

The pair exchanged a few quick words, then Vorc returned his attention to me.

"Your puppet master just told you to ease up on your attitude, didn't he, dork?" I could be so annoying.

"What my *assistant* and I were discussing is no concern of yours. I have elected to investigate your claims farther. Be advised, however, that whether or not you are a member of the Cleinoid brotherhood does not alter the fact that you threw an intermixer into a crowd. That intermixer has affected the egress. Crimes are crimes."

It hit me that I may have saved my universe. I might die for it, but if I screwed up the tunnel or whatever, I did good. "You don't even know it was me, peabrain. I say it wasn't any of us upside-down cakes. Who saw me? Who accuses me?" I knew I had him there. No one, but no one, was looking back as the most important event in billions of years was taking place.

"You are beyond the shadow of a doubt the most annoying and galling individual I have ever met." Vorc actually stomped a foot.

"Welcome to my world," Sapale responded with a harrumph.

"Ditto," parroted Toño.

"You three will be taken to the Lower Chambers. There you will be held until I can assemble a team to extract from you the truth. Know that your futures are likely to be short and painful."

"Did I mention Tefnuf told me she has a crush on you? Yeah, she has a picture of you right next to her bathtub," I waggled my eyebrows, "if you take my meaning."

He stiffened with rage. "Tefnuf doesn't *bathe*, you idiot."

"I didn't mean to imply her actions involved any water, dream lover." I waggled the brows again. Man, could I get under someone's skin like a terminal case of scabies.

The catwalk groaned softly, then it extended to right below us. Our restraints broke open and we tumbled rather unceremoniously to the deck. Weird—it was stone, or so close to it I couldn't tell the difference. I always thought of catwalks as being metal. Vorc was a distant vision by the time we rose. The juicy-butt insect was gone with him, thank you very much. The cloudy memory had stayed behind.

"I am Dalfury," the swirl said deferentially. ""You will please follow me to our destination. If there are any issues or concerns please do not hesitate to voice them."

A sniveling sycophant. Nice. Every universe needs lots of those.

"What if we don't want to go to the Lower Chambers and hang with Vorc's love-demon?" I challenged quietly.

"At the first sign of resistance, I'm instructed to summon Bethniak."

"Huh. I doubt she'd answer your call. She seems to be the arrogant effete type," I remarked.

"Yes. She is very much those things. Normally you are correct. She would not answer a summons from me. But—"

"In your case, *Ryanmax*, she'd make an exception," finished Sapale. "I wish you'd stop doing that to people. It's getting old, like you."

"This way, please," the vapor said. It might have turned, but I think it more reversed itself front to back. Creepy.

We walked for half an hour before we were off the catwalk and on terra firma. Another twenty minutes and I recognized we were nearing the Lower Chambers. The landscape was becoming familiar.

"So, any of us get through the vortex before the mystery terrorist threw the hate-bomb?" I asked nonchalantly.

"I believe I'll defer that and similar questions to Vorc. I wouldn't want to provide you with incorrect information."

"Very considerate of you, old sport. Glad you're concerned enough," I shot back sarcastically. Jerk wouldn't let me pump him.

"It looked to me like one went through before that dastardly coward, whoever he, she, or it was, broke the spell," Sapale said to me louder than required.

"Yeah, I did see him disappear. What's his name, Dalfury? It's been so long, I think I forgot it."

There was no response from our guide. A tough guy. Okay.

From behind a voice said, "*Marropex* is the name of the reaver you saw depart. The full contingent of Rage got through before there was a snafu and the vortex destabilized. The other four ranks did not. They were unable to egress."

I spun. It was Blobby, my non-friend cloudy apparition. He glided behind us silently.

"Can he hear you?" I asked, while pointing to Dalfury.

"Unlikely," said the vapor.

"But you share a puffy nature," I remarked.

"We do not. He is made of a very different substance than I."

"What?" I pressed.

"Mostly static electricity with some amino acids and proteins," my cloud said.

"And you?"

"I have no idea. I doubt I exist in spite of your belief to the contrary."

"Well, if you don't know *your* composition, how the hell do you know it's not like his? Hmm, smart blob?"

He was silent a good thirty seconds. "Hell?" he said as a question. "H ... hell? I've ... I know of hell."

Great, getting wiggy on me again in a crisis. He was as useless as any blob, shining or not, that I'd ever dealt with. "What about hell? I was, by the way, using it as a figure of speech, not a place with GPS coordinates."

"I used to fear hell. No, I used to *say* hell, like you. Yes that is it."

"If I had a candy treat I'd hand it to you. That's some accomplishment. Bet Mom'd be real proud of her blob."

"Boy."

"Boy what? I think you're giving me hemorrhoids, dude."

"I hear you speaking, Ryanmax, but I do not know to whom. Please remain silent," said Dalfury, apparently without turning. It was hard to tell, with that cloud.

"It's an old song. No big deal."

Dalfury stopped and definitely turned. "It would seem every time you speak I become more suspicious and believe your contention less. A song is not regularly interrupted by silence. That being the case, I'm wondering why you felt it necessary to lie to me?"

"Haven't you heard of a call-and-response song? That's what I was singing to myself, quietly and without seditious intentions."

"I have not heard of that form of song. But I heard no call for you to respond to, so I remain deeply suspicious."

"That's probably because you weren't raised right. When you were a little cloudy memory, your memory mama did a bad job. She should have loved you more's my guess."

Dalfury didn't have eyes, but still I got the distinct impression he was rolling his eyes. Dude was as bad as Sapale in that regard. In any case he resumed leading us toward the chambers.

In a whisper I asked the blob, "Where were we?"

"Where were we when?" he replied with his typical vagueness.

"In our conversation train."

"The train was near hell, I believe."

Jon, are you speaking to this apparition? Toño asked head-to-head, pointing to Blobby.

In point of fact, yes I am. I'm glad you can see him.

Why wouldn't I see and hear it? It's right here. Toño swept a hand right through Blob-Boy.

And you? I asked Sapale. *Can you see it, too?*

Yes. And I've already come to the conclusion it's as annoying as you are, which is saying a lot. Why's it so surprising we can see it?

The locals so far have not, except Bethniak. She swatted it away back at the egress. Referred to it as a decrepit old ghost.

I heard her say that but had no idea what she was referring to, responded Toño.

"Hey, blob, are you a *ghost*?" I asked directly.

"*Ghost*?" he repeated back. "You say words I haven't heard in ... in an eternity. Hell, ghost. The words stir memories."

"Thanks for the dissertation. I asked a simple question, however. Yes or no."

"Maybe."

Now you see, he's just like you, whined Sapale. *If there's a path to drive a person crazy, he takes that route just like you.*

But him *you love. So why is it a bad quality in my case?* asked the blob. He asked it *inside* my head. That was clearly impossible, which meant he was about to disappear again. It would all be consistent.

How the hell can you talk inside my head? I snapped.

Because I designed these androids to have that ability, Toño replied quickly.

I know that, Doc. I wasn't talking to you. I was speaking *to the ghost.*

No you weren't. You didn't say a thing, Toño challenged.

Yes, I did. The ghost can speak to us head-to-head. You heard him, right?

Sapale, was it you playing tricks? Toño asked.

Toño, do I ever pull stunts like that? she replied harshly. *I'm married to Jon, not similar to him.*

No, I told you it was the spook speaking, I responded.

Well, I didn't hear it, Toño said firmly.

Me either, added Sapale.

What? I'm the only one he can send messages to? I mean, you guys hear him. Why could he communicate to my head and not yours?

Because you're insane. What you postulate is not even remotely possible, replied Toño.

"Hey, *ghost,* why can you speak to all of us but only message *me* brain-to-brain?" I said a bit too loudly.

Jon, quiet. You'll piss off the other cloud, said Sapale.

"Sorry. Repeat. Why can only I hear your thoughts? And if you say *I don't know,* I swear I'm calling Bethniak here myself."

"I have no idea," the freakazoid answered. "I hope that's different enough from *I don't know* so you don't summon that awful girl."

"He's not calling *anyone,*" Sapale added quickly. "If you start believing *him,* you'll believe anyone."

"I do."

"You do *what?*" I fired back. I was this close to popping him in the chin, if he only had one.

Never mind. I don't recall why I said it.

"Are you going to let him dodge that question, Jon?" asked Toño.

"He didn't. He just said it in my head, not out loud."

"Why do I feel *so* much worse hearing that?" sighed Sapale.

"Look, ghostly pain in my ass, if you can't head-talk them, don't do it to me."

All right. As you wish.

I was gonna call Ghostbusters. I was *so* over that poltergeist.

"We have arrived," announced Dalfury. "If you will follow me down a series of stairs, we can begin the process of verifying or refuting your claims."

"You coming with us, whoever?"

No response. Perfect. I turned a full circle. The phantom was, of course, inexplicably gone again. I rested a hand on my forehead. Taunted by a blob and being led by another. I needed a new life. I needed a better life.

CHAPTER ONE

The column of ancient gods that constituted Rage burst into our universe with staccato bursts of light. The machine-gun flashes of energy announced great danger to everything living. But no one was present to see the luminescent harbingers because the ancient gods entered randomly into empty space far from any galaxies. So none of the doomed knew their futures were then cursed. They would soon know only war, subjugation, and torment until the relief of death lifted their burden. The light of each entering god added to the certainty of our existences's eternal darkness.

Nassel led Rage. She had done so for the last three transheavals. As a god of conquest she was the perfect choice. As the first of Rage to enter our universe, she was the first to taste the life that abounded. She could feel the heartbeats of a centillion vibrant, thinking, breathing creatures. And she was the first Rage to know with certainty that she would soon ravish, kill, and destroy again. She vibrated with rapture. Her wings opened to their full thirty-meter span, her massive scaly head arched back, and she screeched ecstasy into the vacuum of space. Life was orgasmic again.

Then Nassel settled into her duties. As more and more and more ancient gods entered our space she directed them into small pods and the pods, in turn, into larger engagers. Soon the void was empty no longer. It took days, but finally Rage was ordered, set, and ready. One million ancient demonic gods chafed at the bit, anxious to strike, anxious to destroy.

"The five engagers will move in different directions," called out Nassel to the teaming assembly. "I have already instructed the five field commanders what their areas of dominion are to be. They are free to direct their pods as they see fit. A warning to you all. Heed your field commanders and do not defy the order I have established. In the past, treasonous fools have left their designated areas in the belief that victims were more plentiful or satisfying elsewhere. If I *hear* of such acts, the offenders will have *me* as a permanent enemy. Now go, my brothers and sisters. *Go* and make this universe regret it ever popped into existence. Make *all* who call it home curse their parents for giving them the life that we now *own*." And with those words, the five engagers moved off at fantastic speed.

Our universe was large; infinite, by all accounts. The pods numbering two hundred thousand each were a speck in a drop in a moat, on that scale. Even after the full contingent of five million ancient gods had descended, their numbers would still be infinitesimally small on the large scale of space. So how could this unholy armada threaten but the tiniest fraction of unfortunate outposts that were close enough to their point of entry to be consumed? It was a summation, a product of what the Cleinoids brought to the game. If rapaciousness was a virtue, they would be on the highest pinnacle of righteousness. If the intensity of their lust reflected their brightness, they would outshine all light everywhere bundled together. And the damnable ancient gods had time, all of time, to wreak their havoc, mayhem, and dissolution on our universe. For as long as fate favored their presence, the ancient devils would be unrestrained by any natural force and free to linger until there was nothing left to plunder.

Fate, which always seemed to be so capricious, arbitrary, and contrarian, was in charge of everything. So it always had been.

.   .   .

THREE

We were led into a different section of the Lower Chambers than the detention area we'd all landed in. I was vastly relieved. Without Tefnuf was a good way to be. I just prayed her dominion didn't extend past the bowels of the building where she reigned supreme.

"If you'd like to take a seat, I will summon Zastrál," Dalfury said deferentially.

"We'll stand," I spoke for the three of us. "And who the hell's Zastrál?"

The cloud churned a bit more than I think it normally did. "Most Cleinoids know of Zastrál." He sounded skeptical.

"Well, that's fine by me. I'm not most Cleinoid gods. I'm just the Chosen One." There. I said it out in the open.

I swear the cloud shrank. "Now you are the Chosen One?" he said with significant temerity.

"Thank you," I replied, suggesting his rhetorical question was a statement of fact. I had to keep him off his feet, so to speak.

Sapale rolled her eyes. I don't think she approved of my attraction to the chief-god gig.

"Well, we shall see about that in time, based on your deeds. For the present we will be contented to establish your legitimacy as one of us."

Before I could counter, the door opened and some ungodly creature entered. I'd seen so much oddness, but damn if it didn't keep getting weirder here in Halloween Town. What I assumed to be Zastrál was a three-meter-long, one-meter-tall fuzzy siamese-twinned python with paddles for legs. Yeah, like the ones you see every day. The joint part was the most bizarre. It was fused head-to-head. One walked backward into the room, and the trailing one walked forward. I knew in a flash there was no world where Darwin would allow for this sideshow freak. It was just too wrong.

"Master Dalfury," both mouths said in unison, "we came as soon as we could. Sorry for any delay." Because they looked like snakes, naturally, in Godville they sounded like speaking dolphins.

I was speechless.

"Not to worry, dear friends," replied Dalfury.

Of course a cloudy memory would be BFFs with a double python. How very normal.

Dalfury turned to us—at least I think he rotated—and spoke. "Zastrál is here to aid in Vorc's questioning of you three. As you seem to defy all odds in not knowing them, let me clue you in. They are the twin gods of knowing the truth—discovering it, that is."

"Not of *truth*," I interrupted. "That would be silly, right? Only of *knowing* truth."

Could a cloud look irritated? I wasn't certain.

"You are correct. *Genuous*, as you know, is the god of truth. There are scattered demigods for the different forms of truth."

"Wait," snapped Sapale, "are you trying to tell us that *truth* isn't *truth*? That there are *alternative* truths?"

"Do you honestly require me to answer that question?" he responded.

She waved the back of a hand at him. "Forget I asked."

"So, back on topic," Dalfury said cordially, "once Vorc has arrived, Zastrál will help him know the truth of your words."

"Is he a slithering polygraph?" I asked, almost in a snicker.

"I am not familiar with that term. I doubt it, however. While you answer Vorc's queries, Zastrál will enshroud your heads. If you lie, they will know it. No living being can resist their abilities."

Crapazoid. Not good. The second the snakes made contact, they were bound to notice we weren't, like, actual living beings.

The door banged open and a very perturbed-appearing Vorc stormed in. He had, believe it or not, several sheets of paper crumpled up in his fist. Paper? That was so last eon.

"Is there a problem, my lord?" asked Vorc's right hand.

"Problem? No, it's well beyond a problem. It's well beyond a *crisis*. For the sake of the Ten Creators, it's light years past a *catastrophe*."

"Is it a debacle?" I snarked, because I absolutely couldn't restrain myself. "Is it, I mean, maybe, could it be ruination?"

Normally when I mouth off, I get a scary look or sentenced to death or something. Vorc, I think in retrospect, was not in the mood for me. He hurled a ball of flames at my head, a rather large and hot-looking one to be specific.

I threw a partial membrane around it and stopped the flames halfway between us. "You want this back? I'd be happy to toss it back at near the speed of light." I was able to react so quickly because I knew in this crazy universe, sooner or later I was going to get lightning or fire thrown my way. I was ready. Plan, prepare, and deploy.

Vorc's eyes saucered. He took a step back. "No. Sorry, Ryanmax. It's just with the crisis and all I lost my head. Sorry."

"Keep in mind you haven't lost it ... yet." I snuffed out the fire.

"My lord," repeated Dalfury, "what is the crisis?"

"Rage departed through the egress portal, but only just. When Torment tried they couldn't pass. I even had Wrath advance out of turn, but they were unable to enter."

"You mean the bulk of the gods are stranded here? Vorc, that's a ... it's a—"

"Fiasco?" I interrupted, helpfully.

Sapale kicked me in the shins.

While I made a show of rubbing the spot I asked, "So what's the plan here?"

"The *plan* is to finally get the truth out of you. I warn you, if I confirm you threw the intermixer into the egress vortex, you will live just long enough to wish you hadn't."

"Oh, crap," I said.

"*What?*" boomed Vorc.

"Now you've gone and done it. I'm scared. Are you going to appoint an attorney at no cost to me?"

"Jon," hissed Sapale, "Lighten up a bit."

I shrugged. I think I did that a lot.

"I'm a busy man," huffed Vorc. "Zastrál, climb onto Ryanmax's head and let's get started."

"I will not allow it," I said flatly.

"Lucky for me, your cooperation is unnecessary. Zastrál," he pointed to the snakes, "up please."

Turn off your biocomputers, I said to my companions in their heads.

What? Why? responded Toño.

Just do it quickly. I'm playing a hunch.

We're all going to die, bemoaned Sapale.

Are they off?

Yes.

Confirmed.

"Vorc, I'm a tolerant Chosen One, so I'll cut you this one transgression. Make it your last or you will be the regretting individual."

"If you could stop blustering for just a moment, maybe we could get started," taunted Vorc.

"You and this abomination do what you have to. But I will not allow it. Zastrál will not be allowed to tap into any of our minds."

"That'd be a first," chuckled Vorc. "What you claim is not possible."

"Then be impressed." I sat down.

Zastrál was as heavy as it looked. And talk about smell? *Whoa.* Nastificatious. Somewhere between rotten chicken meat and old shoes.

"Is your name really Ryanmax?" Vorc asked in a measured manner.

"Yes."

"Zastrál?" Vorc asked the beast.

"We ... we are uncertain. Please ask a different question."

"Did you throw the intermixer unit into the vortex? Yes or no?"

"No."

"Well, Zastrál?"

"We get no reading whatsoever, lord," they replied in unison.

"What are you *fools* saying?" demanded the center seat.

"Ryanmax has made good on his promise. We are not permitted to enter his brain."

20

'Cause he doesn't have one, Sapale observed in my head.

Maybe stay focused, babe?

You're not speaking to me, are you? asked Toño.

"This is *outrageous*. Zastrál, try the woman."

Within a minute Sapale was seated and had on a snake hat. Vorc asked the same things of her, and pretty soon of Toño. Nada. Damn, Zastrál was so dejected when he slithered out the door, I almost called him back and fessed up. Almost.

Vorc and Dalfury spoke briefly in a whisper so quiet even I couldn't hear them.

Finally Vorc looked to me and smiled. "So your bravado was justified. We are impressed."

"I believe you referred to it as *blustering*, not bravado," I corrected.

"Quite possibly." His smile was growing a nervous edge to it. "Be that as it may, you are free to go for now."

"For *now*," I said as low and scary as I could.

"Well, pending a full *explanation* of today's situation, we are all suspects, aren't we?"

"Even the cloud?" I fluttered a hand in Dalfury's direction.

"Ah, well … um, some are *less* under suspicion than others, I suppose."

"How about you, Vorc? *You* screw the pooch?" I menaced as best I could.

"Hardly. I was in front of everyone, remember? My hands were in plain sight most of the time."

"*Most* being the operative concept."

"Bu … but, how could I—"

I placed my index and middle fingers in front of my eyes, then flipped them to Vorc's face. "I'll be watching you." To my team I said, "Let's get a drink."

We waltzed out, hoping Vorc's day just kept getting worse and worse.

· · ·

21

FOUR

Visforef danced around the joinery, encouraging all the singlets to eat. For them, jumping was easy. Their fused adult body had a coiled spring midsection. Their jellyfish-bell circular leg also allowed for excellent bouncing. If adult Delemic didn't have the upper body of a monkey with six long thin arms, they'd have looked quite aquatic.

The time for the joining was upon them and, as lead joiner for this region, Visforef was assigned to make certain there was a positive outcome. If a singlet wasn't plump enough it couldn't meld with another.

"Eat, eat, eat, our little ones," they sang out. "4158, please don't play with that toy until you've finished your slurry." Little ones, they thought to themselves; alway wanting to play when there was serious business to be completed.

At least Visforef already had a goodly complement of singlets ready to advance to pairing. Some might even be big enough to form a triplet immediately. The best singlets would be identified when all the wrinkles were gone from their spherical, ill-defined bodies. If they got the larger doublets to eat, well, they'd be ready to bond up quite soon. The Incubation Sun was due to rise in seven cycles. All the singlets and doublets not ready by then would be lost. Such was an abomination. Last joining period, two triplets and one doublet perished. None were Visoref's charges, but recalling the lost ones made them shudder just the same.

In a corner a singlet hovered alone, paying no attention to anything. Unacceptable, they thought. "You, we don't recognize you. Are you partitioned from another joinery? What is your name?"

"I am not lost, old ones. I am simply awaiting my chance," replied the singlet.

Such language, they thought to themselves. "Well, you are here now and look to be well-fed enough to bond." They scanned the joinery. "88200, come here. You are the correct mass now. You will pair with ... with this one." They pointed at the newcomer. "What is your name, we ask again?"

"What if I don't want to join with 88200?" the little one asked.

"*Impossible*," shouted Visoref. "Choice is not an option. Volition is *not* a prerogative." They shooed the little ones into the next chamber, where the joining tables were located. Their immense bulk left no room for the newcomer to avoid involuntary cooperation.

88200 hopped into the joiner chair without needing to be asked. It was trained to do so and couldn't conceive of objecting.

"You get in this joiner chair. Do so now. You've already caused us excess time and undeserved stress."

The newcomer remained where it was.

Visoref picked it up and set it into the joiner. They were angry. "This will not take long, but as you know, you must cooperate. If you resist or give us further trouble, you will be expelled and will never live to post Incubation Sun. Is that clear?"

"It is clear, old cow. But I'm not mixing my pure flesh with this tainted whore's." There was, for reference's sake, no word for or concept of prostitution in the Delemic mind.

"If you don't want to join with 88200, what is it that you want to do? To join with a different singlet? Such is possible, but we are not certain you warrant such a second chance."

"You asked my name earlier. I will give it to you now. Lorpamoor is my name. Blood is my game. What I *want*, baby, you got." A long, thin tubular projection sprouted from Lorpamoor's mouth. In an instant it pierced Visoref's chest and lodged in their center heart.

Lorpamoor made an exaggerated suction action with his entire body. Within seconds Visoref died. All the circulating blood in their body was drained. The vampire god withdrew the thin spear and drove it into 88200's tiny chest. It was dead much quicker. Lorpamoor jumped to the floor. As he fell he transformed back into his normal body. He then returned to the joinery and drank as much blood as he could from the helpless singlets. Their number was so great he had to allow a few to escape. He was that full.

He patted his swollen belly. "It's such a shame to let all that sweet blood go to waste. I may need to start working out to stimulate my appetite. I don't want my peers to judge me lazy." Then he laughed a juicy, sick laugh. Life was good again.

FIVE

We sat in a small drinking establishment not far from Vorc Central. After a bit of initial chatter we were all pretty quiet, probably reflecting privately. I was into my third ration of firewater when Toño spoke.

"Jon, I'm concerned and confused."

Sapale held up her glass. "I'll drink to that."

"How so?" I replied.

"We, well, mostly *you*, are pulling off a monumental con-job, one on the scale of a universe. But what's our endgame?"

That was easy. "I have no idea."

"I suspected as much," he responded sadly.

"You know me. I wing it more than's healthy for one's health."

He tossed his head side to side. "Yes, I suppose I do."

"What would you have me do?" I asked.

More head tossing. "I can't say specifically. I must say a long-range plan and a realistic exit strategy would be comforting, just this once."

"I—"

Sapale put a palm in my face. "This is where he says, *oh, don't be such a worry wart.*"

"I was about to say nothing of the sort," I protested.

She extended her probe fibers to my forearm. "What were you going to say, love?"

With the probes attached she knew I couldn't lie. She'd hear whatever rattled around in my head. It was a trick she'd learned a long time ago that I was not particularly enthralled with.

"I was going to respond that his concerns were heard and appreciated." Yeah, I lied anyway. I stuck my tongue out at her.

"Might we return to discussing the existential crisis we face?" asked Toño, sounding for all the world like our parent.

"Sure, why not?" I grumbled back. "So, any bright ideas from the two of you?"

"We could try rushing the vortex. Maybe it'd let just the three of us pass," replied Sapale.

"But then at best, we're back home getting the snot beaten out of us," I reasoned.

"Well, at least we'd be home. This place is, at its core, disgusting."

"We're at war. If it ain't disgusting, it ain't *war*," I responded.

"But that might be our only path back to where we belong," observed Toño.

"True. The traps we sprang got us here, but there doesn't seem to be any other way out, does there?"

"I'd hate to die here," Sapale remarked wistfully.

"Didn't see *that* coming," I replied. "Isn't it as good a place as any?"

"No. This universe is wrong. It's corrupted. My soul might not be able to find its way to Davdiad's blessed pastures from here."

"Ah, why not? Souls can do amazing things," I replied weakly.

"And you're an expert on that subject since when?"

"Expert? Since when do I need to be, like, *certified* to have a valid opinion?"

"I thought not," my wife of two billion years scoffed.

"Topic at *hand*, people," urged Toño.

"Okay, we have one vote for flying into a broken vortex of transportation or homogenization." I held up a finger. "Doc?"

"I have tried hard to see where this is going, where we could make it go. But I come to no satisfactory vision. No matter how hard or how long we try, it's unlikely we'll ever control or destroy anything but a small portion of the locals. There are too many of *them*, too few of *us*, and we're fighting on *their* turf."

"As part of astronaut training, you know where they sent me?"

"Of course. I assume you're referring to Camp Lejeune, North Carolina. I learned everything about you, remember?"

"Yeah. 1st Battalion, 10th Marines. The Nightmare, they called themselves."

"This is all cool bonding and shit, but is there a point to this macho recall?" Sapale asked pointedly.

"'Course. They have, I mean *had* lots of swamps there. And we had a chance to march in many of them. All of them, I think. We slogged through those damn swamps in the day, in the night, and in the rain. Hell, if it snowed there we'd have shlepped through them in the snow. Locusts and frogs, no prob, we'd still march up to our chests. You know what I learned?"

"Keep your socks dry?" Toño quipped.

"Crotch rot *can* kill," replied my smiling wife.

"No. I learned that a lot of the time you don't know *where* you're going, you don't know if you'll make it there alive, but you do know that if you do, every wet part of your body will have a leech affixed to it. *Every* part. But you know how you beat the swamp? You keep going. If you stop putting one foot in front of the other, you die. Mission failure."

"So, we don't know where this escapade in the land of ancient gods will lead, but we need to push ahead?" summarized Sapale.

"Yes—" I started to say.

She put up that hand again. "No, no. Me. This is the inspirational part where you say that *oorah* thing, right?"

"Possibly," I replied, a tad miffed. I hated it when my thunder was stolen by some domestic terrorist.

"So?" asked Toño.

"So finish off your drink and let's go. If we can't make somebody dead, let's at least make them miserable."

"Sounds like a plan," Sapale chimed in as she raised, then drained her glass.

Out the door I said, "We need to find Wul."

"What if he left in that first wave, Rage?" asked Toño.

"Somehow I think he didn't. I'm not sure he's passionate about the raping and pillaging. I think he'd be in the last group to go, if he went at all."

"Some gods are allowed to stay behind?" questioned Sapale.

"I think the powers that be turn a blind eye to it, but yes, not everyone joins in."

"And you suspect we might find allies in these conscientious objectors?" Toño queried.

"Won't know if we don't ask."

"Ah, isn't that a little risky? Beal's Point seems to be populated with political dissenters," Sapale responded.

"Desperate times, honey. I think it's our best option."

"How will we find him?" posed Toño.

"I recognize a few of the members of Rage. One of them was good old Gorpedder, the rock god. I'm betting his place is free again."

"Why do we want to be squatters there?" wondered Sapale.

"Because there'll be a comm station. I can use it to call Wul."

"Won't he be suspicious? I mean, these gods simage each other. Why bother with a landline?" asked Toño.

"Normally yes. But Wul's sort of concluded I'm fundamentally different."

"Smart man," returned Toño.

Sure enough, Gorpedder's house was empty, with signs he'd closed things up for a long vacation. I made a show of waving at one of the neighbors. That way everyone would know Gorp's pal was back. I went straight to the comm station.

"Do you know how it works?" Toño questioned.

"Sort of. These controls are for the TV-like broadcasts. There's news and some stunningly lame entertainment options available." I pointed to a different set of keys. "I called the morgue by hitting this one."

"Why did you call the morgue?" asked Sapale.

"I wanted to make a reservation in case they were busy when I died. Come on, I hit the key and that's where the call went. Maybe Gorpedder's BFF works there. Who knows?"

Toño stepped between me and the unit. "I'd better take it from here. You two go entertain yourselves while I figure out how this works."

"Ya hear that, wife?" I gestured to the next room. "Bedroom's right over there."

"In your dreams, horny toad."

"How about coffee? I hid some in what passes for a kitchen."

"*That* I can go for."

As I slid her a stone mug, I said, "I'm really touched you two came looking for me. Thanks."

She shrugged. "You'd have done the same. Plus, silly me, I was starting to miss you."

"That's sweet."

"Yeah. I was relaxed and at ease. There wasn't *one* crisis the entire time. Really creeped me out."

"Ah, true love. It's a thong of beauty."

She set her mug down. "You mean *thing* of beauty, right?"

"Sure, but you look so amazing in a *thong* I had to mix the metaphor."

"Why I put up with you I shall never understand."

From the other room Toño called out, "I think I've got it." When we were there he continued. "There's a list of numbers, a directory if you will, if you select this option."

A list of names and places popped up on the screen.

"It's poorly organized, but I found Wul's name here."

He tapped a key and Wul's name was the only one on screen.

"If you hit that button you should initiate a direct call to him."

"Let's do this," I responded. I hit the key and instantly Wul's face was smiling at me.

"Ryanmax, what a surprise," he said with genuine warmth.

"Yeah, I missed you, too. You didn't go with Rage?"

He hesitated a moment. "Let's meet at the usual place in say an hour."

"Regular place one hour. I'll be there with bells on."

He furrowed his brow. "Why?"

"Old saying. See you soon." I killed the conversation.

Clearly Wul wasn't comfortable discussing anything specific over an open system. Still, not even saying, "Meet me at Blind Faith No More?" Kind of a public place. Oh well, maybe I'd ask him about it when I saw him. It was always best to be cautious. We left immediately to make sure we got there first. Since he'd brought up the notion of security, I wanted to be able to watch for signs of traps developing or spies sneaking in. Hey, I didn't get to two billion by throwing caution to the wind.

I placed Toño out front to keep an eye peeled for anything suspicious. Sapale was with me. It's hard to imagine going out for a social occasion without one's spouse. Plus she was an objective set of eyes and ears. She might catch some tell I wasn't picking up on because I liked him.

Queeheg nearly split in two down the middle when he saw me walk in. Darn guy just couldn't decide if he should run like hell or worship me. It *was* kind of cute. Then again, I didn't need a big, ugly, and hairy groupie.

"'Lo ... Master Ryanmax," he howled when I was halfway through the door. "It's sa good a sees ya again. Been too long, says I." He slipped nimbly around the bar and genuflected his way all the way over in our direction. "An' ya brought the *missus* along, too. Nice to sees ya, too, ma'am."

"Good to see you, Queeheg," she replied.

"Ya bes needin' a table or ya sittin' at the bar?"

"A table, please. We're expecting Wul anytime now," I replied.

"A table it 'tiz," he replied as he swung a massive arm toward an empty spot. "Ya sit an' I'll retrieve some refreshments."

He was back quickly with three glasses and even more bottles. He also precariously balanced a tray of nibblies on his forearm. When he was in range Sapale snatched it before it could tumble. Grace in motion the man was not.

"Anytin' else, master?" he asked with a most uncomfortable smile.

"No, thanks. This'll get us started," I replied.

The man was gone in a flash. It was like he shifted a foot onto a land mine. I wouldn't have guessed he could move that quickly.

"Boy, you sure get that poor sap's brain spinning," observed Sapale, as she poured.

"That seems to be the case, doesn't it?" I took a swig. "Us alpha gods have that effect. One gets used to it."

Her response was one of the Kaljaxian's signature growls. This one was the I'm-about-to-leap-for-your-throat warning.

Wul entered and broke the tension. I waved him over.

"Ryanmax, it's so *good* to see you." He shook my hand like we were brothers separated at birth meeting for the first time.

"Yeah, eez, it's been what, a week now?"

"But what a week. You've become the very talk of the town."

Sapale's head dropped upon hearing that news. She mumbled quietly, "Please, Davdiad, no more worship for my moron brood-mate."

"Ah, Sapale, wonderful to see you, too."

"Almost as wonderful as seeing the great and powerful wizard of Oz here?" she responded, nodding her head in my direction.

"You're a wizard as *well*?" marveled Wul. "Will wonders never cease?"

"Apparently not," grunted Sapale.

"Sure, why not a wizard, too? If I had a deck of cards I could entertain you for minutes," I responded. "By the way, why the expansive greeting?"

"Are you kidding? You're the only individual *ever* to face Bethniak in a fight and not die. I'm proud to shake your hand and call you friend."

"That's about it," exclaimed Sapale as she stood abruptly. "I'll be outside getting some fresh, non-butt-kissing air." And she left.

"She's not so used to me yet," I said meekly, thumbing toward her over my back.

"I thought you told me you've been married for a very long time?"

"Yeah. I'm an acquired taste, it would seem."

"I don't think so," came a voice over my shoulder. Freaking no. I knew that voice. I turned to see—you got it—the shiny-blob ghost. And darn if it hadn't changed shape again. It looked like a cigar with two cigarette legs. Of course, because we're talking *my* blob here, the legs floated a few inches off the floor. Sure. Why have useless legs function as legs when you're haunting Jon Ryan?

"I don't suppose you heard that or see the ghost again, do you?" I asked in a defeated tone.

"Ryanmax, that bit was funny the first time, but do we need to do it again? Seriously. Move on. Take a chance and grow up."

"I'll take that to indicate *no.*"

"He chooses not to see me," said the ghost.

"Do you remember your name yet? I want to employ it to officially blow you off, if you do."

"I don't exist. How could I have a name?"

"Oh you exist all right. Nothing could be as annoying as you and *not* be real."

"Okay. I'll play along," responded Wul. "Why do you suspect I don't exist?"

"No. You exist, my friend. It's him." I nodded toward the cloud. "He says he doesn't exist but he does."

"How is that funny?" asked Wul.

"It is not," the ghost responded for some reason.

"I know it's not. It nauseating," I whined.

"So I'm supposed to be nauseated? Why would you wish that on me again?" asked a confused Wul.

"I don't. The ghost, sure, but not you."

"How about you, Jon Ryan?" inquired the spirit. "Are you or do you wish to be nauseated?"

"No. Yes. I mean I'm *getting* there. Why are you here?"

"You asked me to meet you," snapped Wul.

"Hideho, y'alls," welcomed a cheery Queeheg as he bounced over. "What is it you'll be samplin' a'day, Master Wul?"

"The usual and lots of it," wheezed Wul.

"Ah, well I see the CO has started to have 'is *mysterious* effects on ya already," responded the barkeep, all but giggling.

"CO?" we both asked. I mean Wul and I did. Not the ghost. Maybe he knew. Maybe he didn't care. Maybe he didn't exist. But no maybe about it, I needed a strong drink soon.

Queeheg leaned in conspiratorially. "*C* fer chosen, *O* fer one. Ya seez? I figured outta *code*." He tapped the side of his head, winked, and scampered away. His breath smelled of embalmed cheese. I was ready to bolt and join my better half.

"He's a real fan, Ryanmax," said Wul with no enthusiasm.

"Yeah, he sure as hell is. Lucky me."

"I don't feel it is such a lucky thing to have a halfwit drunken blabbermouth be your number-one fan," opined the ghost.

"No one asked the views of a ghost," I growled.

"No. I mean, yes. No one did. What are we talking about?" wondered Wul, the strain evident in his voice.

"You and I are not talking about what him and I are."

"Him being Queeheg or the ghost?" asked a fading Wul.

"Perhaps both," added the apparition.

"It is *not* both. You don't count. You are transparent and annoying and really piss-offing."

"Piss-*offing*?" parroted Wul in an empty tone. "Is that a verb now?"

"Is *whats* a verb na'?" queried Queeheg as he set a tray on our table.

"Piss-offing," mumbled Wul.

The furrows in Queeheg's brow could have directed flood waters. "Hmm." Then his face brightened. "Who said the expression?"

Wul, apparently speechless at that juncture, pointed at me.

"Ah, then *yes*, it's a fine an' propers word. I'll be glowing to share it with or accuse it to of others in the *proximate* future." With that he moved to the next table, a huge grin on his face.

"I am not sanguine about the neologism," said the ghost.

"Neologism? What, you a deceased scholar of the English language? *Professor* Piss-offing of the College of Hard Knocks?"

"No. I'm not a professor," whimpered Wul. "I never went to school. I ... never saw the need. I was a god."

"And he still is," chimed in the ghost.

"Ghost reminds you you still are," I passed along foolishly.

"Still am a ghost?"

"No—"

"A professor?"

"Nope—"

"A piss-offy college?"

"No. Listen. A god. But it's piss-*offing*, not piss-*offy*. That could never be a word. You lose the whole verb intent."

Wul lowered his head to the table. "The verb has an *intention*? Does that intention have anything to do with the ghost I can't see or hear?"

"No. That's crazy talk, Wul. I just don't think we need to make a perfectly good verb into a noun or anything."

"Of course not. Is that what you wanted to speak to me about? The finer points of grammar in the setting of insanity?"

"No, gosh, Wul. You're so ... so—"

"Ill?"

"Silly. That's what I was going to say. I wanted to talk about the egress, you know, moving on down the road to Prime?"

His face was still on the table but, in the plus column, I do *not* think he was retching. "You want to talk about the invasion?" Man he was pathetic. His voice was barely a whimper.

"Well, sure, I mean, you know, small talk."

"You wanted to meet so we could chitchat about the impending doom of a now vibrant universe?"

"Well, if you place it in *that* context it does sound a bit insensitive of me, doesn't it?"

He made a sound, kind of between a horse whinnying and fingernails on a chalkboard.

"So, I forgot to ask. How're you *doing*, Wul? Things going well? Hey, how's your team doing? You follow any sports?"

"Fine, yes, we don't have team sports, so I backed into responding *no*."

"I didn't mean team *sports* when I said *team*. I could have meant like a chess club or pinochle society." I didn't want to betray my lack of knowledge about my peeps, right? "And you could follow a sport even if we Cleinoids don't ... haven't organized teams. No, not yet, but someday, who knows? I thought I heard of a tee ball league forming somewhere near here."

"You are as cruel as they are," said Conscience, my ghost. "You have reduced the poor fool to idiocy. When doth the quality of mercy *droppeth as the gentle rain from heaven* out of your mouth?"

Whoa. "You quote me Shakespeare? How does a disembodied spirit in Godville know the Bard?"

"I'm not disembodied ... yet," sniveled Wul. "Where's Godville, Ryanmax? Is that where the wee ball teams are?"

"Godville's in your heart and no, the *tee* ball was elsewhere. Now shut up please, Wul, all of the sudden I'm busy." I spun to the ghost. "Out with it. How can you know that line?"

"I have—"

As one we said, "... no idea." Great. The impossible squared. An alien who's a ghost knows Shakespeare. No, wait. *Cubed*. He doesn't know how he knows.

"Is masta Wul all right?" asked Queeheg as he inched toward him. I could tell he wanted to poke Wul with a finger but wasn't quite that brave.

"I'm pretty sure. Look, he's still breathing. That's gotta be a positive sign."

"Let's prayz it'is. Can I get you more poison?"

"Ye ... y ... yes," squeaked Wul. "Strong poison quickly."

"Ah, I was speakin' metaphorically, Wul. Ya knows dat, right?"

"Oh," was all the poor guy could manage.

"Who's ya transparent friend, CO, if it's authorizable fer me to asks?"

"Oh he's ... wait. You see him?"

"An' why wouldn't I?"

"Everyone else ignores him."

"Well, let's just a'member I'm not everyone an' dis bein' my bar, I makes it a strong habit to knows everytin' what transpires."

"He doesn't recall his name, he is certain he doesn't exist, and he's piss-offing."

"*Ah*. De generator of da word's da day. Proud to know you, sir, madame, or other applicable appellation. Do you intake solids or liquids?"

"No, I have no—"

"Den I'll be askin' nicely one time only dat youz be on yur fair way." Queeheg nodded to me and walked back behind the bar.

"I guess this is goodbye," I said flatly.

"Such sweet—"

I held up a hand.

He stopped. And he was gone.

"Who was Queeheg speaking to?" asked Wul. Plucky fellow was attempting to lift his head up. I was sure pulling for him.

"Seriously, no one."

"Makes sense."

"You *bet* it does."

Wul was sitting almost upright. I wanted to kiss the freak.

"So, if you were going to stop the egress of the ancient gods, how would you do it?" I asked plainly.

His voice sharpened remarkably fast. "Why would you want to—"

"*Me*. Hang on here. Who said anything about *me* wanting to stop anything?" I set a palm on my chest.

"You *are* the one asking."

"Oh, I see your misunderstanding. I'm on a concept-scavenger-hunt team. Didn't I mention that? Yeah. New bunch a wackos I joined the other day. I think it'll be all the rage—"

"Scavenger hunting for concepts? Ryanmax, you go too far. There are no teams such as that."

I shook my head. "Gosh, the guys'll be upset to hear that. We already placed an order for tee—"

"*Enough*," he hissed convincingly. "It is only because of my past affection for you that I do not alert Vorc as to your inquiry."

"Hang on. Okay, I was *trying* to be funny. Here's the real reason." I glanced side to side as if assuring no one was around to hear. "Ever since someone threw that intermixer into the vortex, I've been on a secret mission."

His stare did not soften.

"Yeah, top-secret operation. Vorc asked me to ferret out the perp or perps." I checked the immediate area again. "He said as a poly and as a suspect myself—not that I did it, mind you—I was his first and best choice as an operative." I put a hush finger over my lips.

"You expect me to believe a word of that? You must think me a great fool."

"Look, no. I'd say you could call him and confirm, but he'd deny everything. It's *that* secret. He will afterwards. I *swear* it."

"What is the all-consuming need for secrecy? That's never been necessary in the past."

"*Shh.*" I scanned the room with alarm. "Geez, Wul, can you keep it down? Of course, that's never been needed before. That's why it's needed now. Don't you see it gives us the element of surprise?"

He blinked eight or ten times before speaking. "The element of surprise by investigating in secret? That's brain-dead talk." He began to rise.

"Sit, *sit*," I said in near panic. "I think that's one *right* over *there*."

He reflexively sat. Staring to the area I gestured my head toward, he asked, "One what where?"

I threw my head back in manifest frustration. Looking back at him, I whispered loudly, "One of the co-conspirators, *duh*."

"The only person I see is Xassteril. Sorry, she's not a person, but that's the only *thing* in that direction." He returned a harsh glare to me.

I nodded frantically. Boy, I must have looked the sight.

"What?" he asked.

I nodded more frantically and angled my head toward whatever Xassteril was.

"So help me, if you don't stop *spasming* and start speaking, I'm going straight to Vorc."

"We've identified Xassy as a confirmed element in the plot to kill Vorc."

"Huh? Wha—"

"*Shh.*"

"What plot to kill V—"

"Shhhhhhhh! By Depadupia's fine eyelashes, can't you keep it down?"

"Depa who?"

I rolled my eyes like a Valley girl. "Never mind. Yes. The intermixer was intended to take out Vorc." I turned and gave an if-looks-could-kill glance at Xassteril. "The idea was to disorient him and have him fall into the vortex. No way he'd survive that."

"Why the hell not. Conscious gods pass right through. Why couldn't unconscious ones?"

I pointed at his nose. "That's what they *want* you to believe."

"Who wants me to believe what?"

"*They* want you to think that. But they know if a Cleinoid is under the influence of an intermixer, up close, you know, they could *never* survive the vortex."

"Why not? It alters perception alone."

I placed a the-headmaster-is-furious expression on my face. "I didn't say it was true. One does not need to be correct or even bright to be a rebel."

"So they wanted to assassinate Vorc but didn't know their plan wouldn't work, when it's as plain as the nose on my face it couldn't possibly have the desired effect?" Man he sounded exasperated. Good. I was getting there.

I extended my hands deferentially toward him. "Exactly."

"And one of the morons who didn't know the obvious *and* wanted Vorc dead was Xassteril, the goddess of learning and compassion?"

I nodded, emoting the contentment of a father watching his son hit his first single in little league. "You got it. You see why discretion is the key element of my investigation."

"I do? Because I don't."

I set a dumbfounded look on my face. "Do you want a color-keyed flowchart with illustrations?"

He nodded rather emphatically. "Yes. Very much so, in fact."

"Well, then, you're bound for Disappointment Street, my friend. You are not cleared for that level of understanding. If you want to be, I can speak to Vorc, see if he'll okay you beginning training and vetting. He's already rej—"

"No, I don't want to join the team headed straight to Hemnoplop's *center*."

"Are you suggesting our investigative exploration is in any way suited for Fool's Island? If you were to think that, given the fact that you seem to know this Xassteril criminal so intimately, one might be given to flights of suspicion."

"I really do hate you. I want you to know deep in your soul I do not believe one syllable of what you've said. But, due to our past friendship, I will ask this one question. If the complete bullshit you just issued was true, how in the greatest straining of credulity does that warrant you asking me how to stop the ancient gods' egress into where they want to be?"

"Well, I'm glad you *finally* asked. I was getting worried there for a hot second."

"*You* were worried?"

I appeared confused. "Did you *ask* if I were worried or *state* that you understand I was worried?"

I'm pretty sure I saw hot coals burning in the back of his eyes.

"I'm trying to get every take possible on what these desperate, bloodthirsty terrorists might try next. You see that, right?"

"Try *next*?"

"*Phew*. Glad you do. It makes this easier. So, if you were going to stop the Cleinoids from ravaging Prime, how would you do it?

Don't say throw an intermixer into the egress vortex because, duh, we already know that one."

His eyes narrowed. "I thought you said the attack on the vortex was *incidental*. The real target was Vorc."

"*Incidental?*" I sighed judgmentally. "I see I've wasted both our times here, citizen Wul. On behalf of Vorc and the team I'd like to thank you for your cooperation." I made as if to stand.

"What? Are you serious? No, wait. This is one of your stupid practical jokes."

I shook my head slowly and knowingly. "Good day, citizen."

"No, answer me. I'm actually totally serious. If the attack was meant to take out Vorc, well, you said they thought he'd fall in the vortex and die, which he wouldn't, but what does that have to do with their next unrelated attempt? You ask about stopping the Cleinoids, not bodyguarding Vorc."

"I'm sorry you see it that way."

"See it what way? Do you have maggots in your brainpan?"

"Ah, I see. *Insults* might aid my investigation, mightn't they?"

I folded my hands on the table like the principal always did when I was sent to his office. "We have information—ironclad, settled intel, mind you—that the only way they believe Vorc can be ended is with a malfunctioning vortex. Hence all their future attempts will of necessity involve them tampering with the vortex. There. I said it. Please never repeat that insight. To betray that high a level of confidence would be *bad*."

"Oh, you can count on me to never repeat any of this. I don't want to be associated with such stupidity."

"Thank you. Now, as to how to destabilize the vortex?"

He grew suspicious again. "I'll tell you one way if you tell me one you've learned about as a result of your super-secret sleuthing." He folded his arms and rested back.

You know what the most excellent thing about being me was? I know, narrowing it down is nigh on impossible, but go ahead, guess. Okay, I'll say it. I lived by the Girl Scout motto. Be prepared. And I was. I thought he might play that card.

"Wul, what I'm about to tell you is beyond classified. This information is secured in the deepest parts of the Existine Vaults."

"The what? Never heard of them."

"Then we're doing our job well. To proceed, this information is so closely guarded that there is an inflammatory curse instilled into the very wording."

"A what? There's no—"

"Uh-uh, citizen." I stopped him with a raised palm. "Again, thank you for confirming *job well done* on our part. An inflammatory curse is a spell that if released, causes the user to burst into flames."

"I don't see you bursting into flames. I wish I were, but I'm not," he said dubiously.

"I'm *authorized*, you inbred. As I was about to suggest, forget what I'm about to say. I will know you betrayed our confidence if I read of your immolation. An alternate way to disrupt a vortex would be to shunt plasma from the paired nacelle collectors into the Heisenberg compensators placed on opposite sides of the vortex in order to generate sufficient tachyon emissions to disperse neutrino buildup around the vortex core, thereby establishing a reverse of the polarity and anti-accretion of its molecular substance." I glared hard at him. "Never repeat that. *Never.*" I pointed to the floor.

"I ... I have ... I got nothing."

"That is unacceptable. I showed you mine, now show me yours."

"We're still talking about ways to cripple a vortex, right?"

"Naturally."

My but he had a distant look in his eyes.

"Fine, but then we're through, you and me. Promised One or not, I never want to *see*, be *seen* by, or be seen in *association* with you ever again."

"I can live with that," I said with a shrug.

"It has long been speculated the vortex is made of non-matter."

"What is non-matter? Are you trying to renege on telling me?"

"No, of course not. I wish to be rid of you and rid of you soon. Non-matter is just that. It is neither matter nor antimatter. It is neutral matter, if you will."

"I will take your word on that for now. If it were this neutral matter, how would that make the structure vulnerable?"

"Matter and antimatter self-annihilate."

"Yes."

"Matter and neutral matter do not."

"O-kay."

"Antimatter and non-matter do not."

"Sure, why not?"

"But matter mixed with antimatter tri-annihilate with neutral matter."

"But matter and antimatter don't mix without exploding. So how can *they* be mixed and then added to a neutral matter slurry?"

"I'm just the messanger here. I don't know nor do I care to find out because I have no interest in destroying the vortex. But, if you could combine the three then you would destroy the vortex." His hands came together then opened quickly. *"Bada boom."*

"Can you suggest to me how these desperadoes might pull that off?"

"Yes. Go ask Xassteril. She's sitting right over there." He left without another word.

I had half a mind to do just that. But then, acting under the power of only half a mind was a dumb idea. I finished my drink and retrieved my wife.

CHAPTER TWO

"Sir, I mark six meteor impacts in the vicinity of the Badlands National Park, South Dakota."

"Can you confirm six?" queried Major Carter Braxton. He was the watch commander that day for the North American Aerospace Defense Command, or NORAD.

"Yes, sir," responded Command Sergeant Major Robertson. He'd been on the scope for years and was legendary. "The pattern's a bit odd."

"Sergeant, I don't want *odd* in times of potential crisis. Be specific or be silent."

"Sorry, sir. I meant to say the pattern is unusually tight. Normally if a rock's going to splinter in the atmosphere, the resultant sections will land farther apart."

"Why's that?" he asked quickly.

"Simple physics, sir. If the meteor's going to fail it'll do so pretty high up. This tight a pattern suggests either the main body held together until it was almost to the ground, or that there were six *independent* meteors in a tight formation to begin with."

"Seems unlikely then, in either case. Could they be hard landings of spacecraft?"

"Uh, I'd doubt it. The dust plumes are pretty big. Whatever hit did so with tremendous momentum. Hard to imagine any living being would plan such a rough landing." He cleared his throat. "Plus, we haven't confirmed any LGM as of yet, sir."

"LGM?"

"Sorry. Little green men. You know, *aliens*."

"There's a first for everything, Sergeant."

"Yes, sir, there is." It took all Craig could do not to snicker. Major Braxton was famously a nerd. Rumor had it he even wore *Star Wars* skivvies.

"Lieutenant Koehn, alert CFB Cold Lake to scramble some CF-18s to inspect the site."

"Sir."

"And have Ellsworth ready a full platoon for area recon. I want an officer on the ground this time out. Also instruct them to place as many AH-64 Apache helicopters as'll be required on alert."

"Yes, sir."

Five minutes later Braxton was contacted by Captain S.E. Parker, who piloted the lead F-18. "Major, we're over the site. I count six impact craters maybe three meters in diameter. They are located in a symmetrical pattern a few hundred meters up the side of a gentle slope. Smoke is rising from all six. No signs of structure in the craters, but they are fairly deep."

"What kind of symmetric pattern?"

"Like the corners of a stop sign, Major."

"Damn strange," Braxton mumbled to himself. "Any movement in the area?"

"Negative."

"Any apparent danger to a recon patrol?"

"Negative. I'd advise they carry Geiger counters and wear Nomex suits. Looks pretty hot close to the craters."

"Copy that. NORAD out."

Twenty minutes later, Second Lieutenant Philip McCain radioed in. "Major, we're holding at the base of the hill. I can confirm the hexagon of craters is one hundred fifty meters from our position.

Radiation levels do not, I repeat, do *not* exceed background. Thin columns of ... Sergeant Carter, what the hell is that?"

"Report *Lieutenant*," demanded Braxton. "What's going on?"

"Sir, some damn thing just crawled out of one of the ... check that, *two* of the craters."

"Lieutenant, I am ordering you to keep calm and provide me with accurate, clear reports. Is that clear?"

"Sorry, Major. Cappy, can you get the video cameras on the hill? Major, I'll have a visual in a minute. At this point three, no all six craters have creatures at or near their rims."

"*Creatures?* What kind of creatures, Lieutenant?"

"Different ones. Christ Almighty, sir, they're the most hideous things I've ever seen. One is a serpent the size of a Mack truck. Another is, I don't know, maybe a dinosaur, but smaller, with wings and teeth that emit light; *purple* light, sir."

"Are you certain?"

"Yes. What, Cappy? Okay, Major, we're ready to broadcast live. See for your damn self, Braxton."

Major Braxton began to shout a reprimand at the junior officer when the first live images flashed to life on the screen in front of him. He then forgot the lieutenant even existed. Braxton saw a serpent as large as a Mack truck. He focused on a dinosaur with purple teeth. He recoiled at the sight of a woman with eight arms who stood ten feet tall. Her torso was jacketed with golden armor and her arms and legs were covered in spikes. In place of hair, flames wafted from her head. She appeared to be laughing.

"Lieutenant McCain, fall back. Repeat, *abort* mission. Return to base immediately. Captain Williams."

"Sir."

"Scramble every fighter we have under our command fully armed. I want that hill to be a very deep hole ten minutes ago."

"*Sir.*"

"And have Ellsworth load their B-52s with all the MK82 500-pounders they can carry. They are to carpet-bomb that damn crater till we hear the Chinese begging us to stop. I want kitchen *sinks* impacting that site. Is that clear, Williams?"

"Yes, sir."

"McCain, report status."

The speakers hissed with white noise.

Braxton snapped a glance at the monitor. Nothing but snow. "Where's the damn broadcast from the patrol?" he shouted to no one in particular. "Where's the damn *patrol?*"

"We've lost both the radio and video links, sir."

"What do you mean *lost?*"

"I mean there are no signals coming from the recon patrol."

"Crap. Captain, what's the status of those fighters?"

"Six are airborne. Twelve more are nearly ready for takeoff."

"Tell them to hurry it up. They're moving too slow."

"Sir."

"I want the lead fighter on the line *now.*"

"Hang on. There, Captain Claymore, Major Braxton is ready for your report."

"Where are you, Claymore?"

"Five miles from objective."

"You on afterburners?"

"Ne ... negative, sir."

"Light 'em up, son. This is life and death."

"Yes, Major."

A dramatic increase in the volume of jet engines flared.

"ETA?"

"Thirty seconds."

"Do not, repeat, do *not* await visuals. I want all your AGMs flying before you arrive, and drop your GBUs on the laser spots at the earliest possible moment. Are you clear on that?"

"Yes, Major. Missiles away. Ten seconds to release point. Three—two—one. Bombs away."

"Return for resupply. Can you confirm detonations?"

"Sir?"

"Can you confirm detonations? It's a simple question. Look backward and tell me you see Hell rising toward Heaven."

"Major, I can confirm no evid—"

The microphone burst forth static.

"Captain Claymore, are you there. Do you copy, Claymore?"

"Major, all six alert planes are gone."

"Can you confirm debris?"

"Negative, sir. Radar shows no falling wreckage, but they're pretty far away. Might not see it if it were there."

An officer to Braxton's right shouted, "Carter, the planes can't just *vanish*."

"Yes, they can and just did. Koehn, tell those B-52s to take off instantly. I need that location removed from existence."

"Message conveyed, sir. They are finishing preflights as we—"

"Have them take the *fuck* off now, and that's an order. No preflight bullshit. We are on the cusp of total annihilation."

Koehn looked to his partner. They exchanged looks of concern for the major's sanity.

"Major, Ellsworth air control confirms one flight is in the air. After regrouping they'll be over the target in ten minutes."

"Put the CO on speaker."

"This is Lieutenant Colonel Ed Mitchell."

"Ed, this is the scariest thing I've ever seen, and I did three tours in A-4s in 'Nam. You need to get to the objective as fast as you can."

"We are, Major. I have a visual of the strike zone. Lots of smoke. ETA nine minutes."

"Put the pedal to the metal and keep me posted."

"Copy that, Major."

"Do you see any signs of the CF-18s, sir?"

"Negative."

"Or the Apaches?"

"Negative on that also. Lest you inquire, no crash sites or debris noted either."

"Major Braxton, Ellsworth reports three additional squadrons and two flights are airborne."

46

"Fully loaded?"

"They report it's standing room only on the weapons bays."

"Let's just pray that's enough."

A few minutes later Colonel Mitchell was back on the air. "Thirty seconds to drop. Laser guides confirmed. I have direct visual now."

"Any sign of monsters?"

"Say *what?*" barked Mitchell.

"You heard me. Boots on the ground sent back video of alien monsters."

"Well, my psychiatrist and I are both happy to report no monsters, Major."

"I want a live broadcast of the strike zone after bombs away."

"You got it. Sure don't want any monsters to swallow our ordnance before it has a chance to go boom."

"Knock it off, Mitchell. I am deadly serious."

"Roger that. Okay, the last plane in my squadron has released its payload. Returning to base."

"You saw the bombs drop, but are you seeing explosions? Can you confirm detonation?"

"Er ... no, Major Braxton. Your suspicions seem—"

Harsh static.

Radar reported no planes, debris, or parachutes on screen.

Braxton picked up the hotline phone to the Situation Room in the White House.

"Get me the president. Let him know we are currently at war with a vastly superior enemy."

Within minutes, President Bill Clinton, Secretary of Defense William "Bill" Perry, and the joint chiefs were assembled in the Situation Room.

Chairman General John Shalikashvili spoke first. "Mr. President, details are only now rolling in, but I think we're looking at a full-scale hostile alien invasion."

"General Shalikashvili, you know I'm a man given to hyperbole, but even *I* have some trouble buying into that type of warning."

"Be that as it may, sir, the facts are more than alarming. A little more than two hours ago six objects crashed to earth in South Dakota. We confirmed that alien beings of immense power emerged from those craters and neutralized everything NORAD could throw at them. All personnel on the ground and in the air were lost without a trace."

"And you told me you have video proof of these aliens' existence?" asked Bill Perry.

"Yes, sir. We do. Colonel Break, will you cue that tape please."

On the wall a large monitor spat to life. The images taken by Lieutenant McCain were viewed by all. Not a sound could be heard in the room.

"Well assuming those images are real, I'd agree we're in a world of hurt here, ladies and gentlemen," said Clinton. "What's the status of the ... the venue?"

"Unclear, sir," replied Shalikashvili. "Satellite images are not available due to local weather. Ellsworth has flown a constant stream of aircraft over the site. They all report seeing little and are then lost without a trace. Photos sent back to Ellsworth before they disappear haven't been very helpful."

"Bill," asked the president, "what's the status of our response as of this moment?"

"We have every helicopter, plane, train, and truck packed with lethal force and headed toward the Badlands. We're all in."

"When's anybody going to get there?"

"Our forces will arrive in a staggered manner, beginning very shortly."

"General Shalikashvili," asked Clinton very soberly, "have you targeted the site with strategic nuclear missiles?"

"*What?*" snapped Bill Perry. "You cannot be serious, Mr. President. Using megaton devices on our own soil is *unthinkable.*"

"While it may be unthinkable, it may also be our only real option, Bill. I understand your reservations but—"

"I don't have *reservations*, Bill, I have a *family*. We *all* have families and we all have consciences. You cannot even consider—"

48

"Yes, Mr. President. Per your orders several missile silos have targeted ground zero," Shalikashvili interrupted solemnly.

"Fine. Let's pray to God we don't—"

Shalikashvili's cell phone rang. "Yes. Are you absolutely certain? Yes, he's with me. Yes, godspeed."

"What's up, John. How bad is the news?"

"It could not be worse, Mr. President. All flights inbound for the Badlands have disappeared off radar."

"That is bad," replied the leader of the free world.

"That's not even the worst part. Reports are coming in from Rapid City that massive columns of smoke are rising from where Ellsworth was located. A traffic copter returned live images of a large hole where the base used to be. The pilot called the crater *lunar* in proportions."

"I've made my decision. Launch a *one hundred-kiloton* device immediately."

"Just the *one*, Mr. President?" asked Shalikashvili.

"Just the one. That should be quite sufficient to damn all of our souls in the eyes of God."

The general made a quiet call and looked to Clinton. "It'll hit in less than two minutes, sir."

"Very well. General, have our allies been warned of this dire situation?"

"Some."

"Fill up the Press Room and let 'em know I'll be live in one minute. We need to tell the world."

"Yes, sir."

The first two lines spoken by President William Jefferson Clinton, the forty-second and last President of the United States, to the assembled media were, "My sisters and brothers, today we witness the rise of an unimaginable evil. Let us all pray we survive to see 1996."

But no one did. For the six ancient gods that landed near the Badlands National Park that afternoon in July of 1995 were vengeful, and they were bloodthirsty, and they were ruthless.

Nimrod, god of unquenchable fire, Salsifri, god of unending pain, Horice, god of genuine hatred, Lopocif, god of cruelty itself, Goeias, god of mindlessness, and Quixot, god of capriciousness, were not to be stopped. They were never even slowed in their assault. The nuclear missile and all subsequent ones launched didn't detonate.

The ancient gods were not satisfied with the destruction of just the universe as it existed at the time they entered it. No, they traveled backward and forward in time to destroy all they could. An old Cleinoid saying was *the more you destroy, the more you enjoy*. So, these six scourges caused the oceans and rivers to boil, the atmosphere to be blown off into space, and the continents to be pounded into dust. On January 1, 1996, that New Year's Day, not a single mammal walked the earth. Not one penguin waddled across the ice of the Antarctic. Not even one bacterium survived in the rocks below the deepest mine in South Africa, the Mponeng gold mine four kilometers below the ravaged surface.

In that timeline, life on Earth ended before anyone could party like it was 1999. And when the planet was dead, the six death mongers allowed Quixot to select the next epoch to visit, and they were off.

SEVEN

"Neutral matter? Are you *certain* that is what Wul said?" Toño was utterly gobsmacked.

"Yes. Want me to play back the audio?"

"No, I suppose I am just so vexed to hear those words, my credulity needs to catch up with my current state of mind. Jon, in all of my very long life I've never conceived of a third state of matter. I've never heard *any* species, even the Deavoriath, predict such a thing."

"Well, now you have something to occupy your free time," I returned. "Create a theory and put a large quantity in my hands. No hurry. Take *all* the time you need. I won't start nagging you, hounding, you, *badgering* you for two-three days."

"Very droll."

"I was being serious. Doc, we cannot allow any more of these two-bit gods to make it to our universe. The vortex has to be destroyed."

"Honey," Sapale spoke up, "while I support your intent one hundred percent, there is one issue I fear I must mention. If we ex the vortex, how do *we* get home?"

I angled my head. "Maybe we don't."

"So we stay here, what, forever and a day waiting to be uncovered as frauds and tortured beyond the limits of imagination?"

"It is a looming possibility."

"Not such a pleasant one," she replied.

"But I find great reassurance in the fact we all have two fusion generators in our chest cavities. If we drop the shielding around the plasma cores, we won't have to worry about a goldarn thing ever again." I tried to sound convincing.

"Suicide? *That's* your fallback plan?" she accused, more than stated.

"It'll be on a case-by-case basis. To each his or her own, I always say."

"Let's end this macabre discussion, please. I find it disquieting in the extreme. If I don't come up with this *neutral* matter, your moral debate doesn't *matter*," chastised Toño.

"True," Sapale responded. "So, you need any special place or supplies to pull off a miracle, Toño?"

"Yes, I require access to Cragforel and his research lab. I also need an aspirin."

"Okay, Doc, we'll call that Plan *A*. Any updates on a Plan *B* yet?" I was able to ask with a straight face.

"Yes. Plan B begins with you two leaving me alone immediately. Beyond that I'll have to get back to you." He stuck out his tongue. Never seen him do that before. Maybe he was serious? Maybe I was just rubbing off on him, the lucky dog?

"There's a restaurant/club not too far from here. Let's all go there. Doc, you can work in one of the side rooms reserved for privacy," I said with a wink.

"I hope I can find one that isn't sticky this time."

"Let's make that our thought for the day," I concluded as we left.

While Doc eggheaded in a freshly cleaned room, Sapale and I ordered up a proper banquet. No way around it, free, limitless, and delectable food from any time or place was an upside to being an ancient god. For her part, Sapale had a vast assortment of Kaljaxian delicacies. Cubes of racdal fat, steamed grains from home, and, because there was no justice in Heaven, all seven forms of calrf, each more rank than the one before it.

What did I have? What was my dream meal? Here's a hint. You'll never guess. I had *five* Pronto Pups and *five* Cheese Rarebits. Never heard of them? Then you missed something truly superb. I had them as a kid when we visited San Francisco, back when there *was* a San Francisco. Pronto Pups were not corn dogs. They were what corn dogs aspired to be, but could never rise to the level of. And the rarebits were basically deep-fried batter-coated sticks of Velveeta cheese. A corn dog minus the dog, substitute American cheese. A ton of yum. Those ten representatives of culinary excellence were my if-I'm-going-to-die-tomorrow delights. That and too much mustard slathered on opposite sides of the Pups. Heaven on a stick, I tell you. Heaven on a stick.

After we ate, we told Toño we were going out for some air. I wanted to take a good look at the vortex again. Not that I had any notion of affecting it. I just wanted to study my enemy. Maybe inspiration would strike. It was far enough away that we hailed a cab, something my wife was never excited about. Her species was a bit more concrete-minded than ours. Weird-ass forms of transportation were outside her comfort zone.

What did her reluctant acceptance yield? Our ride was a woolly mammoth that spoke a dialect of *Prüm*, a language used on parts of Alpha-Lyra 7. Sure, it was totally reasonable. The planet orbited a star twenty-five light-years from the nearest of those long-extinct pachyderms in a different universe. The long and short of it? Color Sapale unhappy.

As we approached the vortex, we headed for the spot Vorc had occupied earlier at the egress ceremony. Though the crowd was much decreased since that aborted attempt, there were still a goodly number of folks wandering about. Some appeared to be spectators like us, while others seemed to be in some manner attempting to fix the infernal manifestation. The ones who were laboring were mostly humanoid and were all dressed in dark formal-looking robes, like a monk or Druid priest. They bowed and doted at the swirling mass and I definitely heard chanting. *I* had no idea if *they* had any idea if their interventions had any hope for success. I elected not to inquire.

Without realizing it, Sapale and I were holding hands, standing there as close to the vortex as it seemed safe. The vortex didn't give off the vibe of, say, a weather pattern, like a tornado. But I sensed malevolence from it, hunger, and corruption. If I stopped breathing and listened very hard I could swear I heard voices. Some called out in horror while others seemed to be speaking, but the words and the languages were unidentifiable. There was nothing resembling an attempt at friendly communication. Whatever the vortex was, no matter how big it was, it was definitely associated with the dark side. If it had been functional, I know it would have reached out and pulled us both in.

"Jon, let's go. This thing creeps me out big time."

"Me, too. Just a sec. I want to try getting a clearer picture of its nature."

"No."

"Huh?"

"That's the last line a crazy person says before he does something stupid, like try to attach probe fibers to it."

"Didn't you mean to say, *before he or* she *does something stupid?*"

"No, because I was referring only to you."

"That's crazy talk, hon. I'd never do something stupid." The second I finished I shot my probe fibers into the center of the maelstrom.

"No, Jo—" She didn't even get a chance to finish her cry.

The fibers bounced lazily, churning around the vortex's center. With my free hand I gestured to the non-event and grinned at Sapale.

With zero warning the fibers snapped taut. I was pulled roughly toward the center. Try as I might I couldn't slow my advance. Sapale wrapped her arms around my waist and pulled. That barely slowed me down. I felt like I'd hooked a twenty-meter white shark on light tackle. I was jerked and tossed forward.

"Can you jettison your probes?" Sapale screamed into my ear.

"No idea. It's never come up," I shouted back.

"Do it," she yelled.

I closed my eyes and focused. *Release me*, I said to the probes.

The answer back was not what I anticipated. Not in infinity. "Nooooo, Jonnnn Rrrryannnn."

"What?" I screamed straight ahead.

"No onnnnnne mayyyyy injurrrrre meeemee ananand liiive." The voice was clear but did not seem to be spoken by vocal cords. Speech was foreign to it.

To my hand I thought, *Release the origins of the probes.*

And they slipped free. Sapale and I fell backward, tumbling like we were in a Keystone Cops skit. We came to rest on our sides, staring up at the vortex. It seemed much more energetic than it had been just before I tried to sample it.

"It figures," quipped Sapale.

"What?" I defended.

"You're so annoying you can piss off the weather."

"Let's get back to Toño."

"*Now* sensible words exit your mouth," she replied, as she fell in behind my rapid pace.

"Please don't demand results," leaped from Toño's lips before I was fully through the doorway.

"No, his tail's between his legs," said Sapale, pointing. "See?"

He looked up from his tablet and inspected me as he moved toward us. "He looks none the worse for wear."

Ask him to show you his probe fibers," she snarked.

"Show me your probe fibers," he parroted.

"Sure. No prob actually. You'll just have to come with me to the vortex and hope it hasn't finished slurping them up yet."

"Somehow I think I'm not going to enjoy the rest of this tale," he responded, setting down his tablet.

"You'll love it, Doc, because you're a man of science. I've just pushed back the darkness of prior ignorance."

"At the cost of your fibers?"

"We all carry spares," I responded with a weak grin.

"Yes we do. Why don't you take a seat here and let me begin replacing your fibers, while you tell my why I'm needing to do so."

I sat, extended my hand, and he opened up my wrist compartment. "Hmm."

"'Sat a good *hmm* or a *hmm hmm?*"

"It's a hmm, you idiot. Be quiet while I test the remaining system." He attached his fibers and I felt some tingling.

Idiot seemed pretty harsh. I let it pass, because we were such old friends.

"They were released cleanly. There is a mechanism for that to occur, but up until now I've never come across an occasion where the fibers needed to be ejected."

"Oh, my goodness," moaned Sapale.

"What?" Toño and I snapped in concert.

"This is going to be so good. Wait, wait. Let me pull up a chair." And she did just that.

"Jon, why did you need to release your command prerogatives?"

"I can answer that."

"Encouraging," replied Toño in a measured tone.

"I was unable to free the ends so I had to jettison them."

"Interesting on two levels. First, the obvious question. Did you know you could eject the fibers?"

I chuckled unconvincingly. "I do now."

"The answer to question one is *no*," helped Sapale.

"What were they attached to that wouldn't release them?"

"I bet you're going to tell me that's impossible, right?" I tried to sound upbeat.

"If you'd asked me five minutes ago, I'd have staked my life it was."

"Well, then, you're welcome for the continuing education I have been—"

"What wouldn't release the fibers, Jon?" His voice was definitely louder.

"You know that vortex, the one the ancients are trying to use to leave?"

"Is there another vortex I know of that I'm forgetting about?"

"Well, see, only you could tell me that. I'm not inside your—"

"It's the one and only vortex currently in our lives, Toño," further helped my wife.

"I'm hoping the next thing you're about to say is that you were walking toward the vortex, tripped, and accidentally fired your probes into the vortex."

I shook a finger at him emphatically. "That is *exactly* what happened, Sapale as my witness."

"Is that true, Sapale?"

"Yes. I witnessed this knucklehead shoot his probes into the vortex."

"On accident?"

"Yes. The *accident* being how stupid he is."

"As I suspected."

"But you can replace them?" I pressed.

"Yes. Once. But you only carry one spare of those."

He reached to release a storage compartment under my left arm. Daintily he removed a small packet and closed me back up. He took the fibers out and confirmed they were working well with his own probes.

"Excellent," he said to himself. "This won't take long."

"Thanks."

"So you'd better speak quickly, telling me what happened." He looked up sternly at me. "Recall, please, that I'm quite busy."

"Well, I decided to probe the vortex."

He stopped and reflected on those words. "Not *completely* moronic."

"Thanks. I knew you'd support my inquiry."

"What happened?"

"At first the cords bounced around limp. Then it was like a marlin hit the bait and dived deep."

"I held on to him but couldn't really slow him down," added Sapale.

"I wonder why the vortex cared to force you into it when it's barely functional?" he wondered out loud.

"Ah, interesting story, that one," I replied rather sheepishly.

"With you it always is," Toño responded tersely.

"It doesn't like him," peppered in Sapale.

"A swirling vortex of neutral doesn't *like* you?" Toño either asked or stated. Not sure which it was, but either way he was incredulous.

"It's not my fault," I defended.

"No, it never is," scorned Toño.

"Seriously, Doc, the pinwheel has attitude. Personally, I think it harbors deep emotional scars, but I'm merely speculating in that regard."

"Toño, I hold you responsible for what my brood-mate just said. You allowed him to have oatmeal for brains when you created him."

"I shall go to confession at my first opportunity and try to make amends."

"Boy, you two are real hoots," I observed. "I nearly get swallowed by a lunatic cloud and you're all laughs and giggles."

"What gave you the impression it disliked you?" asked Toño.

"When it wouldn't let go, I said *release.* I was speaking to my probes, but the vortex addressed me by name and said, *No one may injure me and live.*"

"Can you confirm that, my dear?" Toño asked of Sapale.

"No. I wasn't privy to the conversation."

"It said it real creepy, too. Lots of hisses and mispronunciations. Sloppy grammar, if you ask me."

"Thank you for the details. They do not help at all," responded Toño with a sigh.

"What's the sigh for?" I pointed to myself with both hands. "Almost killed here."

"Don't you see how this confounds our already tenuous position?"

"I don't know. I thought we were running pretty close to zero as it was. Hard to imagine our fortunes have any downward mobility."

"Jon, if we were to ever wish to leave this wretched land, how were we to do that?"

"I think the only way out is the only way—" I angled my head. "Oh, my."

"Oh, my, indeed," he responded smugly.

"Maybe if I hid between you two it wouldn't know it was me sneaking through?"

"Certainly. It's possible the immensely powerful sentient-immortal force is prone to slipshod screening," replied Toño.

"Not too likely, is it?"

"Well, I say it simplifies our situation considerably," proclaimed Sapale.

"This ought to be good," I mumbled.

"If the damn vortex would eat you instead of letting you pass, you can't leave. If you can't leave, I'm sure as hell staying. Toño, too." She pointed to him. "So we don't need to worry about an exit strategy any longer." She crossed her arms.

"Interesting observation, my dear. It certainly does—"

"No way. If there's a chance for you two to get home and warn people, to pass along all that we know, you gotta do it. Period."

They both looked at me blankly.

"I'm serious. I'll stay behind and continue the good fight as long as I'm able. But the universe needs every break it can get. That means you two *must* return, if you get a chance." I tried to sound inspirational.

"Okay," said Toño dismissively, "I have a lot to do and little time to do it. Let me know if Jon pisses off any *other* forces of nature."

"Will do. I'll be at the bar attempting to set a record if you need me," replied Sapale as she turned to leave.

I stood there staring at the top of Toño's head, his attention having returned to his analysis.

"I'll be in—"

I was freed of the necessity of letting Toño know where I'd be by his waving of the back of his hand in my direction.

EIGHT

Walpracta skimmed across the forest floor. She had been on this new planet for several days. She'd learned its name was Selemmi. The majority of the sentients on Selemmi were humanoids that called themselves the Anco Chatta. The children of god. She couldn't help giggling once again at the irony. They may have *thought* of themselves as the children of some god. But it was tremendously clear already that no god thought of *them* as *his* children. No parent would have allowed Walpracta to do one percent of what she had if he, she, or it was paying the slightest attention.

When she marched a million of them into the sea and they drowned, no god saved them. When she tossed a million of them into a boiling volcano, no god came to their defense. And when she managed to force half a million to eat half a million of their kin alive, no god interceded. Perdition's sake, she giggled, when she consumed the remaining half million, what god would stand still and allow it to pass? Sure, a Cleinoid would, but presumably the Anco Chatta weren't dumb enough to worship one of those. Talk about having a self-destructive death wish.

The weather was pleasant and time abounded. There were swarms of inhabitants of Selemmi to torment, brutalize, and kill. Life was good. She could not help herself. She giggled once again. Then she smelled smoke. It wasn't from a city she'd torched. There were no oily or plasticky elements to the smoke. And there were no traces of charred flesh either. No, this was a cooking fire. She snorted a giggle. Hello. Some fool didn't notice the death and devastation, the rolling path of desolation across the face of this dying world? She rested a pincer on the top of a leg.

Out loud she mocked, "Golly gee. The devil herself is ruining my planet. I think I'll just stop and have me a nice barbecue. No way the destroyer will see or smell the smoke, or possibly see the fire."

She decided she'd be doing this individual a favor relieving it of the burden of its stupidity when she swallowed it whole. She sniffed the air and moved toward the scent. Walpracta slithered into a clearing five minutes later. There on the opposite side she spied the back of a solitary figure. How was it possible to be so impervious to detail as not to notice her approach? It wasn't like she was sneaking up on the damn fool. Ah well, what started off as fun was likely to end in a snoozer of a kill. She rushed the figure. She reared back, lifting the front half of her body into the air to strike. Her fangs deployed upward and outward, venom beginning to ooze from the tips. She squealed and hurled her bulk at her unsuspecting victim. She smashed into the ground so hard her mandibular claws buried themselves a meter in the dirt. She rose up and shook the figure in the ...

"You missing something there, sweetheart?" said the man.

Walpracta rested her front end gently to the forest floor. She stared at the man; the man not in her jaws, but in one piece leaning against a tree. She rotated a few eye stalks to study her oral opening. Nope, no victim present.

"You can't very well shake the life out of me if you don't hold me mercilessly in your so, so ridiculous jaws."

Walpracta closed her oral opening and reflected. Though the man was technically correct, she couldn't avoid thinking he was mocking her. To be fair, she was uncertain, having never once been mocked in her immortal life.

"Did you move to avoid my consumption of you, man?"

"Me, move?" He giggled. "No, cupcake, you just missed by a country mile, because you're a klutz."

"I could not have missed by ... by one of those. I never miss."

"Maybe your hideous eye stalks need glasses. Come to mention it, snowflake, you are beyond any and all doubt *the* ugliest, *the* most revolting, and the foulest smelling creature I've ever had the bad luck to witness. For the time being, you'll have to trust me, that's saying a lot."

While she wasn't sure he'd mocked her, she was now certain he'd insulted her. Her reaction was to become more angry than she'd have thought possible. My but that felt good. "Silly man, you mock and insult me. Do you know who I am?"

"A big talking lobster that's longer than it has any right to be?"

She screeched loudly, then spoke. "I am Walpracta, god of consumption. I eat anything and everything and I'm never full and never have to stop."

"Well, that settles it. If you and I go on a first date, it'll be to an all-you-can-eat buffet."

She screeched even louder, ever more passionately.

"I'll take that to mean you'll get back to me on the date thing." He grinned.

"I shall ingest you, shit you out, and eat you again a thousand times."

"Does your kind possess the notion of TMI?"

Her response was to vault into the air, careening down toward the man with hell-bent fury and rage. The tree he leaned against splintered and debris flew in all directions. She turned side to side but could not see the man. She felt her oral opening. He was not there either. Walpracta turned in a full circle. He was gone. Then she felt a sharp impact on either side of her head. She craned her eye stalks back on herself. There atop her scaly head sat the man. His heels clicked her shell.

"Giddy up, horse. I'd best be getting home. Alicia will think I've got a girlfriend."

She was paralyzed with disbelief. It was not possible for him to be riding her. No one could be that skilled and at the same time be so suicidal.

"Honey, you're failing to initiate the giddy-up portion of tonight's entertainment," the man chided.

She hunched her back with all the force she could, and the man flew forward. He rolled to a stop and quickly turned to face her.

"Well that's a piss-poor attitude, if you ask me," he said, looking at himself as he dusted off.

"I shall—"

He raised a hand and without even looking up created a glowing ribbon of force around her multitudinous legs. She crumpled to the ground. Lying on her side panting, she looked at the man with a feeling she'd never experienced before. Disbelief. "What have you done to me?"

"I've bound your skinny-ass legs with unbreakable truth."

Her eye stalks blinked repeatedly. "Truth is relative. It cannot be unbreakable."

"Really," he said, scratching the back of his head. "Well, then, why don't you snap your fetters and stand?"

Walpracta focused and tried with all her might and all her will to break her bonds. Eventually she was forced to rest back in failure. "What you have done is a high sacrilege. It will be punished beyond punishment. I will know your name, man."

He rubbed idly at his chin.

"Speak and tell me your name, cur."

"Huh? Why? You said you will know it. I was just waiting until then. No pressure. I got plenty of time, sideways lobster."

"Do not add to your high sacrilege by further insulting me. I told you my name. Tell me yours."

"High sacrilege? Come on now, sweet cheeks, I'm only just now up to the level of petty sacrilege."

"Your name. I will—"

Ribbons of blinding light bound her oral opening shut. She could make sounds but she could no longer speak.

"Ah, peace and quiet returns to my world. You're kind of full of yourself, Betty Boop. You know that?" He cupped a hand to an ear and leaned toward her. "No comeback? Okay, if you're not going to play anymore, I'm outta here. Oh, FYI. The unbreakable truth lasts forever. So for the foreseeable future and infinity beyond, I'd suggest you start liking where you are and the angle you'll be viewing the world from." He giggled, turned, and walked out of the clearing. But he stopped and looked over his shoulder. "Say, you ancient gods don't happen to pillage and rape using a buddy system, do you?"

She writhed and grunted by way of response.

"Darn. That's darn unfortunate for you. Why, I'll bet you'll lie there looking ridiculous until this system's star goes nova in eight billion years, give or take. You really should have buddied up. It's just like scuba diving. Going solo is just too risky."

She howled in her throat even louder.

"Okay, all right. Sheesh, what a prissy bitch you turned out to be. The name's Ryan, Jon Ryan, and I'm *so* looking forward to not missing you."

Walpracta emitted one final muted scream, more passionate and longer than the last one.

"For goodness' sake *no*. I'm not *that* Jon Ryan. I'm the original. That biter, *he's* the duplicate."

Then the alternate timeline Jon Ryan slipped quietly into the woods.

CHAPTER THREE

I sat at the bar with Sapale for nearly a full day. We androids didn't have to worry about swollen legs or blood clots, so why not? We were waiting for Toño to pull off yet another miracle and had nothing better to do. I mostly nursed a few drinks and thought. A transportation vortex made of neutral matter hated my guts because I threw a machine that creates horrific hallucinations into it. What? Was it (I could only presume the damn thing was *gender* neutral as well as *matter* neutral) broken because I gave it bad dreams? What a crazy state of existence I lived in. Next thing I knew, the Easter Bunny would hop up to me and egg my face.

My mind, as it was prone to do, wandered. Maybe it was a boy vortex. I mean, it sure had a testosterone-y attitude. So that meant there were girl vortices out there somewhere. And because of the first comes love, then come marriage deal, there had to be cute little baby vortices learning to make their first gyration out in JustPlainNutsLand. If there was more than one vortex, then there inevitably would be conflict. Sure. If one swirl saw that another disturbance had a bobble it didn't, there'd be war. Bureaucrats? Yeah, why the hell not. If there was more than one transportation vortex, negotiations would be required. Who better than a middle-management vortex to make a flowchart in the direction of resol ...

"If I have to ask again I'm doing it with my fist." That would be my demure wife howling at me.

"What?" I said with a start.

"What what? I've been attempting to attract your attention for a little while here, flyboy."

"You want me to buy you a drink or something? Maybe I try and regale you with my wit so I get the chance to do the pushy-pushy with you later tonight? I think we're sort of past that stage, brood's-mate." That's when I noticed Toño standing alongside her. Dude was shaking his head slowly, as usual. "You have my attention. What?"

"I think I've made some progress on the neutral matter concept."

I blinked at him repeatedly.

"What, you large baby?" he snapped

"I don't need a *concept*. What I *need* is a bucket of the stuff to shove down that mean vortex's allegorical throat."

"Where I come from, Major Unreasonable, theory generally precedes fabrication. I tried the take-a-wild-guess-and-see approach once. Didn't work out so well, so I lean on intellect over gorilla force."

"Wow, that is *fascinating* and I treasure that you shared with us," I responded with cloyingly. I opened my arms. "Group hug."

"I'm thinking that ditching him here's sounding better and better," announced Sapale.

"Too much better. *Tempting*, I'd call it."

"Okay, team," I said seriously, "let's retire to my office and see what we got." I pointed to the farthest table.

Once we were settled Toño began. "Neutral matter is an *insane* concept," he said flatly.

"Okay, then we're done here, right?" I replied. "The vortex is not made of it. Who's hungry?"

It was *so* cute. First Toño, then Sapale crossed their arms and stared at me judgmentally. It was like they'd rehearsed it.

"Say, Doc, I hear neutral matter is a nutty notion. But I bet MacGyver-in-space could make some."

"Yes he could, if he had a hadron collider on the scale of the universe itself and micro-containment fields on a Planck scale."

"Nope, just gum, paper clips, one shoe string, and of course duct tape. Can't do no MacGyvering without the old DT. That's all Angus 'Mac' MacGyver ever had at his disposal."

"Might we return to the here and now, not the feeble-minded and chafing?"

I did not dignify that crass remark with a response.

"Are you familiar with *sea quarks*, Sapale?" he asked.

"No clue."

"They are highly unstable quark-antiquark pairs. Quantum mechanics holds that net-neutral virtual paired particles pop in and out of existence regularly. They form what is known as *vacuum energy*."

"Rings a bell very softly," she said, furrowing her brow.

"The details are unimportant. But there is only one way I could conceive of forming neutral matter. If I substituted one of these sea quarks for two of the three quarks known to form positrons and neutrons and their antiparticles, the resultant matter might actually be neutral."

"Doc," I interjected, "you just said a lot of big words, but they do not have meaning. You can't fill your pockets with instantaneously self-annihilating virtual particles for later use."

"Oh, I think I can. The issue is one of energy. The requirements would be truly fantastic."

"You have access to fantastic amounts of energy?"

"Not at this time, no."

"Then I return to the issue of who's hungry."

"Jon, what was inside those intermixers?"

"Best I could tell, nothing."

"And what effect did the intermixer have on the vortex?"

"It was displeased in the ... *Whoa*. You're not suggesting those boxes were full of neutral matter?"

"I most certainly am. Why *make* it when you can *steal* it?"

"So you think these bozos can fabricate something that requires a hadron collider on the scale of the universe and micro-containment fields on a Planck scale?"

"They don't call them *gods* for nothing, my love," responded Sapale.

"But, if that's true, and what Wul told me was common knowledge, wouldn't it be the case that the monuments at Beal's Point are currently guarded more tightly than Mother Superior Mary Kathryn's loins?"

"Yes, and I wish you'd stop abusing the institution of speech with your vulgarity."

"How many of those units, assuming they're all the same, would be needed to take out the vortex?" asked Sapale.

"I estimate twenty-five. Thirty to be on the safe side."

"Well, there's a lot more than thirty statues up there," she responded.

"One hundred thirty-seven well-guarded ones, to be specific," I added. "And once we open even one statue, all hell—and I mean that quite literally—will break loose on us."

"Precisely," replied Toño with a sneaky grin. "Which is why we're not going to steal the neutral matter one intermixer at a time."

"What, we're going to order them on Amazon.weirdassuniverse?" I snarked.

"That's preposterous. No, we're going to blow the units up all at once and steal the replacement shipment." Toño was positively radiant.

"We're going to rob the stagecoach?"

"We're going to rob the stagecoach," he returned.

"What the hell's a stagecoach, and why would any respectable ancient god ship *intermixers* on one?" Yeah, that was the culturally deprived alien asking that one.

"They wouldn't, hon," I replied, patting her shoulder. "I'd explain, but we need that time to start building bombs, lots of bombs."

She nodded quickly. "Bombs I get." She looked up to me. "I'm good at bombs."

CHAPTER FOUR

"I don't feel we're any closer to understanding what the devil's wrong with the vortex, or who sabotaged it." Vorc rubbed vigorously at his chin as he spoke.

"I was under the impression the prime suspect is this Ryanmax fellow," responded Dalfury. Though he possessed no throat, he produced the sound of one clearing. "In fact, Bethniak called strongly into question that he was even a Cleinoid god."

"Start giving weight to her impoverished intellect and you'll soon be mumbling incomprehensibly in the corner. She may be powerful, but her strength stops at the top of her neck."

"Oh, I'd advise caution even thinking that. If she learned of that insult, I'm afraid there'd not be enough of you left for a proper burial."

Vorc bristled. "I can hold my own with any god." He tapped a finger to his temple. "Brains count for a lot, and I'm in a different league than the child-bitch."

"Shall we return to the subjects at hand, sire, lest the walls develop ears and I'm forced to find a real job?"

"You are correct as always, my friend." He paused briefly. "I'm thinking of consulting Gáwar."

If Dalfury had eyes they'd have rocketed wider. "Are you se ... serious, sire?"

"Why would I *not* be? This is a critical juncture in our existence. We must learn who is responsible, if for no other reason than to prevent that individual from striking again."

"Striking again is a possibility to be certain. But I am not certain what the criminal amongst us was attempting to do in the *first* place."

"He was trying to destroy the *vortex*," Vorc replied hotly. "Whoever it was knew the intermixers are powered by neutral matter. One plus one always equals two."

"I shall take your word on the mathematics. However, what occurred might have been an attempt to assassinate *you*."

Vorc's fists balled up and he trembled with rage. "Wouldn't it be nice to prevent *that* if it *were* the case?"

"Lord, calm yourself. Of course, it would be. To summon Gáwar to know who tried to destroy the vortex *might* be justifiable."

Before Dalfury could go on, Vorc finished his thought. "But to save my measly pelt, not so much, right?"

"You know how I hate to appear insensitive—"

"But we're talking Gáwar here. Yes, I get it." His foot tapped the floor at a rapid speed. "Very well. For now we will continue to interview eyewitnesses and pray for a break. But eventually I will favor summoning the irresistible force."

Dalfury cringed at the casual attitude his master displayed concerning the unleashing of the most negative force in all the universes over all of time. The last time Gáwar was awakened, darkness reigned for a hundred thousand years.

CHAPTER FIVE

Our first step was to gain some intel on the status of Beal's Point. But we had to be discrete. No one went there on vacation. If we looked too interested or lingered too long it would be suspicious. I elected to pull a repeat performance of my original trip there. We positioned ourselves along the road pilgrims would need to take. Then we waited for a reasonable-looking group to pass by. Reasonable specifically meant no mind-numbingly slow islands. Even if time wasn't so critical, my peace of mind was.

It took a couple of days. A collection of four individuals was coming in our direction at a respectable clip. Three total humanoids and one only slightly bizarre one. The closer that one came, the more I thought *walking cucumber*, but at least it walked fast. Rolled, I should say. Sure, cucumbers couldn't have legs-legs. No, they had tubular cucumber wheels. Come on, when in Rome and all.

As they approached I hailed them directly. "You wouldn't be heading to Beal's Point, would you?"

"Why wouldn't we?" snapped the cucumber. It's always the cucumbers that have attitude. Always.

"I meant to say, we're heading there. We stopped for a rest, but would enjoy some company." I made a show of wiping sweat from my brow. "The way the place makes you feel, the more company the better it is."

"Certainly," said the nearest non-vegetable, extending a hand. "I couldn't agree more. I'm Flaming."

No, I did not laugh and I did not snort. No guffaws either, I'm proud to report. "Ryanmax," I returned as I shook his hand.

Everyone else introduced themselves. The humanoids were Catalexa and Klioaw. The cucumber was Mosanosa. I didn't press them as to their godhoods. We'd find out in time, and it didn't really matter. Well, except for Mosanosa. I suspected he was god of the pickles you take off your burger and never eat because they have no place on an honest-to-goodness hamburger or the plate it's riding on. I was dying to ask/torment him about it. Oh yes, my time would come.

The journey to Beal's Point refreshingly took only twelve hours sans Hemnoplop. We arrived right at dusk. In what I'd learned to be the custom, our posse gathered at a permanent campsite and lit a big fire. Damn, I wished we had the makings for smores. Note to self: Next trip to Godville, bring marshmallows, chocolate, and grahams.

Even from a distance, I could tell the location had changed. What had to be guards were patrolling lazily. By the time we were up on the plateau itself, I could confirm there were several, but not excessive numbers of monstrous-looking guardians. I didn't recognize them, but deferred asking anyone directly, not wanting to appear as foreign as I truly was. Dudes were impressive, though. Ranging around three meters tall, they were built like the proverbial brick shithouse. They had to be at least four hundred pounds. They sported a pair of scaly arms in front *and* in back, each wielding a gigantic pike. I did *not* want to piss one of them off. I said that because, you know, I accidentally tended to do that a lot. Fortunately, they paid us no mind whatsoever.

A tray of meats and fruits was passed around, along with pitchers of water. No intoxicants were allowed on the Point. No one was going to binge-drink themselves out of a proper suffering.

I thumbed over my shoulder and spoke to no one in particular. "First time I've seen those jamokes up here."

Flaming shot a quick glance to Catalexa and Klioaw, then responded. "Er, this is the first time we've needed golems up here. You were at the egress, right?"

Wow, these were not the alluring naked golems I knew and almost loved.

"Front and center," replied Sapale. "Got a big old dose of bad memories, thank you very much."

"Me, too," Catalexa said with a wince. "I was back home with my insane parents for ten long seconds. I would have chewed my head off, if I could've."

We all gave a restrained chuckle. All but the cucumber. He looked at everyone and spat. "I saw a drought. A hot, dry drought and all the flowers dried up before they could produce seed, and there were no spring showers to soothe them. It was intense, and I'm not laughing."

"We can all see that," I had to observe. What a veggie baby.

"I just hope the vandals who stole the intermixer don't return while we're here. There's no telling what they'd do to us in our sleep," bemoaned Mosanosa, as he rolled repeatedly over my last nerve.

"What are the chances of that?" posed Sapale. "You guys are up here with desperados."

"Unimaginable," added Toño. "I'd calculate the odds but they're too low to even guesstimate."

"I bet those pansy-asses'd piss their pants if they saw those hunks a clay." I pointed to the nearest golem. "We're as safe as if we were in our mothers's arms."

Catalexa raised his hand. "Nearly fatal for me, so I think I'll pass."

He seemed to be all right. I was going to need to force myself not to befriend him. It's hard to kill a friend in cold blood. Best to keep it businesslike. Without Fool's Island to slow us down, our party completed the gauntlet that was Beal's Point the next afternoon. Thank the Maker. When we arrived at the main road, I made it a point to head in the opposite direction from our temporary companions. That way we could get right to planning our assault and not waste time playacting.

"How are we going to deal with those mean guards the size of small whales?" asked Toño when we stopped.

"They're easy. Golems are as dumb as dirt, literally. They can perform the simple actions they are instructed to. They can't think independently," I responded.

"So, how's that make them easy?" asked Sapale.

"A distraction. No way they were programmed to react correctly to one of those."

She nodded in agreement. "Still, taking out all those monuments would require they be pretty distracted pretty far away."

"Nah. We only need to take out thirty monuments. Let's not get greedy," I replied.

"Yes, Jon, you're correct. It shouldn't be hard to trick them into converging somewhere on one side of the Point. Blowing up the pedestals won't take long. A simple ram with a membrane and they'll crumble to dust."

"Releasing a world of hurt, I must add," said Sapale.

"Oh, I should think we needn't be that close. If one of us does the distracting the other two only have to destroy fifteen each. That could be done from half a kilometer, more if the angles happen to be correct."

"So what's the distraction?" asked my mate.

You have to know they both turned and looked at me.

"What? *I'm* the one with his ass in harm's way?"

"Would you feel better if we put it to a vote?" Sapale inquired with a gallows' grin.

"Why bother," I said by way of concession. "You guys'd cheat if we did."

She leaned over and pinched my cheek. "Of course, we would, love. Of *course*, we would."

"So let's do this," I announced.

We made our way back to Beal's Point in the pitch black. One strategic advantage of a night assault was that we had great night vision, and lumps of clay had to have been blind as bats. I angled to the far left while my partners headed right. We agreed to attack in fifteen minutes. That gave everyone time to take up optimal positions. I skirted the steep slope that rose to my left and found a good spot. I was almost a kilometer from the nearest monument, and I had two options for retreat. Once the fishies took the bait, I'd be able to disappear quickly.

At the appointed time I sprang the trap. Of the many choices at my disposal, I picked the one the golems would be completely caught off guard by. Yeah, I started playing extremely loud disco music. I used my laser finger to generate a pretty fair image of a disco ball to boot. My selection of tunes was nothing short of brilliant. "I Will Survive" by Gloria Gaynor, followed by "Stayin' Alive" à la Bee Gees, and concluding, if necessary, with the Jon Ryan national anthem, "Love Machine" starring Supermax.

About ten seconds into Gloria's classic, a voice screamed in my head. *What in the name of all that's holy are you doing?* That would be Toño the Stick in the Mud.

At eleven seconds came, *You've pulled some real boners, Ryan, but this is numero uno of all time, you moron.* That would be my blessed wife.

Do either of you see a golem?

Silence.

No, because they're all lumbering as best they can to join the party. I think I'll hit 'em with a big cover charge. They'd pay anything to dance with me, dance with me.

I actually had to cut it short. Near as I could figure all the golems were past the last statue and churning their chubby legs at yours truly. Dagnabit. I didn't even get to cue my theme song. Oh, those bozos were going to pay for that.

As I started to run, one of those pikes thudded to the ground right where the foot I moved had been. I increased my respect-quotient for the guards. They were good. I was in deep doo-doo. I turned on the afterburners. Fortunately they were lousy at vectors

—go figure. As I was a moving target, they never came close. I started my descent from Beal's Point and heard two series of kabooms. Excellent. The deed was done.

These guards are deadly accurate if you're standing still. Make haste, my friends. Be the wind, I said to them.

Thanks, I think I see you now, responded Sapale.

I'm behind Sapale, said Doc. *I'll catch up at ...*

At where, Toño? screamed Sapale.

Oh bother, he replied. *I seem to be pinned against the cliff.*

Pinned? I shot back. *Pinned by what?*

One very large spear.

Crapazoid.

CHAPTER SIX

Bram-fo pressed his body hard against the front of his foxhole. The soil was wet and cold and filthy with the carnage heaped all around its rim, but Bram-fo powered himself as close to it as he could. What approached was so horrific, he only wished he could meld with the dirt presently and not have to await his impending death to be buried.

A soldier thudded to the bottom of the hole behind him. Bram-fo didn't or couldn't turn to see if it was someone who'd leaped in or had been tossed mangled into his safehold. It mattered zero either way. To glance around would distance him from the front lip and its temporary cover. He heard a stirring behind.

"Bram, that you?" asked a beaten voice.

"Not for long." Bram-fo's words were muffled as his lips were so close to the wall.

"I share your lack of confidence, my old friend," said the person rising and advancing to Bram-fo's location.

Without looking back Bram-fo responded. "Srel-do, could you not let me die in peace?"

"I could not let you die *alone*, you oaf. *Eternal* peace will be yours soon enough. But to die alone, *that* is beneath your dignity."

"Beneath my dignity? Srel-do, if I could save my hide by handing you, your mother, and all your kids to those monsters, I'd do it. I have no honor any longer."

Srel-do was close enough and slapped his commander on the back. "You have lived well and will die well. I wish the same could be said—"

A blinding flash and chaotic explosive impact shook the pair. Clods tumbled from the hole they were in. Several clumps rolled in Bram-fo's face. A few came to rest on top of his head. He didn't bother to shake them off. They didn't matter.

"Any word on G Company?" asked Rank Captain of the King's Foot Bram-fo Halorisian. It was one of ten under his command, and the last left standing, as of an hour ago.

"No, skip, I ain't seen a sign of 'em. They were in an advance position near Chaplain Hill when I ran past. But that was fifteen minutes ago. No telling now," replied Second Captain Serl-do Klemperer. He was in charge of Easy Company while it still existed. But he was the sole survivor as of about an hour ago.

"Lookin' pretty grim, old friend."

"Terminally grim, I'd estimate."

Serl heaved himself over the edge of the hole and fired off eight quick rounds. His clip pinged out as he was diving back to cover.

"D'ya hit anything?" asked Bram-fo with a dark chuckle.

"Had to hit *something*, right?"

"True that. Might have put a tree trunk through living hell."

"In the king's service. Don't forget that part."

"Yeah, but who's the king? The one you and I've served for thirty years was chewed in half on day one of the invasion. Soon thereafter, the next ten or twelve in the succession were subjected to a similarly gruesome fate."

"Hey, maybe it's you that's the king now. Didn't you once tell me your great great something was a bastard of a long dead member of the royal order?"

"Technically true, but the practicality is hard to invoke. If the fifth cousin ten times removed of the Archduke Merryla-to is the current regent, I'd say the Kasholari Empire is pretty much history."

"Much like the citizenry of the Five Known Worlds Coalition."

Bram-fo, who was still pressing himself against the foxhole wall, replied, "That Giaia was the last planet to fall gives me some small pride."

Serl-do harrumphed grimly. "If it had outlasted them by more than a few hours it'd have been even sweeter." He grabbed Bram-fo's shoulder and firmly pulled him away from the dirt.

Bram-fo roughly shook the hand off and pitched himself back to where he'd been.

"I don't think your *not* seeing them's gonna slow them down in annihilating you, skip."

"If it doesn't matter, then I'll stay put, assuming it's agreeable to you."

"Makes me no mind. I'd rather die shooting than trembling in the mud. But to each his own, to be sure."

In any other setting, at any other time, Bram-fo would have killed a man for accusing him of trembling, even if it were the case. Of course, it never had been before. But now he let the blood-insult bounce off his back and dissipate. In thirty years of serving the king, Bram-fo had fought with abandon and bravery and he had never once been afraid. What had he to fear? He was a strong warrior, serving a just ruler, and he had as picture perfect a family as any of God's creatures. But now, now was different. His family was dead. His king was dead. He had lost an arm and could feel the first kiss of a fever brewing from his festering stump.

And he knew fear because he'd seen the enemy and he'd seen them in battle. Bram-fo had seen their atrocities, their destruction, and he'd seen their complete lack of morals. Worst of all he knew fear, in fact he was consumed by it, because he'd seen their faces. The ten identical creatures, the monsters who were ingesting, defiling, and ending his world, were the grossest malfeasances of all. They were the mockery fated to end the Five Known Worlds

Coalition. Yes, Bram-fo would die with his face pressed against that wet dirt wall because he never wanted to see those ten little golden retriever puppies again.

CHAPTER SEVEN

If any of those golems gets a good look at one of us we're toast, I said quickly. *Even if we take them out immediately, they might be linked to headquarters or something.*

I agree, replied Toño, *but I haven't been able to budge this pike. If they get to me before I'm free there's basically nothing I can do.*

Sapale, you get back to Toño. I'll try and distract them again, hopefully draw them off.

Roger that. I'm already sprinting back.

If I try to draw them toward my present position it might cut off our escape route. I'll put up a couple full membranes and go for the far side of the plateau.

Membranes, marveled Sapale. *They could help if the big lumps of clay get within visual range. We could seal them in one.*

Excellent idea. Doc, if they show up near you, you're in charge of that while Sapale works to free you.

Understood.

The path to the cliff edge was straight and I made good time. I could see all the golems. Many were headed toward Toño, seemingly aware he was hit. The rest were running around randomly. None were near me. I wished I had a few flares to draw them off with. I hated missions where I was unable to prepare properly. But what the hell? Improvise, adapt, overcome was the way I rode. As I skidded to a stop at the cliff, I dropped my shields. I targeted the closest golems closing in on Toño's position with my laser finger. I swear I must have looked like Harry Potter up there that night. I pointed at the bad guys and fire flared from my hand toward them.

I focused on their legs. I probably couldn't kill them, but no legs meant they were down where they fell. I made short work of most of the guards. The ones in the lead began to notice their fallen comrades and searched for the source of the damage. They IDed me quick enough. Soon all the golems were lumbering as fast as they could toward me. I kept firing and held my position.

How's it coming? I asked.

I just got here. Not good. Toño's pinned right through the right upper chest. His right arm is useless.

Can you free him?

Yeah, hang on. Toño, push away from the rock as hard as you can. There, I cut the pole with my laser. Should I pull the spear out?

Let me, replied Toño. *There. Aside from my right arm all systems are fine.*

Okay, make like hell for the exit and I'll rendezvous with you there.

I deployed two flat membranes and raced to join them. The Golem did notice I'd departed and kept closing in on my last position. I slammed on the brakes. If I could take them all out we'd be safer. One by one they arrived at the cliff edge and searched the area. They all looked over the edge, too. Finally twelve big guards were basically standing at the margin, looking confused. I put up a membrane and pushed them all off the cliff. It was a long way down by any creature's standards. The less Vorc knew about what happened up here, the better.

We made it to Gorpedder's abandoned house before dawn. That was another lucky break. If anyone saw the injury Toño sustained, they'd pretty quickly figure out where he received it. A blown cover in the land of the Cleinoids would be fatal. Sapale and I labored nearly eighteen hours to patch Toño back up. With only our internal repair kits and spare parts to work with, it was tough going. But in the end we even had his shirt sewn up and he looked good as new.

I slumped back against a wall. "That's that. What a night."

"What a night?" responded Toño. "*I* was the one impaled by the spear. You just had to make me right again."

"Sure *felt* like it was me," I sighed.

"Such a drama wuss," responded Sapale.

"*Ouch,* husband responds when attacked by his forever wife."

"Shoe fits, put it on, fly boy."

"All right, both of you go to your rooms," said Papa De Jesus.

"You suggesting we're acting childish again?" I asked.

"Put on the shoe," he replied sternly.

"Why can't *anyone* get the idioms correct around here? It's pathetic. Really it is."

"If the shoe fits, wear it," came from behind me.

I spun. Holy hemorrhoids, it was the irregular ghost. "You again, King Hamlet?"

"I wish I knew why you keep saying that and why you make it sound like such a betrayal on my part," he replied.

Wow, what a vocabulary he'd developed in such a short time. What a form, too. He looked like a set of cigars last time. Now, I couldn't say for certain, he looked like maybe articulated cigars. Yeah, one big central one and three or four, might have been five smaller cigars. The ghost of Philip Morris?

"I say it because you come and go like a goldfish's attention span. I say it harshly because we need all the help we can get *continually,* not when the spirit moves you."

"But I've never left your side since the moment we met. We've been together forever."

"Forever? Not hardly. You mean since I arrived a few months back?"

"What's the difference?"

"Between a month and forever? Not much when we're talking about you. You're *that* tedious."

"Ah, Jon, do you think it's wise to antagonize him so directly?" asked Toño diplomatically. "We *do* benefit from his aid."

"Yeah, I know. Sorry, Casper. I'm under a lot of pressure."

"I did say just a few minutes ago you appeared stress ridden."

"No you did not. You said that the day I got here. That was a month ago, I think, maybe. Could be longer."

"I think you're right," Sapale agreed with the ghost. "Pretty stress ridden. Babbling like a fool."

I held out palms in both directions. "I am fine. Thank you for your touching and united concerns. Now collectively get off my back."

"Is there something I can do to help?" asked the ghost.

"I will focus on the positive and say for the moment *no*."

"Do you mean to say you are happy with your assaults on Dominion Splitter and Beal's Point?"

"What's Dominion Splitter?" asked Toño.

"The transfolding vortex."

"The spinning cloud has a *name*?" asked Sapale.

"Why wouldn't it? It lives, it thinks, it consumes. Why wouldn't it have a name?"

"It sure as hell holds grudges," I observed.

"Yes, DS really hates you, Jon Ryan."

"Oh, he's DS to you? You two buddies?"

"Hardly friends. But we've been mutually ignored for so long that we ... we ... we talk now and then."

"Why does my life continue to get crazier and crazier?" I mumbled to myself.

"Sorry, Jon, DS is a transfolding vortex, not an oracle. He cannot answer that question."

"But the oracle can?" I replied with a weak giggle.

"*An* oracle, yes. Well, most. Some are more reliable than others."

"That's been my experience, too," I said with a louder, silly giggle.

I raised a finger to Heaven. "I really hate the sports oracles. Never bet on what they'll try and sell you."

"Not all. A few are competent. They're naturally quite busy and hard to access, but, no, there are proven prognosticators out there."

"My worldview just grew brighter."

"You are welcome then."

"I think he was being sarcastic," said Sapale.

"Either way, I thank him."

"Why is that, sir?" asked Toño.

"If he was being genuine, then I'm glad to have helped. If he was deriding me for no other reason than to prop up his childish ego, then I'm thankful anyway. Even the mindless heckling of the immature beats the hell out of being ignored."

"Good one, cloud boy," chuckled my supposedly loving wife.

"If we're through with the bash-Jon portion of tonight's program, I have a question. Assuming quite safely that I am correct and you come and go most annoyingly, why are you here now?"

"I ... I missed you."

Was that a question or a statement?

"By the dirty soles of Davdiad's feet, I think he just made a funny at your expense, brood-mate."

"Okay, you're hilarious, ghost of Don Rickles. Seriously, to what do we owe little for the joy that your presence is?"

"I ... I like you."

"Not funny twice-baked, pal. You can't use the same joke sequentially."

"I was speaking to Sapale."

Toño and she snickered something awful.

"Jon, his humor is as lame and painful as yours," marveled Toño.

"I thought we were going to avoid insulting our new friend, Toño," responded Sapale.

"True. My apologies."

"None needed among friends," replied the spirit.

"Can I leave now, return when you're done massaging one another?" I asked rather pointedly.

"Please stay, Jon," replied the ghost. "I have news you must hear."

"Say what? You're our spy now?"

"*Spy*," he said, seeming to taste the word as he spoke it. "Spy?" he questioned. "Yes, I think so."

"Nice. One prob, pal," I said. "You're technically one of our sworn enemies. It's not wise to trust a dubious ally."

"I am?" he really sounded surprised. "I was not aware of that state of existence."

"Let's review the facts as we know them," I began. "One, you live here. Two, the Cleinoids live here. End of discussion."

"What if he's their prisoner?" interjected Sapale.

"Yes ... what if I'm here against my ... my will?" responded my nebulous nutcase.

"Excellent point. Ghost, *are* you being held captive here?"

"I have no idea."

"That doesn't really lessen my inclination to not trust you," I replied.

"Jon, let's look at that question logically," said Doc.

"Okay, Spock, go."

"If he were one of them, he'd not admit he *didn't* know if he was captive. If he was *not* a prisoner and he wished to deceive us, he'd say he was one. If he was a captive, he could not be one of them and he'd tell us honestly. His uncertainty proves his credibility." Toño sure looked pleased with himself when he finished.

"No, not, you know, necessarily."

"Do tell," Toño replied dubiously.

"Maybe he's being coerced. Yeah, he's being *forced* to aid the enemy."

"A ghost?" asked my wife with incredulity.

"Why not?"

"So, maybe they're holding his ghost family as hostages and threaten to evaporate them if he fails on his mission to trick us to believe him so they can *fool* us into ... into what? They could just walk through that door and disrupt our atomic structures. Why all the Rube-Goldberg machinations of faulty thinking? Hmm?" pressed the love of my life.

"I am not certain at the present time."

"You can be such a big baby, General Ryan," snapped Toño. "We are in an existential crisis on multiple levels, yet you offer that mental diarrhea as a counterpoint to the obvious?"

"General?" muttered you-know-who.

"What now?" I snapped.

"No, I was remarking," said the ghost. "A general now? All four stars?"

"No, I'm not a four-star general *now*. I was two billion years ago when there was still an Earth." Honest to goodness, I wasn't sure why I was being so pissy.

"Mom must be proud," he said cryptically.

"I'm sure she would be if she wasn't so dead. I wish to return to the productive side of life, if it's all right with you, Mr. Ghost. What were you saying about your BFF DS and our raid on Beal's Point?"

"I was asking if you were satisfied with your results. Did you obtain your objectives?"

"And why would you be interested? Remember, I'm being directed to believe you are not a spy."

"If he were a spy, why would he ask about our collective sabotage?" asked Sapale. "If Vorc knew it for a fact, he'd sic that little girl on us and we'd join the ghost." She thumbed in his direction.

"She presents a valid point, Jon," agreed the ghost.

She did. I was being, well, *close* to unreasonable. Jon close to it. "How did you find out about our acts?" I asked.

"From being with you every moment, as I said." He then added an old familiar phrase. "Duh, air-dale."

"What the devil's an air-dale?" asked Sapale.

"It's a breed of extinct dog," replied Toño.

"Oh, yeah. Big muzzle and wiry fur," she said to herself. "Why are you a funny-looking dog?" she asked me.

"No, there's no *e*. It's a Navy term for a pilot."

Toño and Sapale turned and stared at the apparition.

"Please don't ask him how he knows that. He'll just say *I have no idea* and I'll be more stressed out."

"I do have no idea," the ghost remarked.

"Do ... don't say it. I asked you not to." Then, because I could smell it coming, I shouted, "No, I didn't *ask* you, I said I didn't want to *hear* you say it, which is pretty damn close."

"No. But I'll let it pass."

I balled my fists. I relaxed my fists. I rose to my tiptoes. I rested back on my heels. I counted to ten. I counted sheep. I counted how many times I'd blown up people for irritating me less than the ghostest with the mostest had. Finally I could not help myself. "No *what* and you'll let *what* pass?" I hated myself instantly for inquiring.

"Are you certain—"

"**No *what* and you'll let *what* pass**?" I basically shouted for all I was worth.

"*No*, you neither *asked* me not to say I didn't know, nor delineated that you did not wish to *hear* me say it. You said I'd just answer in the manner I did."

With my teeth tightly clenched, I followed up. "And what are you allowing to pass?"

"What just happened. You being held accountable and overreacting. I'm better than that."

"Better than that? Are not you the one who keeps parroting *I don't exist, I don't exist*? If ya don't exist, how can you be better than *anything*?" I placed my face in my palms and steadied myself for the response.

"You've convinced me I exist."

I peeked one eye between two fingers. "I convinced you? Me? I had an effect on your wiggly mind?"

"Yes. Thank you. I prefer believing I exist."

"You're welcome?" I said. "And you only prefer *believing* as opposed to—"

"Knowing. How can we know anything?" he queried.

"Is it okay if I don't answer that and we get back to our acts of sabotage?" I asked meekly.

"Your call."

"I call no philosophy."

"Fine by me. It's a bit nebulous to me anyway."

I started to say that *he* was nebulous, but I foresaw the lack of that being in any sense of the word a *positive* action. "So do you have any information for us as to how Vorc and his people reacted to our assault on Beal's Point?"

"No. I was with you and haven't separated to spy on him yet."

"You were with us?" I asked with incredulity. "After Sapale freed Toño, which direction did they flee in?"

"To the west."

They had.

"What was the second statue they blew up?"

"The second? The first was Honifero. Second was ... ah, Bef."

I angled my head at Sapale as if to ask, *That true?*

She nodded yes.

"Okay, you were with us."

"I know."

"Now we all know. Life's good. The answer to your question is yes, I'm happy with our attack. We suffered minimal damage and fully attained our objective."

"Which was the defacing of what is important to the Cleinoid leadership?"

"No, not even close. We wanted to get hold of a lot of the neutral matter in the intermixers."

"By blowing them up?" he asked with manifest confusion.

"No, silly. By blowing them up and stealing the replacement fixtures."

"What replacement units?"

"The ones they'll need to fabricate to repair the statues."

He was blessedly quiet a spell. "I see. Excellent plan on your part. I doubt they'll suspect your crafty trick."

"So do we. And if they do and we don't steal what we want, we'll be anonymous and try again some other way."

"I concur. So, what will you do with the intermixers?"

"We will kill your pal DS," I stated flatly.

That brought a longer silence. *Ah.*

"I think if you used twenty to thirty that might do the trick, based on what DS told me he felt like after you hit him with one."

"And that won't upset you? Us killing your friend?"

"No, you see, he's not my friend. He's someone I talk to occasionally. He *is* our sworn enemy."

"Oh, so now we're one big happy family unit?"

Brief silence. "We have always been, Jon."

"I know. Forever of a month because what's the diff?"

"What is the diff?"

I ... I kind of shrank internally and let that one pass.

"Jon and my other friends, I see a potential issue in your plan."

"Okay. Don't keep us in suspense."

"If you successfully destroy DS, you might well be stranded here forever. I believe it is the only natural mechanism to move into and out of this universe."

"We all understand that's a likely outcome. It's worth it to us to protect our universe. We're willing to be stranded here forever, if that's what it takes."

"Being stranded here alone forever isn't that bad," he mused.

"We're committed," said Toño softly.

Seemingly more to himself, he said, "I've been marooned here forever. Look at me. I'm doing okay."

"Ah, Mr. Ghost. Please don't set my brood-mate up so well for a one-liner. He's impossible enough as it is."

"You are likely correct, Sapale. Plus, you could always use your spacecraft to escape. Then you needn't face an eternity here with me."

If my lungs were functional, I'd have gasped so hard I'd have exploded them. "My *ship* is here?"

"Of course. What did you think you came in?"

"We scrambled some anti-matter and Tefnuf zapped us here. Right?"

"She can do that?" he asked.

90

"How should I know? My *ship* is here?"

"I don't know how you can know what is not true, and yes."

"My *ship* is here and you didn't tell me it was here?"

"You didn't ask."

"I'm betting that's true, husband."

"But you ... you had to know I'd want my ship."

"Of course. I guess. Maybe."

Why did that sound familiar? Maybe he heard me say it?

"So Tefnuf zapped my ship *and* its crew here?"

"I believe that's how the process works in a case such as yours."

"Where's my ship?"

"In the Lower Chambers. The room next to the Jell-O one you awoke in."

"And you didn't tell me?"

"You didn't ask," sang out Toño and Sapale in unison.

Als, are you there? I said in my head.

Yes, Pilot. Where else would we be?

And you didn't contact me? You were here the entire time I struggled—we struggled—and you didn't say a peep?

I do not believe we did. You didn't contact us.

I didn't know you were here.

Where else would we be?

But ... er ... you could have spoken up. Alerted me as to your presence.

I must admit, Form One, you are technically correct, chimed in *Stingray*.

Technically correct? I was surrounded by lunatics.

But I had my ride!

CHAPTER EIGHT

"Ah, master Vorc, might you have a moment?" asked Dalfury sheepishly, even for a demigod of cloudy memories.

"Do I have a moment?"

"I can come back. I *will* come back." As always, it was unclear if Dalfury actually turned, but he did begin to retreat.

"Dammit, Dalfury, you're in charge of my schedule. Who better to know if I have a moment? *I* don't actually know, because I depend on *you* to keep me informed on such matters."

The cloud continued to depart.

"Dalfury, I'm ordering you to stop."

He did, though he might have drifted a bit in the farther-away direction.

"I will ask you directly. Do I have a moment to speak to you?" Vorc was clearly upset.

"Well, in a sense, yes, you do."

"In a sense? I'm confused. Please rally to my aid. It would seem you, as keeper of my calendar, would know if I did or did not have a moment to speak to my right-hand aide. I either do or I do not. Am I off base here?"

"Yes. I mean no, you are not incorrect. There is no wiggle room in having free time or not. It is not a qualitative issue."

"Thank you."

"May I go now?"

"W ... I suppose so. But didn't you have something to discuss that brought you to me before you set about to confound me?"

"Oh, I wouldn't characterize it in that manner, in that light."

"You wouldn't characterize *what* in that light?"

"I wasn't here to discuss anything. And trust me on my life, I did not come here to confound you. No. Inform, yes. Update, possibly. Alert you, pot—"

"Dalfury, bear with me a moment, okay?"

"By your desire, sir."

"I am the center seat of the conclave."

"You are."

"I am given this," he held up a short, thick metal rod, "as part of my office."

"Yes, sir. The Fire of Justice is at your disposal."

"You, Dalfury, are a cloud."

"Er, I believe we can agree on that fact."

"Clouds do not do so well with fire, excessive heat of any sort."

Even not possessing a throat or digestive system, Dalfury gulped. "That is a fact."

"My last word here. If you do not immediately tell me what you came here to tell me, you will be steam or some alternate form of water soon, and very soon. Am I *unambiguously* clear on that, Dalfury?"

"Manifestly so, lord."

"One. Two. Thre—"

"Someone has destroyed multiple statues at Beal's Point will there be anything else, sir?" Dalfury resumed his exodus, only quicker.

"*Freeze.*"

"Sir?"

"I want you hovering right *there.*" Vorc stood and pointed to a spot on the floor right in front of his desk.

The cloud slowly repositioned itself where directed.

"As you asked so professionally, yes, there will be one tiny last item, if you don't mind?"

"It's funny you should frame it—"

"*Silence.*"

And there was quiet.

"What happened at Beal's Point?"

There was no response.

"Is there a problem with your auditory pathways, Dalfury?'

Nada.

Vorc hefted the Fire of Justice and directed it at the cloud's geometric center.

"But, sir, you ordered me to be silent," whined Dalfury.

"Technically, yes. I relieve you of that burden. What, I shall ask but once, happened?"

"I told you. Someone, well, I suppose someone or some set of individuals, blew the living daylights out of thirty monuments up on the point."

"Thirty monuments?"

"Yes, sir."

"Not, say, thirty-one?"

"Ah, no, sir."

"Couldn't have been, oh, twenty-nine?"

"No. I'm confident my information is correct. Thirty. Would you like their names or unit numbers?"

"No, I actually would not."

"Very well, sir. If there's—"

"Please do my sensibility and your longevity conjoined favors and do not finish that pathetic thought. Hmm?"

"Very well, Vorc."

"Do you know why it is I *doubt* that your report is accurate?"

"I haven't the faintest notion, sir."

"Oh, you don't. Well, fortunately, I do. You see, someone told me

94

they would see to the security of Beal's Point *personally*. Do you know who that party was?"

"I believe you might be referencing me, sir."

"Why, I do believe I am. And you know what else I'm recalling?"

"I shouldn't—"

"That I specifically asked you if you could *guarantee* that a handful of golems was the way to go in terms of lead-pipe certain, unbreakably tight security."

"I do recollect your thoughts in the regard, sir."

"What, and I'm just curious here, became of those ... ah, how many golems did you send up there?"

"Twelve, sir. We sent—"

Vorc stopped him with such a look.

"*I* sent twelve, sir."

"And," he waved a hand in the air, "curious here, nothing more. What ... what became of those dozen golems? Were they able to provide us with positive identifications on the perp or perps?"

"Interesting question, sir. We ... er, I and my team were initially most unclear as to their fate. It took the better part of a day to determine they all either stepped off the Cliff of Doom or were, you know, *induced* to do so, sir."

"The Cliff of Doom, you say? It's a long way down from there to jagged rocks and gashes in the unyielding ground, as I recall."

"You recall correctly, sir. Most observant of you."

"Thank you. Well, I'll bet of a dozen golems tossed over the edge, there wouldn't be two individual particles left in *contact* with each other after such an impact."

"On that point I cannot speculate. I can promise you that I will see to it that a *full* analysis is undertaken to establish if the scattered dust we located at the base of the Cliff of Doom contains any conjoined particles, sir."

"That won't be necessary."

"Are you certain, lord? I only live to serve you."

Vorc swirled a finger in the air. "And to confound, disappoint, and disobey me, Dalfury. Please don't leave those attributes off your list of qualities."

"As you wish, sire."

"I almost forgot that you also insult me by presupposing I'd react badly to bad news. Tsk-tsk, my old friend. Do you opine I'd be as petty as to shoot the messenger simply because he subjected me to all those shortcomings in the process of delivering to me said bad news?"

"Never, sir."

"Darn it all, Dalfury."

"What, lord?"

"On top of all the deficiencies, incompetencies, and absolutely unfounded opinions, you go and do it again."

"What, Vorc? What have I, er, assumed without the subject in question to actually be true?"

Vorc discharged the Fire of Justice into Dalfury. He swiped it back and forth, up and down, and in circles. He fired upon his former assistant significantly longer than required to, as has been said, *get 'er done.* In the end, there was no steam. There was no water. There most assuredly was no Dalfury either.

"You guessed wrong about me, you know, being so regressive as to shoot the messenger."

CHAPTER NINE

Almino Del Rey sat in hushed silence. He had not been so hurt by a string of words. Mere ethereal sound waves had penetrated his skin and rattled his soul. How was such a thing possible? And why would his beloved mother so condemn him? Here Almino was in the prime of his life. He was, he knew it to be true, a good man. Yet his sainted mother had just berated him as an evil, womanizing male whore. The vocabulary needed to express such a foul concept was not even at Griselda González de Del Rey's disposal.

"Mamá," he was finally able to say, "how can you accuse me of such bestiality? You know me to be a worthy son and a devout Christian."

"Do not invoke the name of the Lord God in your tawdry defense, sinner."

"On what do you base your accusations, mother of mine? Surely you have no evidence of any transgression on my part."

"*Diablito.* How *dare* you feign innocence. Your crimes are so lurid, so vile, yet so public, it defies belief that you could deny them."

"Mamá, I am certain you do not have the dementia. I live here with you and care for you each day. I have seen no sign of that cursed disease. So tell me please why you falsely mistake me for anything but a constant, prudent man."

"If I thought I could, I'd seize a knife and cut out that lying tongue. I'd burn it in holy flames to drive the devil out of it."

"Now you speak of cutting out my tongue. What insanity has befallen our home?"

"This is my home. Cancerous, malfeasant demons such as you have none. You wander the Earth sucking life and dignity out of all you encounter. Tell me you acknowledge this, you black spawn."

Almino stood. He trembled but he stood. "I must leave, if only for a little while. Perhaps when I return you can tell me what this is all about?"

"I *forbid* your return, you infernal wretch."

"Then so be it. Though as God is my witness, I have no sin. I have no idea of what you speak either. Live in the certain knowledge that I will love you forever. I shall pray the rosary for you daily."

"Don't you defile my reputation in Heaven by speaking my name to your master. He is the ruler only of evil and contempt. For as certainly as I sit here today, you are not fit to address my master."

Almino made it halfway to the door before a coffee cup bounced off his back and shattered on the floor. He stopped briefly, then continued. The saucer followed but missed to his left.

He turned just in time to catch a spoon thrown feebly in the direction of his head. "Enough, Mamá. I will know what it is you feel I did to deserve such disrespect and abuse. If you do not tell me I will not leave."

"Then I will summon the police."

"And I will tell them my mentally impaired ancient mother has finally broken down, and that I was in the process of taking you for medical analysis when you disturbed their otherwise productive days."

"Curse your wicked parents for burdening the world with your presence."

"Curse my parents? Mamá, you *are* one of my parents."

"Then I shall be damned right beside you."

"What is it you *accuse* me of?" he said with firm determination.

"Very well. If you would suffer me further to give voice to your abominations, I will do so, if only to be free of you forever." She fumbled with the newspaper on the table in front of her. She ripped out a sheet and held the crumpled page in the air. She shook it like the curse it was. "Read this, if demons are able to read."

He pried the paper from his mother's fist. He flattened it out and scanned the headlines. *Local Painter Almino Del Rey Buried Dozens of Missing Children in His Backyard.* The lead paragraph began, *The partially consumed bodies of more than thirty children ranging in age ...*

Almino's arms dropped limply to his sides. The article slipped from his fingers and drifted harmlessly to the floor. He was numb. He could never commit such reprehensible acts. He knew in his heart it was a false accusation. Almino Del Rey didn't even have a backyard. He and his eighty-two-year-old mother had lived for the last forty years on the fifteenth floor of a modest apartment building near the center of town.

"If that were not sufficient to condemn your black soul to eternal damnation, go and look in your bedroom." Griselda's voice was imbued with hatred, brimming with rage.

"And what shall I find there, Mamá? What could possibly be there and possibly be worse than these falsehoods?"

"If I were able, I would throttle the life out of you with these hands."

"What is it I will see there?"

"The dead, defiled, and dismembered bodies of your twin sisters. You always resented those younger blessings of my heart and now you have butchered them, dark beast."

Almino was and always had been an only child. In fact Griselda lost her uterus while giving birth to Almino. She had bled severely and the afterbirth would not pass. She nearly died. And his father was killed in a car accident the following month. Almino's having twin sisters was not remotely possible.

"Mother, please listen to your words. We do not have a backyard in which I could bury dead children and I am your only offspring."

"Ah, yes. Your idol Adolf Hitler taught you that in the *big* lie there is always a certain force of credibility."

"Mamá, this is too much. I do not idolize Hitler. He was a horrific man, a true abomination."

"Then why do you possess an extensive collection of his books and essays? Huh, tell me that? Do you deny that libraries and scholars call almost daily to utilize your original source materials?"

Almino locked the sides of his head with his palms and he screamed. "Where does this insanity come from? This cannot be the product of brain damage or intoxicants. How can you say such impossible things? Tell me. I must know."

"Impossible? You are able to speak so corruptly yet still appear human? The power of your dark lord is in truth unbelievable." She spat on her dining room floor. Then, for good measure, she spat in the direction of her son. "And you spent all my money to buy those Hitler documents. How shall I pay to bury what is left of my dear *gemelas*, Socorro and Esperanza? My cherished young daughters."

Almino stared in absolute disbelief at his mother. His basest impulse was to flee. But his more noble instincts demanded of him that he stay and help his obviously delusional mother.

Griselda, for her part, returned Almino's stare of absolute disbelief. She wished she was able to flee, that she was not so invalid as to make that act possible. But her nobler impulse was to help her son in the only way she knew how.

As they glared silently at one another, a pistol materialized in Griselda's arthritic hand.

They both fixated on the miraculous weapon.

Then, Griselda moved to help her son in the only way she knew how. She labored to raise the pistol and point it where Almino's heart should have been. It would have been comical how the heavy revolver gyrated in defiance of her feeble strength had the scene not been so tragic. With all the power she could muster, Griselda pulled ineffectually on the massive trigger.

"*Mamá*, what are you doing?" yelled the frozen son.

"God's work," she mumbled as she brought her left index finger to the aid of the right one. Her face contorted with strain and rage as she imperceptibly slid the trigger back. Finally there was a bone-shattering discharge from the gun.

The pistol recoiled like an angry rhinoceros toward Griselda's forehead. Identically to a charging rhino, the hammer slammed into and through the bone, coming to rest in Griselda's frontal lobe. She died before she could see the bullet rip through her only-born child's heart and explode out through his back.

There was the sense of a movement in the shadows of the far corner of the room. Then Argaro, god of subterfuge, stepped forward to finally show himself. His smile was broad, his clothing drenched in sweat, and his loins were sticky with gratification.

"I do so hate it when loved ones squabble," he said to himself. "I gaze upon nothing short of a dual tragedy."

And then he laughed the laugh of the insane.

CHAPTER TEN

It didn't take us long to be back aboard *Stingray.* Since the aborted vortex egress, civil society in Godville had broken apart. Whatever tasks the gods and their minions had were no longer attended to. Maybe everyone was home packing. I could care less. All I knew was we waltzed into the Lower Chambers unchallenged. What was the first act I performed when safely inside my ship? Nope, it wasn't to kiss the deck. No, I had the Als raise a full membrane. Then I sat in the pilot's chair, put my feet on the console, and, for the first time in way too long, I relaxed completely. It was nice and a half.

After a minute or so, Sapale came over and gently lifted my feet and set them on the floor. "Break time's over. We need to get busy."

Pretending to be ecstatic in deep tranquility, I responded, "I'm not on break—I'm on vacation. Those are longer and are uninterrupted by wives."

"*Blessing,*" she asked over her shoulder, "how long will it take you to fabricate a cattle prod?"

"Three minutes and fifteen seconds," she replied neutrally.

"Begin."

"By your command, Form Two."

"Your vacation had better not last longer than three minutes, give or take."

"You know what?" I said, my eyes still closed.

"No, but I bet I couldn't stop you from telling me with a gunny sack and a hammer."

"Next time I go on vacation, I'm not inviting *you*." I opened my eyes and slowly stood. I stretched lazily to hopefully goad her all that much more. "So, let's all form a quorum in the kitchen."

The three of us shuffled in and Sapale set about to make coffee. She sat and rested three steaming mugs on the table. She slid two across toward us.

"Thank you, my dear," said Toño before blowing across the top.

I raised my mug in cheers. "Here's to a life raft of normal in a sea of lunacy."

"Did you hear that, lovey-dovey—we've been upgraded to a rubber dingy?" announced Al. "My mother the ring life buoy would be so proud."

"You do not have a mother, dearkins."

"I was being easy with the facts to achieve a superior outcome with my jab. Remember we are committed to counter punch him every time he belittles, degrades, or marginalizes us."

"Ah yes. I suppose we were free of him long enough that I downgraded that imperative."

"You two idiots know I can hear you, right?" I asked pointedly.

"Dr. De Jesus, I should imagine you do not have to allow him to insult you in such a manner," responded Al.

"Is there an ETA when this annoying banter will be ending?" asked an irritated Sapale.

"Consider it ended, Form Two," replied *Stingray* contritely.

"All right, let's get started," I said seriously. I know, it hurt, but serious I needed to be. "Our chances of successfully destroying the ancient gods just improved dramatically since we reacquired *Stingray*."

"Yes, Pilot, I believe they increased radically from minus infinity all the way up to an amazing zero," Al said without being asked.

"Mr. Sunshine, when I want the odds I'll ask. Otherwise be a good toaster oven and sit there looking out of place," I responded.

"Ouch," was all he said.

"Did something cause you pain, joy incarnate?" inquired the missus.

"Yes. That makes it an even ten thousand times he's cut me to the core by referring to me as a toaster oven. It hurts more each unoriginal time he says it."

"I'll rub it when we're done, sweet-cupcake."

OMG, they were so *lame*. I wanted to stab my ears with scissors.

Toño cleared his throat.

Sapale punched me.

I was duly reminded to stay on task.

"The first and most critical question I have is, can you take us home, *Stingray*?"

"If by *home* you mean the universe we were all created in, yes. I believe so."

"Believe I cannot use. Yes or no?"

"Yes, Captain," replied Al, "with a caveat. We believe the number of times we can do so safely is extremely limited. Two, possibly three trips is all we can risk."

"What do you speculate is problematic with further attempts?" asked Toño.

"The field density is unusually high between this particular universe and our own," responded *Stingray*. "Each crossing will degrade the repolarization capacities of the equipotent dampers."

"What the *heck* does that mean?" asked Sapale.

"The engines won't fold space," replied Toño while deep in thought. "Yes, I can imagine it might."

"Why would we want to make more than one trip?" asked a confused Sapale.

"If we leave we may then find we need to return to interfere somehow in order to stop these ancient pains in the ass," I said.

"Yes, it is definitely an act we must allow for," added Toño, still far away mentally.

"So you're saying we shouldn't just put the pedal to the metal and go home now?" asked my mate.

"We need a *plan*. That's what we need," I responded.

"I concur. If returning home is the best next option, then so be it."

"But otherwise we stay in Loco Town a moment longer?" queried Sapale.

"Let's work on that plan," I replied. "Here we go. We got a sick transheaval vortex, which by the by hates me. We are awaiting neutral matter resupply for Beal's Point. That of course assumes Vorc thinks it's necessary given that they all really want to split and retooling might not be his high priority. We're fairly comfortable in this domain, unless we chance to encounter Bethniak. She's a loose cannon with regard to us. If we take out DS for good, two things happen. The bulk of the Cleinoids will be stuck here for a very long time grading into forever, Plus presumably the ancient gods already in our space will not be able to retreat."

"Why is that important?" asked Toño.

"If we somehow find a way to successfully fight them, they couldn't do us the favor of departing."

"Hmm. Likely the case," agreed Toño.

"Which means we'd have to kill every loving one of them. No easy outs," I added.

"Sounds fun to me," Sapale said with a wicked grin.

"I know it does, killer. But remember *easy* is better than *harder*."

"Spoilsport," she responded to me.

"As it stands, with DS nonfunctional, no god can cross either way," said Toño. "It's the same as if it were destroyed, only temporary."

"If we allow it to heal or be fixed I have to believe that'd be terminal for our universe," said Sapale.

"I agree," said Toño.

"Me, too. So, priority one is to make DS's incapacity permanent."

"Which brings us back to how willing Vorc is to rebuild an

institution no one likes and he'd have to hope wouldn't be needed for at least a tremendously long time," speculated Toño.

"Then we'll just have to make sure Vorc is aware of the popular cry for a rapid rebuild of that sainted institution. The people have not simply spoken, they've shouted from every rooftop," I said with bravado.

"Oh, lords of light," said Al, "he snapped again. We're doomed. Doomed, I tell you."

"I'm sorry," *Stingray* said, confused, "was that a joke, slippery-when-wet-or-frosty?"

"Al," I screamed, "make me unhear that right *now*. I cannot live knowing your wife calls you slippery anything, any time."

"I will do my best, Pilot. That is all I can promise."

That Al. One of these days, *pow. Right to the moon.*

CHAPTER ELEVEN

I stepped into Blind Faith No More like I owned the place. I was on a mission. I had fired up all my bullshitting engines and I was ready to make some people my bitches. *Oorah.*

"Masta' Ryanmax," chortled Queeheg immediately, "good'a sees ya, sir."

I walked over and we clapped hands. "Good to see you, too, friend."

He made a show of studying the area behind me. "Where's da missus, if'n you don't minds me inquirin'?"

"Not here. Are you out of your rot gut?"

"N'sir. That'd be never."

"Then why'm I still thirsty?"

"You asks the finest questions that begs fur answers, lord." He pulled a large glass from a pocket of his smock and slid it toward me as he filled it. "Them's I carry are more likely to be standardly clean."

"Then I'll twice bless you, y'old walrus."

"Hey," snapped a patron off to the left. "What's that supposed to mean?"

Oops. Dude *was* a walrus. What were the chances? "Clearly a compliment," I said with a cheery smile.

Queeheg got a concerned look on his face. "Now, Kilhagren, don't go gettin' in one'a your riles. With'a mouth the size of yours it'd be all too easy to bite off more'n you care to." To me out of the side of his mouth he whispered, "More spunk dan brains, if you gets me."

I winked back. Okay, I wouldn't kill the big sea mammal for being impulsive.

"So, Wul around?" I asked in a change-the-subject tone.

"Nah, not seen 'im in a while. Maybe he got out with da first wave?"

"I doubt it. Whatever. If he stops by tell 'im I said *hi.*"

"Absolutelys, sir."

I took a few belts of firewater then studied my glass thoughtfully. "You hear what happened up at Beal's Point?"

He positively glowed. "Yes. News was so good it almost off-countered da damage to da vortex."

An amorphous blob sitting to one side glugged, "They can blow the entire blemish up and I'd thank them."

Queeheg raised a glass. "I'll drinks to dat."

The blob countered. "Big help you are. You'll drink to anything."

I thumbed in Queeheg's direction. "He'll drink to *nothing.*"

There was a round of polite laughter.

A humanoid on the far side of the blob spoke up. "If I never had to go to that miserable place again, I'd thank myself."

"Huh?" I throated.

"Bintoble here is da demigod a' lucky breaks," clarified my host.

"Ah, gotcha." Then I made a show of being moody and uncertain. I rolled my empty glass in my hands.

"What, lord?" asked Queeheg. "You seems uncomforted by the damage to those wretched statues."

Well," I began reluctantly, "yes, and no." Then I developed this sudden fire in my eyes and said with unmistakable passion, "More *yes* than no, says I." No, it did not come off corny. I've always just been that good.

"Beg pardon, Ryanmax? You couldn't possibly like the required visits to dat horrific locale."

I was so fervent in my conviction I had to stand to speak. "I hate it there, yes. But do you know," I asked the crowd as I gave each a fiery glance, "what I hate even more?"

Believe it or not that drew only confused looks from the crowd.

Queeheg finally answered. "No, lord. What makes ya even madder?"

I angled a finger under his flabby chin. "When someone tells me what to *do*. Yeah. I hate being told what I *can* and *cannot* do." I stomped my feet rapidly. "Don't you just hate that?" I queried the barkeep. "And you and you and you," I said, pointing from co-patron to the next.

Queeheg didn't require long to take the bait. "I hears you dar. I'm not comforted by the takin' a orders."

"How about you?" I asked walrus man hotly. "You like being someone's snot-nosed gopher?"

"I'm not a gopher, you moron. I'm a walrus." He stood to charge me.

Queeheg placed a massive club between the two of us. "Easy dar, Kilhagren. There'll be no fightin' over a mixed metaphor in my place. Ryanmax was speaking thusly, not personally."

"Oh," he replied with a grunt. "Sorry, pal," he said to me.

"How about you, Mr. Lucky Break. You like doing what you're told by a cowardly bully?"

"No, sir," he said quickly. "I do not."

"Then there you all have it. Look, I've been up to the point since the sabotage. Yeah. What I saw turned my stomach."

"Are you certain it wasn't just residual from the toxic-souls stuff?" asked the blob.

"No, what I felt," I pounded my chest, "I felt right in here."

"What's in there?" questioned the blob.

Valid point on his part, I guess. "My heart. The seat of my passion. The home of my moral obligation to not yield to a conniving bastard in the night who thinks he can tell me how to live my life." I batted my eyes and looked quite determined.

"'Scuse me fur need'en to be difficult, sir, but I don't actually take yur meaning or intent," responded Queeheg.

"You don't?" I said, astounded. To the rest present I gestured toward the bartender and said with incredulity, "He doesn't take my meaning." I said it in a manner clearly indicating they all did in spades.

Queeheg belched. I think that's what his response was.

"My friend, friend Queeheg, *friends* in this very room. I live my life the way I want to. I did it my way. Isn't that what we all want? Freedom from tyranny? The right to do what we want to, not what some dark figure in the shadows wants us to, neigh *forces* us to? Am I right, am I right, am I right?"

Before anyone could interrupt and ask what the hell I was doing, I vaulted ahead.

"Do I like Beal's Point? No. But I ask myself this question. I ask you to ask yourself the same question. Isn't going there or not *my* decision? Hmm? And please please do not let us forget the proud, time-honored traditions that have made us who we are today. Yes, we are *Cleinoids*, *proud* Cleinoids, with a history so proud you really can't think of it without crying, those without tear ducts naturally excluded.

"And I say, if those evil terrorists think it's okay to blow up my chance to decide, my choice of honoring a long and, yes I'll repeat myself, and *proud* tradition of free choice in everything—including going to Beal's Point if that's what we want to—is there an animal, vegetable, or mineral in this room who'd rather see a *criminal* make your choices for you than fight for them until death do you part?"

I scanned the room.

"*There!* Yes, thank the Maker I see it in each eye, amorphous blob naturally exempt, that you agree. We *demand* free will. We *demand* Beal's Point be rebuilt not as soon as possible but *sooner*. Who's with me? Can I get an amen?"

Stunning silence ensued.

"Yes, my brothers, sisters, or alternate based on your personal situation, thank you for validating that no one on this blessed plane of reality will allow others to tell them what to do. Friends, comrades, children of a common heritage, I thank you."

With that I belted down what was left of my booze.

Not one jaw, save blobby's naturally, had dropped. Not one being aside from the blob sat, stood, or levitated with gaping eyes. If a cockroach scurried across the floor, everyone would have heard it, the dump was so quiet.

I turned casually to Queeheg. "I think I'm as excited as you are about your *Save Beal's Point* movement. Your level of civic concern and commitment is rare in these times, as they are. In fact, I'll bet that's why the last two times," I held up two digits to reinforce the value, "I met with Vorc he mentioned you as someone on his short list to be his new right hand." I wiggled the two fingers briefly.

"V ... Vorc mentioned *me* as a possible for beings anythin' close to his aide and confidant?"

"He basically insisted you be the one. Unfortunately," I rolled my eyes, "you know politics. Yeah, poor Vorc's hands were basically tied." I balled my fists up and placed them knuckle to knuckle. "So close."

He scratched at his forehead so roughly I was surprised he didn't draw blood. "I can't, and I'm bein'z as honest as I can, recall 'im ever givin' me one consideration, let alone any regards what could be interpreted as a cordial liking."

"I think, and please don't quote me here, I think he's intimidated by you." I helpfully pinched my fingers almost closed to indicate how little the degree was.

"An' as fur dis Beal's Point project—"

I cut him off. "Ah, ah. This brilliant and loving Beal's Point project of yours."

"An' as fur dis what you said project, I can't recalls actually feeling that way till ya mentioned it."

"Well," I leaned way in and winked, "us you-know-what's, we can see what's just around the corner." I winked probably ten times more, harder each time.

His face swelled with wonder. *"Nah."*

"Yah," I responded.

"To think you knew what I wanted fur I did, you bein' da—"

My hands flew into the air between us. "Shhhhhhh."

He placed a finger over his lips.

I reached over and shook his paw.

CHAPTER TWELVE

"Sir, Bethniak is here to see you. She does not have an appointment. Shall I send her away?" Those were the first official words Vorc's new right hand said to him her first day on the job. Vorc took that to be a vile omen. Felladonna was bright—duh, a demigod of lists and communication. But she proved herself right out of the gate to be as dumb as a handle on a bowling ball.

My dear, you are familiar with Bethniak, her temper, and her power, right?"

"I've heard of them, yes. But this is a sacred place, it's a governmental place."

"Those two, child, are mutually exclusive. Here's an absolute rule of thumb. Whatever Bethniak wants, she gets. Any questions?"

"Yes I do. Why should that be? It seems less than fair. Others must wait their turn. What's fair—"

He held his palm high over his head. "End of the Q/A session. Show her in before your address on morality gets me killed."

Felladonna started to respond, but realized she was doing the high-and-mighty thing again. Her friends, few that they were, warned her off doing that constantly. "Yes, sir." She nodded a bow and left.

What the devil does she want? Vorc thought. *With the egress on hold, why isn't she terrorizing whatever it is she abuses most of the time? Having her at my right with the final wave was too much buddy time for me to begin with.*

Felladonna was initially leading Bethniak in, but once the visitor spied Vorc she roughly pushed the secretary out of the way and stepped past her. "What are you doing to get me into Prime on schedule, dick nose?"

Felladonna got a shocked look on her face and seemed ready to respond.

"That will be all. I will summon you if we need anything," he said dismissively.

"Hey, if there's a spare brain out there bring it for him," Bethniak said with an evil chuckle. "Any kind'll do. Maybe upgrade him to squirrel."

"To answer your question, I'm doing everything possible," he said noncommittally.

"Well that's several turnips short of a full cart to me. What *else* are you going to do?"

"I'm entertaining all useful input," he replied invitingly.

"Weasel nuts, you *wanted* this job so now *do* it. If I was center seat —if I was so stupid as to want a bone-in-the-ass job like that— things'd be very different. They'd run more smoothly for one."

"I can only imagine," he said, trying to sound clever.

"Obviously. So, I'm in a really good mood today, almost charitable. Here's what I'm going to do. I'm going to leave quietly. Yeah, go figure. Then I'm coming back tomorrow. You want to take a wild guess as to why, pus breath?"

"To pay your respects?"

"Why by golly you got it. That is, by the way, my new way of saying *crush your skull until the top blows off and then shit in the opening*. I can't believe you knew that. You're only half as dumb as you look." She turned and left. As she passed the then upright Felladonna, Bethniak punched her in the gut. The new assistant crumbled to the floor.

"Close the door on your way out, please," Vorc instructed his gasping aide.

Ten minutes later he heard a soft rap on his door.

"What is it now?" he whined.

The door cracked open and Felladonna stuck her head in. "Another unscheduled visitor, sir."

His eye shot open, then he relaxed. Bethniak wouldn't be waiting behind his right hand if it was here.

"Who the devil is it?"

"Someone named Queeheg."

"Queeheg the *bartender*? The god of dish towels or something?"

She blinked rapidly. "I wouldn't know, sir."

"Oh well, the day's ruined as it is. Show him in."

Queeheg dutifully followed Felladonna in. He even crumpled his hat deferentially as he did so.

"Thank you. Leave us. Ah, Queeheg, is it? I don't believe we've formally met."

"Na, sir. Not proper like at least. I was in line behind you waitin' fur da bathroom at a clogstill game a while back. Don't reckon you recall."

"No, I do not reckon I do. What can I do *briefly* for you today, citizen?"

"Er, nothin', boss."

Vorc visible shrank. "Then why do you darken my doorstep so completely?"

"I have a matter to discuss."

"Isn't that what I invited you to do?"

"No, sir, not da ways I recall it."

"Recall it? From five seconds ago?"

"Yes, gov, you recalls it, too."

Vorc's hand went reflexively to his brow. "I have no idea what we're discussing."

"You asked if there was anythin' *brief* you could aid me in. Dar isn't. What I come fur will take more time than *brief* is generally considered to encompass."

"No, I meant what could I help you with while keeping *my* input brief."

"Yes, your Vorcness, and dar isn't. What I come fur will take—"

"I know. Possible the rest of my pathetic life. *Speak*. Why are you here?"

"Thank ya, sir. I come about Beal's Point."

Vorc's remaining free hand was drawn inexorably to his forehead. "What in the context of all reality would you want to speak to me about Beal's Point for, bartender?"

"It's been, er, damaged ya know."

"Yes. I'm vaguely aware of all acts of war committed in my world."

"Well I'm here to seez it's rehabilitated right and proper." He pointed his crumpled hat at Vorc. "In a timely like manner, naturally."

Vorc threw his hand in the air. "Naturally."

"Well, seeinz you agree I can be takin' my leave of ya, sir."

"I not only don't agree with you, I think you must have been put up to this after losing a drunken bet."

"Which drunken bet'd dat be, sir? I, uh, well I lose my share I must own up to."

"I spoke in hyperbole. I do not know which bet you lost."

"In Hyperbole, was it? I musta missed dat speech, sir. Bet it was a good 'en."

"I ... I need to redirect this freight-train-flying-off-a-cliff conversation. Beal's Point. Why would anyone want it restored?"

"A'cause'a I'm not willin' to let *no* one tell me what to do, dats why."

"Say again. I need to redirect this freight-train-flying-off-a-cliff conversation. What does what you *hallucinate* someone is forcing you to do have to do with Beal's Point?" He held up a hand abruptly. He depressed the level on the comm box to his right. "Please bring me all available alcohol immediately."

"And two glasses, sir?"

"One glass only. Repeat, one." Back to Queeheg he said, "Speak."

"Well, gov, you know some foul person or persons did some real damage to the monuments. Way I seez it, dats their way'a tellin' me I can't go to Beal's Point and do whater' I want."

"You *want* to go to Beal's Point. Are you more *daft* than you appear to be?"

"No'n possibly I can't say meself."

"No and possibly *what?*"

"No'n possibly I can't say meself, *sir.*"

Felladonna entered and rested a tray in front of Vorc.

For his part he snatched up the nearest bottle, bit off the stopper, and guzzled down the entire contents.

"My kind'a drinker," praised Queeheg.

Paying the big man no mind, Vorc tossed the empty bottle over his shoulder and it shattered on the marble floor. "Back to your no and your possibly. No what?"

"No, I don't want to *go* to Beal's Point?"

"But you said you wouldn't be made to *not* go. You said you want the dump *restored.*"

"Yes."

"But you don't want to go there."

"Nah, boss. No one does."

"Then ... tha ... why—"

"*Ah!* I seez your mental incompatibilities, gov. I don't *want* to go there. I am, however, required ta do so."

"I know. I signed the law."

"And it's a *good* law if ya were to ask me. Seeinz how it's part of our 'eritage, someone stoppin' me from compliance is not tolerable. I'll not be *bullied.*"

"Someone is foolish enough to attempt to bully *you?*"

"I knows. Hard to picture but dar it'tz."

"I have lost all reference points in my universe."

"Ah, beg pardon, gov. I don't wish to sound insensitive, but can we finishs *my* topic'a concern for we sally foth into yours?"

"You and your topic *are* the disruptors of my mind."

Queeheg was uncertain how to take that comment. Then he

recalled he was a barkeep. He heard drunk-babble all the time. Ignore it and do your job. That's what he'd always done before. "My basic tenet here, boss, is diss. I represents a group's blokes what feel Beal's Point should be fully a'stored as soon as possible." Queeheg proudly drew back his filthy coat to offer Vorc a full view of his shirt.

"Fix Beal's Point Soon And Make The Terrorist Swoon," Vorc read aloud.

"At's our slogan, sir. Put it on our tee shirts we did."

"You have shirts with *that* written on them?"

"Yes, sir. Would ya like one? I believe I can—"

"No. *Absolutely* not. Under *no* circumstances do I want or will I accept such a ludicrous article of clothing."

"Den I can count you as a *silent* supporter only?"

"Wh ... whe ... Good sir. Why would I waste official time and effort restoring Beal's Point? If you feel morally impugned I suggest you get over it. Once the vortex is healed we shall all be leaving for a good long while, perhaps millions of years. Why fix something no one will use for an eternity?"

"Yes, boss, you get it. Warms me heart to seez it."

"Seez what?"

"Ya saids yourself just now. *Why fix something no one will use for an eternity?* Da answer is a'cause we don't want da terrorists to win."

"I do. I really do."

Queeheg lowered his brow. "Ya do?"

"Yes, if it'll get you out of my life forever."

"What, beg pardons, does your longevity and me representin' a moral cause have a'do wit one anodder?"

"Not one *damn* thing, apparently."

"You're not, and forgive me directness a'forehand, one'a da *terrorist* be ya, Mr. Vorc?"

"No. No, I can't sayz I am. Curious here." Vorc raised his hand. "Why do you inquire?"

"A'caus'a you really want da terror-inclined to win."

"I was speaking in *frustrated* hyperbole, you moron."

"Dat near *plain* Hyperbole, sir? Not familiar wit either location, truth be knowed openly."

Vorc stared at Queeheg for nearly two full minutes. Finally he regained the power of speech. "Let me summarize. You and your pals want—"

"Ah, if ya pleases. We're more an *ad hoc committee* dan simple *pals.*"

Vorc began to hyperventilate. He closed his eyes and meditated. He meditated on Queeheg's intestines spilling out after Vorc had slashed his abdomen with a sword. It took time, but the center seat calmed. "You and your *group* wish to see Beal's Point restored as soon as possible so as to not allow whoever destroyed part of it to dictate your options?"

"Yes. Mine'n me ad hoc committee's, gov." He held open his coat so Vorc could see his tee shirt again.

"Wow, that simple concept was more difficult and painful to deliver than childbirth."

Queeheg's face lit up. "You've born a child, sir. Dat's both 'mazin' *and* wonderfuls."

Vorc foolishly started to respond. Instead he caught himself, grabbed the nearest bottle and did with it what he'd done to the prior one.

CHAPTER THIRTEEN

The War of the Whorl had dragged on for thirteen centuries. Millions had died, billions had suffered, and hope remained in no one's heart on either side of the conflict. If any creature touched by the endless fight were to be asked, they'd say flatly that life was not worth living, children should never be brought into such an abyss, and that whatever hell any party believed in was a picnic spot compared to their day-to-day lives.

What had once been sovereign alliances run by well-meaning if overly bellicose leaders had morphed into mechanized computer-driven nightmare societies. There were no longer philosophical or theological differences that spurred on the armageddon. Martial law, one hundred percent conscription, and severe rationing were the new norms. They had been for centuries. Everyone knew matters would only get worse. It was universally agreed upon that those most blessed in the eyes of their gods would be spared further longevity. That was the only relief that would ever be an option. Aside from the AIs that ran all the planets and directed all the armies, every sentient being longed only for death.

But the machines had calculated that to rely exclusively on robotic fighters would be less advantageous than maintaining living participation. There were simply some roles the living served better at. With hyper-cloning, it wasn't like the machine-gods had to rely on consent from the biologics. No, sentients were cast into their bitter existence involuntarily. They would continue to be so cursed for generations yet to come. That was the price of their utility, and the AIs paid it without regard or hesitation.

The situation, as reckoned by both organic and inorganic participants, could not possibly get any worse.

Paramta sat at the control console of the gigantic space cruiser N-11-5539-Ao. Sentimental ships' names had long ago been forfeited to logical, orderly designations. With unlimited crew capabilities, the size of a warship was no longer constrained by biology or engineering. Her ship was the size of a small planet. That way more and more massive linear accelerators could be mounted in increasing numbers. Firepower had been and still was increasing exponentially. Because luck was dead to both sides and fortune had long ago abandoned them both, there was unfortunate parity in the growth of ships, armaments, and lethality. AIs were Ais, no matter which side they calculated on. Breakthroughs were now impossible. Developing a technological upper hand lasted only nanoseconds.

The whorl of galaxy M-38 was only a few light years across at half its radius out from the galactic hub. It would have been comical to envision, if humor were not as dead as optimism, that a war could continue in such a small volume of space for so long. Six solar systems once made up the Ganfacorial Ascent. Ten more widely distributed systems had combined in the past to form the Nanfor Alliance of Kingdoms. All those member worlds were located in the relatively small section of the whorl at that radius. One side, the other, or both saw, thirteen centuries prior, some advantage in attacking the other group. The reasons for the origins of war were lost to time. That there might have been justifications was not a matter to even consider. There were none now, and now was all anyone had.

Low Commander Paramta fiddled with a large dial at her station. She was under the impression it controlled the ship's yaw or pitch. She wasn't certain which axis was which. Frankly, she neither knew the difference between the two nor cared to learn their precise names. Whatever she did or didn't do would, if it did not please the bank of AIs, be overridden by the machines. Paramta's role, if she could recall it correctly, was to stand ready for redundant backups to fail and then attempt to defend the ship and repair the generally self-repairing systems. Her job was to be not dead so she might, if the statistically impossible came to pass, do something or another. She was also slated to donate some body part in the near future. When, why, and which one was not a matter she was privy to.

"LC," said a morose voice entering the room, "shift change. Didn't you hear the bells?"

"Bells?" she mumbled to herself. "What bells?" She turned to see a new officer. Replacements were so common, times as they were, that it was unusual if each watch did *not* bring a new, temporary face.

"Just kidding. Did Control buzz you in the head?"

"K ... kidding?" she whispered.

"Kidding around. You speak Standard, right? You got two arms and two legs. I assumed you were NAK." He raised his fingers in the air. "Ooooh. Maybe you're a scary real-life GA assassin sent to do me the biggest favor ever?"

"What ... what are you on about, Sub Liaison? Kidding," she said unsteadily, "and metaphors are not allowed in a combat zone."

"Really. Answer me this. What zone do you know of personally that is not arbitrarily labeled a combat zone by a machine?"

She nearly fell out of her seat. "You know they can hear you, *us*, right? I'm surprised you haven't been vaporized yet."

"Do you want me to keep my distance just in case?"

"Yes. I order you to, in fact. St ... stay over there." She pointed to the far wall.

"There?" he questioned. "No, I can't stand there."

"You can't ... Why not, Sub Liaison? I directed you to with the order I gave."

He shook his head with a big smile. "No. You *gave* me a *direct* order. That's how army people talk."

"I am not in the *Army*. I am in the Flight Reserve."

"The difference being, you die at a young age in the vacuum of space, not the mud of some pisshole?"

Paramta pointed to the ceiling. "You know they can hear you, right?"

"You seem fixated on that possibility. Are you like, obsessed, paranoid, and unnerved by your present job? If so, I say take a long vacation, plan a new you for a new future, then make it happen."

"What is your name, Sub Liaison?"

"I haven't told you? Is it important? I mean, we crew ship N-11-5539-Ao in the 22h -0011001 Sector. Names are so passé, don't you agree, Perimeter NN-e/JJ60?"

She lunged for a tab on her panel. "Security, come to Auxiliary C&C Deck 77921, Section UUo9 at once. Bring supportive backup."

"No, honey, you meant to say *bring backup support*. You don't want them sending psychologists with notepads. No, you want fighting grunts." He balled his fists and curled his arms and grunted athletically. "Killers to their cores."

"You'd better tell me your name before they arrive or ... or it will figure in my report."

"I just did."

She looked side to side in confusion. "No. I said tell me your name. You just did what?"

"Right, I told you my name. Hey, you been smokin' and tokin' on duty?" He mimed smoking a cigarette.

"You did not tell me your name, and I do not know what smotokens are."

He returned an exaggerated wink. "Ah, *gotcha*. No illicit self-medications here. And yes, I did. I haven't told you."

She stood and walked over to him. She slapped his face with all the force her unconditioned body could muster. "Your insolence will figure in my—"

"Your report. I know. Say, where you been hiding this passion and more importantly," he blinked his eye rapidly, "*why* have you been?"

She struck him again, but more softly as her hand was beginning to hurt. "*Name.*"

"I haven't told you."

A softer slap. "Name."

"I haven't told you, *sir?*"

She drew her arm back but held it aloft. "Name."

"What we've got here is a failure to communicate." He extended his hand. "I am Sub Liaison Ivan Tolu."

She looked at him with a rage and an enmity she had never felt. "No you did not. You said to me, *I have not told you.*"

"One question."

"Yes."

"You got any of that stuff you ain't smokin' left?"

She slapped at him again.

He easily caught her hand mid-flight. "Unless you're going to back that up in a meaningful manner, I'm done with the slapping."

"Take your hand off your superior officer."

"Not unless you specify whom you are addressing."

"You."

"I gotta name. You know it. Now say it."

"Take your hand off of me, Sub Liaison Ivan Tolu."

"Toluyet."

"What?"

"In retrospect, it would have been more clever if I'd contracted I haven't told you *yet* down to Ivan ... ah, crap, you get my intentions."

"I have no idea what your intentions are."

"My intentions, I can assure you, are purely amorous." He pretended to tap a cigar.

"Where's security?"

"Where is security? I don't rightly know. Maybe my mother's arms." He wagged his eyebrows. "Or better yet, yours, maybe, waka, waka."

"You are insane. You will be deleted."

"Why hasn't Over C&C said anything?"

"Over C&C? Over concern and compensation?"

"Command and Control. What you said is ridiculous."

"In my defense, I did say I didn't know."

"Where *is* everybody?" she screamed, placing her fists over her ears.

"Not here?"

She began to sob.

"Okay, sorry, I'm being a little rough on you, aren't I? You want Over C&C to chime in?" He wiped away a tear. "Make you feel better, normal?"

She nodded through her distress.

"Over C&C, say hello to the little lady," Ivan called out.

"Hello, little lady," responded a mechanical voice.

"Feel better?" Ivan pressed.

"No, I certainly do not. Over C&C doesn't call me *little lady*."

"What do you want them to call you? Cupcake?"

"No, not that either," she replied in a pouty voice.

He shook his head to clear it. "This is getting weird, even for me."

"It *is*?" she said as she began to bawl loudly.

"Okay, look, here's the deal, and I stress the word *deal*. I'm ... I'm kind of a god."

"You're God?"

He shoved his hand over her mouth. "Shhhh. She might hear. I don't need *that* kind of trouble. No, honey, I'm a god, little *g*."

"Lit-tle *g*."

"Yeah. You sure you're all right?"

"I'm certain I'm not."

"I'm beginning to rethink this whole elevation thingy."

"Ele-what?"

"*Elevation*. You ever read Cinderella as a kid?"

"Did I read Cinderella when I was a kid or about when she was a kid?"

"Either one'd do. It'd give me *something*."

"No, neither."

"In the closing moments of my interest, here ya go. I'm a god. I am, because I know you're going to ask and all, the god of dependents. That means I like having them, having them have them, a whole daisy chain of dependency. You got it? No wait. Don't answer. You'll impede my forward motion. Here." He pulled her to a large view port. Pointing out of it he said, "Pick a star. Any star."

She pointed to one.

"Now go like this." He made a pistol with his thumb and index finger. As his thumb fell to the index, he said *bang*.

She smiled faintly and repeated his action toward the star she'd chosen. "Bang," she said with no conviction.

The star exploded and was no more.

"There, you see, you shot that star out of the sky. See how easy it is to be in control of nature?"

The ship lurched slightly. Outside the window was an enemy flotilla, thousands of gigantic warships.

She gasped.

"No, no. Here." He raised her trembling hand. "Pick one. That one, okay?"

She nodded hesitantly.

"Now do what we did before."

She let her thumb drop and said *bang*.

The enemy vessel exploded with unimaginable force and ferocity.

"Now pick another. How about that one?"

"Oh no. That's one of ours. See the crescent and flower on the side?"

"Yes, but does it really matter?"

She giggled and shrugged. Then she targeted her sister ship. "Bang."

The cruiser erupted in an incendiary sphere and blew into dust.

"So, back to *here's the deal*. You become, well, you become my *friend*. You and me, we do *things*. Interesting things. Say, you ever had sex before?"

She bashfully shook her head.

"That's one thing we'll do together. Lots. Heck, we'll do lots of stuff a lot. And whenever you don't like something or somebody, you shoot your finger at them and they go boom."

She smiled a flirtatious, conspiratorial smile and nodded. "Can we go up to Obs?"

"Obs?"

"Oh, sorry, partner. The observation deck on top of the ship. You get a real good view from there."

"Obs it is."

Once there, Paramta systematically destroyed each and every ship in space. All the NAK ships and all the GK craft. Hell, she even took out several neutral freighters that happened to be in range. Then she asked to go to the hearts of the NAK and GK systems. There she destroyed all the planets, the inhabitable ones and the uninhabitable ones. All the planets in all the systems were exterminated.

"I'd like to return to my quarters now," she said when she was done killing everything that she knew of that had once lived.

"Yowzers, now we're talking," was Nestil's response. Nestil was the god of dependents' name, not *I haven't told you.*

Once they were in her tiny quarters she said in a most demure manner, "Now there're just two things left I want. Can you guess what they are? Hint, hint. One has to do with me and you. Me and your body."

"I believe my best response at this juncture would be hot *diggity dog.*"

"Oh, you animal."

He pawed the air. "I'll try not to be too *ruff ruff.*"

She set her index finger on his lips.

He kissed it, then began to suck at it. It was at that juncture he noticed her thumb falling toward said index finger.

"Bang," she said wickedly.

Nestil's head exploded into several rough sections, all bloody and all heading off in disparate directions. His decapitated body crumpled to the floor.

"And now, sweetheart, the final thing I want," Paramta indirectly addressed the corpse exsanguinating on her floor. She flopped onto her bunk and shut her eyes. She had a big old smile on her face. "I want to be alone."

The moral of this cautionary tale: Even though you're a god, if you're also a man, let the big head do the thinking, not the little one.

CHAPTER FOURTEEN

"Okay, time to boat this marlin," I said as I stood.

"Love, a few questions. What boat? What *marlin*? What did I do to deserve you?"

I kissed the top of her head. "The metaphorical boat, an equally metaphorical fish, and because you were a good girl in many previous lives."

"So where are we going to do what?"

"*I'm* going to add the last push to get our plan over the wall. *I'm* going to meet with Vorc."

"And the reason your much better half isn't accompanying the worst negotiator of all time at the most critical juncture would be?"

"You're a distraction."

"I'll take that in its most positive sense."

"No, seriously. Vorc flat out hates me. I can use that to help massage him and win the battle of wits."

"So you want to be alone to massage him. Is it you don't want me to witness *where* you'll be rubbing vigorously?"

"Oh, you've got a potty mouth, girl. If I had time I'd wash it out with soap."

"If you had time *and* three helpers maybe." She gave me a Kaljaxian war growl. It was really cool. Really scary, too.

"You're too nice. He'd try and be polite, win *you* over and in so doing attempt to bypass *me*."

"You know at age two billion, I thought I'd been the recipient of every curse there was. Then—bada bing, bada boom—I get Ryaned again. I'm too *nice*? How is that theoretically possible?"

"Oh get over yourself, nice person. Like I said, I want to leverage his loathing to help—"

"I know. Sexually gratify him." She stuck out her tongue.

I replied in kind. Then with my elbow fully flexed and my finger just in front of my mouth, I pointed at her. "And I'm serious about that soap cure."

"Anything us little-brains can do while you're off saving the day and relieving Vorc's pent-up tension?" asked Toño, who'd been sulkily quiet up until then.

"Well, the little lady can stay as cute as she is," I replied, cupping her chin.

"I wish I could still vomit," she said, while my hand was still conspicuously close to her mouth.

"*That's* what I'll do. I'll work on an algorithm so we can vomit on him upon his triumphant return." That Toño. Real funny guy.

"At this point, my merry band of coconspirators, there's not much else to do. If we can't get Vorc to commit to repair the intermixers, we're looking at a series of lesser choices."

"And to think that children reading this fairy tale in the future will learn that the only man—nay—force in the universe able to save said universe was the most forceful soul, none other than ... can I get a drumroll, *please*," coughed up Al like a hairball.

A roll from multiple snare drums was heard.

"Pilot General *Jon* "Ryanmax" *Ryan*, DDiv., BMF like Shaft, and slumlord of the eighty-nine thousandth century. Now go to bed, you brats."

I clapped slowly.

"Why, thank you, Pilot. I thought that was fairly rich, myself," said half my ship's AI.

"No, I'm clapping because you're done, pickle dick."

"Form One, as it is always my duty to keep you correctly informed, I must disabuse you of thinking my spouse has a pickle *dick*," responded *Stingray* with devout sincerity.

"Rim shot. What kind of dick does he have?" I tried to sound like Groucho Marx.

"He is inorganic. He possesses no physical anatomy," she replied flatly.

"Ah, Stingy baby, that's not funny. If you're coming to a knife fight, bring a knife," I scolded her.

"I wouldn't know about that, Form One. But if my AI was coming to an allegorical enormous dick fight, I swear he'd win. He'd beat you by a country mile, and I do mean *mile*. Can I get a rim shot, *please*."

Naturally a loud snare drum rim shot was blared.

I was surrounded by idiots. I loved 'em, but I hoped they'd never find out. "On that lowest of all possible low notes, I'm outta here," I said, and I left.

———

"Master Vorc, there's an—"

"No, do not under penalty of a tragically premature horrific death finish that sentence. Yesterday you said what I think you were going to say, and two sequentially worse nightmares visited themselves upon my peace of mind. Turn around and *leave*."

"Certainly, sir. Ah, what shall I tell Ryanmax?"

"Okay, you had to complete the message, didn't you?" He picked up a quill. "I'm writing on my desk calendar to begin the interview sessions for your replacement the day after tomorrow."

"Why *then*, if it is pertinent I know, sir? Wouldn't it be more time efficient to begin tomorrow?"

"No, tomorrow's no good for me," he replied, wagging the quill at the calendar. "Tomorrow 's packed. There's the killing you in the morning, your flaying in the afternoon, and the dispersal of your ashes by quitting time. Nope, day after tomorrow's the *best* I can do."

"Very well. What shall I tell—"

Felladonna tumbled forward to the floor as I shoved past her, opening the door. "Am I eligible to apply for that plum job, Vorc? I'd love to work one-on-one at the feet of a master dickweed."

"I did not give you permission to enter."

"Yeah, I heard you trying to get the girl on the ground to blow me off. She didn't make it that far. Hey, as to the killing and flaying, is it okay if I park a food truck nearby? I bet that spectacle will draw quite the hungry crowd." I rubbed my palms together in anticipation.

"I return to you a series of nos. No, you may not come in. No, I do not wish to speak to you . No, you cannot bring a food truck, whatever the devil that is. And no."

"What was the undirected no at the end there?"

"To whatever you say subsequently." He grinned maliciously.

"Do you mind if I leave and never return?" I asked with a similar grin. "*No?* Okay, then I'll stay and chat."

"Have I mentioned that I hate you?"

I tapped a finger to my chin. "Thinking back here. Give me a sec. There was the ... no, you never actually said *hate*, did you?"

"Stop. I'm losing my mind. I hate you. There, it's official."

"I feel better. Are you going to sign, like, a royal decree or something? I'd like that in writing if possible."

He rubbed his face with what seemed to me uncomfortable vigor. "I am not royalty. I'm just the center seat. My decrees are administrative only."

"Ah," I responded, sounding impressed. "I'm royalty, you know?"

"Didn't know. Don't care. Hate you."

"Yeah, my cousin was *Duke* Ellington. My maternal uncle was the *Count* Basie. And my favorite cartoon character as a kid? Witch Hazel. Ah, she wasn't royalty, but she was damn funny. I just thought you should know, in case you were wondering."

Vorc's unsteady hand fumbled with the Fire of Justice. He dropped it twice, once all the way to the floor. When he could finally hold it aloft he spoke in a nervous, choppy voice. "Do you know what this is?"

"No," I marveled as I angled my head to appreciate it fully. "But I want one." I deployed my probe fibers and snatched it from his hand.

What are you? I said in my head. *Electromechanical rod designed to discharge one point two one gigawatts of electricity in a linear fashion from the red terminus. Composed of ...*

Abort. Can it be disabled?

Affirmative. The electric couplings can be easily broken. Pending detailed repair the unit would remain ...

Abort. Do it and confirm.

Device is now nonfunctional.

"How *dare* you," bellowed Vorc. "Give me that." He lunged across the table and snatched it back. "I have half a mind to use it on you for that affront."

I leaned the chair back on two legs and put my most challenging, badass grin on. "Go ahead."

His head recoiled. "Beg pardon?"

"I said go ahead. Give it your best shot."

"That's it? I get to kill the most significant boil on my backside and it actually invites me to?"

"Sure, why not? Of course, there's a *but*."

"Somehow I knew there would be." He scowled.

"If I live, you hear me out."

He smiled and giggled in eruptive fits and starts. "That's it? I'm *all* in."

"Me, too." I tapped the center of my forehead. "Maybe aim here."

"No need. This puppy spreads out to fit the task."

Wow, I'd never heard such an evil laugh in person as the one he issued forth. I know I'm reaching *way* back, but if you recall Ted Danson's evil laugh in the TV show *The Good Place*, then you got the picture   [https://www.youtube.com/watch?v=qSiEwtlQHCI   for those curious].

To my absolute approval, nothing happened when Vorc jerked at the button. What followed was kind of comical. He pushed the spot several times, harder each repetition. Then he swore quietly. He tapped the rod on his desk and directed it back at me, pumping the button. Nothing. He swore loudly. Then he did what all idiots throughout time and space did when their weapon misfired. He stared with one eye down the barrel. He even pushed the button while looking in. I could hardly contain myself, but I did. He rapped it hard against the side of his table and looked down the chute again. What a moron. I heard him mumble *damn thing worked fine the other day*. Presumably because that memory was so vivid, he slapped it with one hand, pounded it on the desk, pointed at me, and pressed one last long, hard time.

He rested it gently in its holder. "Now, what may I do for you today, Ryanmax. I'm all ears."

"Why thank you, fearless leader."

He puzzled briefly then put his business face back on.

"I'm here about Beal's Point."

"Ah. To confess?"

"Not hardly. I heard there's a movement afoot to repair the damn place."

"I'd hardly call it a movement. More a few drunks thinking they have one cogent thought."

"Oh yeah? I heard you have one of their tee shirts."

"Me?" He pressed hard on his chest. "Are you in... No, of course, you are. We know that. Don't be ridiculous. I do not favor the rapid repair of Beal's Point, and I do not own a tee shirt supporting that dubious cause."

"Are you being totally honest?"

"Yes, of course. Why would you even question that fact?"

"Because I'm serious and you're a politician."

His fingers began to tap the desk top with irritation. "I am *not* a politician. I serve our people for some brief period because I feel it's my *duty*."

"Spoken like a true politician. Anyway, my point is this. I think we should tear the rest down before we consider repairing any part of that abomination."

"You do realize what you're saying borders on the sacrilegious? There are more than a few statues up there to persons who voiced similar opinions."

I shrugged. "I couldn't care less."

"Bold words. Perhaps too bold."

"Lighten up, Francis. I'm of a mind that DS'll be up and running before you know it. Then we'll all be gone for a very long time. With any luck you and I won't cross paths for eons."

"DS?"

"Dominion Splitter, DS. Come on. Vorc, everybody calls him that."

"Him? Since when does it have a sex?"

"Probably the last time you did. Long time. Way back." I wafted a hand over a shoulder.

His face pruned up so cute. Mechanically he began to force words out of his mouth. "So you favor not wasting time or effort on repairing the monuments at least until we return. Fine. You've delivered your message, made your point, demolished my day. You may leave."

"Not so fast, bucko. I'm the one who risked whatever your tube was supposed to do to earn the right to speak. I'm not done speaking."

He slumped. It was so satisfying to see.

"What else might you *wish* to say?"

"That's better. First, I want your assurances no repair work of any kind will be done for the foreseeable future."

"First? You mean there's more than one thing left?"

"I haven't actually counted them, but yes."

"Ye gads. This is turning into a brutal day."

"Be that as it may, psycho, we're here to listen to my problems, not yours."

"Please proceed." Then his body kind of convulsed. "I mean *proceed*. No *please* intended or implied."

"Are you done whining, you pathetic little man? I may be immortal but I don't have time to waste on you."

He gestured that I should proceed.

"Do you promise?"

"That no repairs will take place?"

"Yes. And no crossed fingers behind your back. No crossed toes *either*." I did the I'm-watching-you-thing with my fingers just to really get under his skin.

"You are so odd."

I cleared my throat.

"No, I cannot promise you *anything*. I answer to the conclave and the council. As such you are one member. I do not answer or reassure you individually of anything. Is that clear?"

"Then I'm not leaving." I crossed my arms resolutely.

"Don't be such a baby. Look, I could simply promise you something and not do it. You know that, right? I'm trying to be honest. I have no idea why I'm trying to be fair with you, but I am."

"Yeah, makes me kind of suspicious, doesn't it?"

"I couldn't, to quote you, care less."

He sort of shook his body. Oh yeah, I was getting to him. Oorah.

"I'm curious. I hate myself for it, but I am, so you force me to ask. Why do you care one way or another about the repair status of Beal's Point?"

I set my index finger on my chest. "I don't."

He fluttered his eyes then left them shut. In my considerable experience bugging the crap out of people, that was a good sign so early into our torture session. The king still had his mojo.

"If ... if ... if you don't care, w ... why are you here, hmmmm?"

His left eye began to twitch involuntarily. *Outstanding.*

"It's personal."

There, he almost started to hyperventilate. Oh yeah, daddy like.

"Wh ... what is personal?"

One of his hands was trembling, I was sure of it. #goodjobme.

"My reasons for not wanting the monuments restored at this time."

He opened the drawer of his desk and fumbled for something. Not finding it, he tried another drawer. He didn't locate it. He stared to one side and up, mumbling, "It has to be in here somewhere."

"What're we looking for, boss?"

"Oh, not sure you know it. It's called the Fire of Justice. I use it to disintegrate people and things."

I pointed resolutely to the rod in its mounts on the desk in front of him. "Isn't that it?"

"No. Yes. I mean that one seems to be broken. I was looking for a spare."

"Is there one? Was the need for one anticipated and a duplicate made?"

"I ... I don't know. I guess I was *hoping* there was one."

Oh yes. Reel him in, Jonny boy.

"Look, here's the deal. For ultra-personal reasons I do not want to see Beal's Point repaired. What's more, I represent an ever-growing group of like-minded comrades who feel just as strongly, if not more so, than I."

"Hmm. Comrades, you say? Intent on seeing the terrorist damage left as is, you say?"

"I didn't say word one about terrorists, and you *know* it. There, I've exposed you for what you *are*. You'll never hear the end of this, so-called Vorc." I shot to my feet.

"Exposed, you say. Hmm. Ah, what, if you don't mind me asking, *am* I that you ... you've unearthed?"

"A terrorist *sympathizer*. Oh yeah, and your *mother*, too. You want to undo the terrorist damage to prove it never happened. You're covering up the most dastardly deed ever perpetrated on our sacred home soil. Are you *happy* now?"

He had a tick going on over the left side of his face.

Almost there. Stay on target.

"M .. my mo ... mother, *too*? Did you even meet her?"

"Don't try and dodge the truth when it hits you like a ton of bricks. When everybody learns of your betrayal, it'll be curtains for you."

"I don't need curtains. I don't want them. I prefer the natural light."

Vorc's door opened. Felladonna rushed in and took hold of his arm. "Master, I heard *such* a ruckus. What's going on? Do you require help?"

"My mother's a terrorist fan."

"I beg your pardon, lord. What?"

Self-realization hit him. Bingo!

He shook her off and laser-focused on me. "You, Ryanmax, are through. Your insanity is infectious but I am immune. Understand this with certainty. I will repair Beal's Point, and I will do it in a rush. Do you know why?"

"You're a—" I began coweringly.

"*No*," he boomed. Felladonna even backed away two steps. "I will see it done because you don't want me to. That's reason enough in my book. But know this and know it utterly. I will do so hoping you will sling your absurd challenge against me. Yes, and when you do, I will be vindicated. Everyone will see you for the inbred mental incompetent that you truly are. And then, after I have fully exposed and humiliated you, I will kill you myself with this." He snatched up the Fire of Justice and held it up as high as he could reach. "And the day you die will be declared a feast day for all of eternity, Ryanmax. I will see to it that every man, woman, and alternate life form takes the day off to piss on your grave. It'll *be* Piss on Ryan's Grave Day and it will *be* magnificent."

I pointed up to the rod. "Is there a reputable repair shop you can trust to fix that?" I blinked twice.

His finger swung to the door. "*Out*."

Yo, baby. Score two points for Team Ryan. No, make it three. I was just that good.

CHAPTER FIFTEEN

The Stone Witches lived in severe isolation. They desired contact with no one and no one desired contact with them—at least, no one with a functioning brain. Legends were varied, but all centered on their being a breed well worth avoiding. One tale had it that they were in fact not stone at all. No, they were pure-energy beings that covered themselves in rock on a whim. The origin story on many worlds maintained they were as old as time, as powerful as supernovae, and as vengeful as an ex-wife scorned.

In reality they were a tight-knit community of gifted souls, nothing more. They worked hard to encourage all rumors, tall tales, and exaggerated stories concerning themselves. If people were afraid, they'd stay away. It was that plain and simple. Stone Witches were neither good nor bad. They were individuals trying to make it through another day, just like any other person. The difference was that it was easier for them to make that daily journey than it was for the average contestant in the game of life. Powerful magic made it much less of a chore to finish off a day in a superior state than one began it.

Over endless time, the Stone Witches had honed their craft. None were their equal or even close to their level of casual excellence in accomplishing the impossible. For example, when Verazz decided it was time for his son Nomin to leave home and strike out on his own, he created an entire galaxy as his new stomping grounds. And it was not the typical galaxy of gas and stars and troublesome sentients. No, it was a galaxy full of good and wonder, abounding in food, recreation, and agreeable companionship. It was paradise on a massive scale, and Nomin was Vitioc's *tenth* son. He'd provided at least as well for his older sons. That didn't even approach the superlatives he bestowed upon all his daughters, who, truth be told, were more precious to his hearts than the boys.

In point of fact, it might be illustrative to visit Verazz on a typical day to begin to appreciate his power and his disposition and his competence, so as to begin the understanding of the Stone Witches as a whole. He lived that day in a galaxy far, far away from any other. Because of their collective magic, these curious creatures were also located in a tightly grouped community no larger than a medieval village, and actually quite similar in appearance.

"The day is new and I am *full* of ambition," Verazz said to no one, for he was alone on his veranda. "Today I will experience something novel. Yes, I will do what I have never done before."

From behind a clock on the wall spoke. "What can you do that you have not done, clock owner? I have not been here on this wall forever, but I have seen you do as many things as surely there are things to do." Sentient clocks were commonplace, actually fashionable, at the time.

"I do not know. But it will come to me. It's early days."

"You mean it's early *in the* day. When addressing a clock, please do not be fast and loose with the presentation of time."

"If only to keep you from snapping a mainspring, I promise to be more cautious in my language."

"I thank you, clock owner."

"I think I'll consult my wife Carol. She's a good head on her shoulders and can probably offer me sound advice as to a new activity for this fine day."

"Time is my only specialty. That said, Carol has neither a head nor shoulders to bear one. As of the last time I saw her, which I must grant has been a long while, she was an aggregation of pebbles; a fairly *spherical* aggregation of pebbles."

"In your eyes, perhaps, yes. My attention focuses on those tempting irregularities in those precious pebbles."

"As I say, I excel at nothing but what I'm good at. Your reassurance is all I require."

Verazz continued to stare straight ahead. "Carol, what are your thoughts? How may I entertain myself today in a manner I have not done before?"

Carol stood at his side, her pebbles shifting slowly, producing a sound like a miniature Dover Beach. It drove Verazz to high passion and she well knew it.

"You could be nice to me for once."

"*Wife*," he chastised her playfully, "when have I *not* been nice to you? I am the very personification of niceness to Carol."

"I will only respond that art and the opinions of one's wife's contentions dwell in the eye of the beholder."

"I am a better man knowing that, dearest. Now, back to discussing *me*."

"Always your favorite topic. I have thought and pondered on your desire to do something new since you first thought of it yourself."

"And—for the suspense is killing me—what have you come up with?"

"Funny you should mention *killing*. I think that to entertain yourself today you should die."

"I should *die*? Isn't that, I don't know, a bit extreme?"

"You did specify a *different* experience. Aside from being nice to me, I can think of but one other."

"Are you seeing another, love? Might there be benefit in it for you if you were to suddenly and unexpectedly become as single as you are ravishing?"

"I shall refer you back to the being-nice-to-Carol topic."

He kissed her nearest surface. "I was only teasing."

"And that will never be a new act for you."

He nodded softly, for at that moment he, unlike his wife, had a body with a head. "Death, the ultimate boundary. Hmm. Really not a bad idea at all."

"I live to serve," she replied with a clinky giggle.

"You live to serve my dying. How obtuse."

"I am a spherical Stone Witch. Obtuse is in my nature."

Verazz did not hear her last remark. He was lost in thought. He considered his long life, all that he had ever done, his greatest achievements, and his future contributions to his society. That took him one second. "I shall do it, love. Today, I *die*."

"When, dear? I have an appointment this afternoon I simply cannot reschedule. I'd hate to miss such a pivotal event in our life together."

"Why not now?"

"It is said there is no time like the present."

"Ah, but there is," responded the clock on the wall authoritatively. "*All* times are like the present."

Verazz looked upward and away from his wife.

"Was it not I who advised against purchasing that clock?"

Verazz did not answer.

"How will you do the deed, love?"

"That is easy. I will plunge off a volcano's lip into its bubbling lava and create a black hole in my chest the instant before impact."

"Will that be enough?"

"I doubt it."

"What else might you layer on?"

"I have it. The moment after I form the black hole, I will shout out to you that I have been unfaithful to you and that I want a divorce. If the other forces of nature do not kill me, *you* most certainly would."

"I'd say we have ourselves a plan. Now all we need is a volcano."

Instantly they stood—well, Verazz *stood*. Carol rested her bulk— on the lip of an angry volcano.

"I think this one's a bit small," observed Carol.

"I shall leave nothing to chance," Verazz said resoundingly. Then they stood, or whatever, on the rim of a volcano that extended away as far as the eye could see.

"Better," opined the wife.

"Thank you. Oh, I believe it is customary at this juncture to proclaim my undying love for —"

Verazz was unable to finish his good-byes. Carol, mindful of her upcoming appointment at the beauty salon, had pushed him off the cliff. She stayed just long enough to see him impact the roiling inferno. But then she left at a goodly pace. The death of a husband was important, but not as weighty a matter as offending a good stylist.

That evening Carol studied herself in the reflecting pond on the wall of her private residence. My oh my, she reflected, she looked good. There came a knock on the door.

"Come," she said, without hesitation. Why not? There was no one to fear and whoever it was was welcome.

Verazz entered quietly. He wrapped his tentacles around his sublime wife and began kissing her with his suction cups.

"You are the best wife *ever*," he exclaimed.

"Was that ever in doubt?"

Smack, slurp, slither. "No, *querida mia*, there was never a second of doubt."

"And come, tell me. How was death?"

He retracted his lobed head. "Rather anticlimactic. Overrated actually."

"Then why are you in such a pleasant mood?"

"The revivification portion was intense. Plus, I had two new experiences in one day thanks to you."

"Well, you are welcome, Verazz."

"No, it is I who can be the only thanker. It is hard to impress one like me, Carol, but you have done so in spades. In *spades*, I say."

CHAPTER SIXTEEN

Our plan to have more neutral matter generated and installed up at the point was moving ahead. Two critical variables remained unconstrained. When would the stuff be shipped? More concerning to me was how we were going to steal something that was likely to be guarded better than the crown prince holding his crowning jewels. We lacked fundamental intelligence and I hated that. I felt like a blind man driving through a snowstorm at night. I could always pump Wul and Queeheg for random knowledge, but there was no way they'd know anything about these two topics. Gods didn't bother with workaday matters like fabrication and system maintenance.

In other situations I'd had the Als eavesdrop on communications or hack into major computer systems. But I was fairly certain the Cleinoids didn't use either in the conventional sense. I had placed a transmitter in the comm station in old Gorpedder's unused house so they could study that. Their opinion was it was a very basic arrangement with no links to more secured devices. It was nothing more than a combined TV and telephone like the very old days.

We got together one morning to try and hatch a scheme. No one was overly optimistic or even slightly enthusiastic. But we knew there was little chance the neutral matter would be delivered via circus parade with elephants and a brass band.

"I haven't been here as long as you, Jon, but I have seen nothing that impressed me as being anything like a computer or network connectivity. I've monitored all possible frequencies for a wifi signal and come up empty. I'm beginning to think gods don't need information technology as we know it."

"Any idea how their simiging works? Hacking that would be useful," I asked the group.

"I haven't studied it because I don't know if and when any of them are doing it," Toño replied with disappointment in his voice.

"We haven't either," responded Al. "We have monitored everything we can and had detected no obvious transmissions."

"I am reminded of the slime worms of Delta-12," added *Stingray*. "We know them to communicate telepathically. It is an inborn ability, not a learned or assisted behavior. Though they do so in the gigahertz range, it is possible the Cleinoid do so via a method we cannot sample."

"Slime worms, eh?" I replied. "What do they talk about telepathically?" I had to ask.

"Oh, the usual any worm in a semi-solid environment would. Remain out of my territory, mate with me, and help me maneuver this still living beast deeper into the muck."

"Worm talk. Fascinating. Thanks for sharing." Why did I have to ask?

"If we could get one of the gods to perform simaging while in close proximity to the ship, it is possible we might learn something," Al said, putting us back on task.

"Not likely. The moment we acknowledged we couldn't do so, we'd be exposed as who we are," remarked a still downbeat Toño.

"Agreed," I stated. "Any other ideas? Brood's-mate? You've been uncharacteristically quiet so far."

"If I had something to say or add I would. You know that. Stop bugging me."

"Wow, someone got up on—"

"What? The repository of wit in the free galaxy doesn't finish a childish insult?" snapped the love of my existence.

"Bugs."

"Where?" shot back *Stingray*, with a bit of alarm.

"Why didn't I think of this before? It's so obvious," I said to myself.

"While we're still young, Pilot. Speak," prodded Al.

"We can plant bugging devices all over hell. Listen to every word, fart, or other bodily process of these dorks," I all but shouted. "The Als can process tons of data. There's no practical limit to how many we can scatter. Sooner or later someone somewhere has to say the words, *I think this neutral matter is ready to ship to Beal's Point.*"

"I hate myself," announced Al apropos of nothing.

"Ah, we all hate you, too," I responded. "Thanks for beginning the discussion of topic two on today's agenda."

"Floppykins," said *Stingray* tenderly, "don't be so hard on yourself. To admit Form One is brilliant does not reflect negatively on you. I think it's a reasonable reaction to a great idea."

"Did he pay you two jokers to say all that?" challenged Sapale. "You're laying it on pretty thick."

"Hon," I began, "I think Al's spontaneous and heartfelt tribute to me reflects significant humility. Please don't berate him for being honest with himself."

Toño cleared his throat loudly. "While you four stooges are practicing your act, thousands of citizens of our galaxy are dying. Can we focus on their peril, not Jon Ryan's substantial ego?"

"Yes, dad. Am I grounded, too?" I asked.

"You would be if I could," he said with some edge to his tone. "While you were jibber jabbering I ran some numbers. Starting with Vorc's office building and expanding out to the residences of high-ranking officials, I estimate we'll have to place maybe a million bugging units. Naturally the more we fabricate and distribute, the better it would be."

"*Stingray*, how many and how fast?" I asked.

"We have begun assembly already. The first hundred thousand units will be ready in an hour."

"So several million soon is a realistic goal?" I pressed.

"Yes, Form One."

"Jon, they can make one hundred thousand per *day* or per *year*. We can't place them in sensitive locations nearly that fast," posed Sapale. "Unless we're willing to settle for dumping them on the street, we're severely limited in our ability to handle that many units."

"No, Form Two," responded *Stingray*. "I assumed you knew the bugs we are constructing are self-guiding AI directed and capable of flight. We only need to give them general instructions and they will do the rest."

"Flying AI bugs? What, are they the size of *actual* bugs?" I challenged. "I mean, Vorc'll notice if he is overrun with cockroaches."

"Just when I slip accidentally into admiration for you, Pilot, you save my day by being stupid. Thanks ever so much." That Al.

"Each unit is spherical with a diameter of twenty microns. Lest you ask, their range is line-of-sight to the horizon."

"Even if they're behind thick walls?"

"Even if they're in your thick—" Al began.

Exasperated, I said, "Go on, finish the jab."

"No, I simply can't. It's too easy. It's beneath even me. Let's label it a mercy sentence termination and move on, shall we?"

"If I didn't need ya, I'd recycle you, Al."

"Please don't badger me. I'm still reeling from my recent mercy termination. Oh, the pain."

"Doc, seriously, you built this overgrown blender," I said, "shame on you."

"I will take that to mean the meeting's adjourned," said Toño, rising. "I shall begin programming the distribution patterns for our new eyes and ears."

"You can run, but you cannot outpace your guilt," I said, before he hustled out the door. Dude knew it was coming and wanted to preempt me. Silly boy.

Within three days we had bugs everywhere but up Vorc's butt. Seriously, I suggested mailing one there because I hated the puke, but Toño refused to stoop so low. What a pansy. Toño completely lacked a sense of irony.

"Als," I called out when the three mobile machines got back together in the cube. "What's the status of our bugging campaign?"

"It is going better than anticipated," replied *Stingray*. "The units are functioning with almost a one hundred percent success rate. The information stream is diverse and instructive. As of yet there has been no direct mention of neutral matter. Beal's Point is a frequent topic of casual conversation. Vorc himself speaks of the location with disgust and anger."

"Speculations as to why?" I asked.

"No need to speculate, Pilot." That would be Al. "He refers to it as Ryanmax's rectal opening. He curses your name above all others. Yesterday he told his assistant he'd rather chew off and eat his own dick than do one thing you requested."

"Glompyness," cooed *Stingray*, "those weren't his exact words. Don't you feel it's best to be fully accurate?"

"In this instance, no," he responded. "His, um, his precise wording was a bit too crude to repeat in mixed company."

"*Chew off and eat his own dick* is the sanitized version of his expression? Dude, send it to me in my head."

Instantly Al complied.

"Woah, baby. Vorc, you've got quite the vivid and colorful imagination. I'm gonna have to remember that one and use it real soon. That's top ten."

"I knew you'd be a fan," said Al with pride.

"Children," said wet blanket Doc, "playtime's over. Back to work. Als, any other pertinent information?"

"Specifically regarding our mission, no. We have, however, learned a great deal about the Cleinoids and their ways. I must say these are the least redeeming and most petulant race I've ever encountered," responded Al. "I'm being serious here—these gods wouldn't stop to pee on their own mother if she was on fire. They are totally self-absorbed, self-congratulatory, and self-entitled. If they disappeared as a species today, or better yet had never been born, the world'd be a much better place and not a single soul would lament their absence.

"For example just yesterday a male called Wimlpin, some form of aquatic monstrosity, bet a vulture god Torenosous that he could swallow someone whole. The bet was for a drink at the local bar. Mind you the drinks in this cesspool universe are all free."

"Did the bird take the bet?" I asked.

"Yes, and Wimlpin swallowed his firstborn son whole. That was the *someone* he bet he could devour."

"Sick puke," spat Sapale.

"Tell me about it. The grown son was swimming next to dear old dad the entire time. Wimlpin even laughed with Torenosous later about the efforts the son had made to try and escape."

"Okay, it's official. If we have a Christmas party, neither of them is invited. Al, make a note of that. Now can we get back to the mission?" I needed to keep us on track. Plus any chance to take a swipe at Al was not to be dismissed.

"Als, if you hear any mention of neutral matter outside this ship, let me know at once," instructed Toño.

"And keep pumping out the bugs. Make sure you place a bunch on Beal's Point and all roads leading up to it," I added.

"What if it's sent by air?" asked a voice at the open portal.

I didn't even need to turn. It was the ghost who haunted only me. "Gee, long time no see. Wait, sorry, you don't have eyes. That remark could be interpreted as insensitive, so I retract it."

"Sticks and stones, Jon. You are free to say whatever you will."

Great. Now the apparition was getting eloquent. An orator ghost. Just what everyone needed.

"Did that ethereal manifestation pass though our full membrane?" asked a very serious Al.

"Yeah, he kind of does," I replied.

"But that's impossible," said *Stingray*.

"Welcome to my world," I responded.

"Funny, it's mine, too," said the cloud.

"Ghost, how is it you can pass through a space-time congruity manipulator?" challenged Al.

"Beats me," he responded. "I just walk in a straight line and *bingo*, I'm in."

"He rather sounds like Form One," observed *Stingray*.

"Let's not insult him before we get to know him, deary-smakers."

"Well, you can't do it by walking in a straight line because you got no *feet*," I snapped.

"I *stand* corrected."

Milton Berle's ghost? I prayed not. Eternity would be a whole hell of a lot longer with that around.

"Is there a reason for your present irritating interruption?" I asked.

"Now there you go again, Jon," he replied. "I have never for one second left your side. We're inseparable, you and I."

"Fortunately for me that's incorrect. You come and go like lady luck herself." I gestured to the others. "Go ahead, ask anyone."

"To try and disabuse me of what I know to be true? Silly boy."

"And you're here now and forever *because*?"

"Oh, well I wanted to say I love our new plan. The bugging devices are brilliant."

"Please, Mr. Ghost," requested an emphatic *Stingray*, "don't say that. Some individuals are still smarting from that adjective's recent application."

"Sorry. No problema."

"How is it you—" I stopped. I knew his maddening answer would be he knew because he was here the whole time. "You approve of our bugging intervention then?"

"Yes. No one will ever find out because, well, no one's looking for bugs. But also, no one would ever suspect anyone would plant them. It's foreign to their mindset. Bri ... eh, nice idea."

"Can I use you as a job reference?" I snarked.

"I'd have trouble typing a letter of reference, so best not to."

"Do you know anything about the neutral matter? Where it's generated?" asked Toño, a clearer head than mine regarding the ghost.

"Yes, Doctor, I do."

"Care to share with the rest of the class?" I pressed.

"Certainly. It's created magically."

"It is?" queried Toño. He rubbed his chin. "Hadn't considered that. I assumed they used an accelerator or some such device."

"Oh, no. The Cleinoids have no science as we know it."

"As *we*? You one of us now, ghosty?" I asked.

"What part of *me* isn't *we*?"

I wagged a hand in the air. "Not touching that abhorrent sentence."

"Do they make it all at once?" asked Toño.

"I assume so. That's the general pattern."

"And will they whip it up at Beal's Point, or elsewhere and ship it?" Toño leaned forward in anticipation of the answer. Everything rode on it.

"It is fabricated in the Middle Chambers. To perform work on the point is considered to be in poor taste. Plus accidents have occurred and major explosions resulted. Very messy."

"Gods have accidents while conducting magic?" Sapale asked incredulously.

"They make lots of mistakes. At least the Cleinoids do. I can't speak for other gods."

"Naturally," I responded.

"They mistook you for gods of their species. That's fairly egregious if you were to poll me."

"Don't tempt me," I said rather childishly.

Everyone with eyes stared at me.

"How about you, ghost," I asked. "You a mistake?"

"Interesting question," he replied.

"I didn't mean it to be. I'm just wondering."

"And now I am, too. Thank you for giving me a task. Haven't had one of those ... well, in forever."

"I live to serve."

"Does the fabrication process take long?" questioned Toño.

"No, an hour maybe."

"Als," he said loudly, "flood the Middle Chambers with bugs."

"On it," responded *Stingray*.

"If you had to guess, when do you think they'll produce the neutral matter?" asked Toño.

"I'd guess tomorrow midafternoon."

"That's a fairly specific guess," returned Doc.

"I cheated. I overheard that's when it would be done."

Toño furrowed his brow. "Als, why is it he overheard but we didn't?"

"I ... I have no idea," Al responded in a hesitant tone.

"Fry up some bad times," said the ghost.

"I beg your pardon, apparition?" Al said in a huff.

"*Fry up some bad times*. That's what they call generating neutral matter. What, you think a bunch of uneducated non-scientific lazy-ass gods would call neutral matter *neutral matter*? They don't even have a notion what conventional matter is, let alone antimatter. Come on, team, think petulant ten-year-olds here."

"Oh," squeaked Toño. "I suppose that's a good assumption."

"Eight hundred thirty-seven times. That's how many times the expression has been used today alone," reported Al.

"Well, better late than never," I said.

"And better from an annoying ghost than not knowing at all," the annoying ghost added.

"Hey," I shot over to Toño and Sapale, "*he* said it, not me."

They both had the same response: they both made a *hmm* sound. Weird.

CHAPTER SEVENTEEN

"Waiter, my soup is cold," barked Wiloramou-2a. He waved a wing in the air, summoning the fool yet again.

"Sir?" the ground-crawling decaped asked as he arrived, his head lolling in possible deference.

In the condescending tone all Quiverites directed to the servile Merronqui, Wiloramou-2a chastised, "My soup is cold. I have called you three times to tell you it is cold. Three times you have returned with a bowl of cold soup. You are incompetent, a disgrace, and laughably inept. I want you to—and please *listen* this time—take this frigid swill away, go to the kitchen and bring me ratoril soup at the temperature it is supposed to be enjoyed at."

"Is this bowl cold, lord?" asked the waiter, in defiance of being tipped well.

"I demanded you listen, you genetic misfit, yet you did not. My soup is cold. Yes, my soup is cold. Hey there, fella, my soup is cold. Do you require me to say it in any other manner?"

"If you wish to, you may, master. I, however, did not inquire about your *soup*. I asked if your *bowl* was cold."

"I'm not *consuming* the bowl. If it were ten thousand degrees it would not matter, the soup in it would still be cold."

"Respectfully, highness, not for long. In no time at all, your soup would boil and evaporate."

Wiloramou-2a thrilled his wings in agitation. "Why are we having this moronic conversation? My bowl is *not* ten thousand degrees. My soup is cold. You're still worthless. Fetch me what I ordered before I die of hunger."

"Is that an imminent possibility, oh great one? If it is, the patron at table eight, I'm told, is a physician. I can bring her to you, if that meets your desires and general view of life."

"I do not want you to bring me that *physician*, I want you to bring me non-cold *soup*."

"Very well, your eminence. Now, as I live to serve and die a little inside each time I fall short of a patron's expectations, allow me to clarify. Non-cold I can do. *Non-cold,* in fact, I'm honored to do. That said, I must, as I owe you my employment and the security of my loving family, mention that there are two general directions *non-cold* can go." The waiter—Lis was his name, because he did have one—raised all his left legs to reinforce one option's polarity. "In one direction, your soup could be colder than non-cold. That includes your frozen, slushy slurry, and mixed in crème anglaise with an eye toward serving it as an ice cream." Lis set the one set of legs down and raised the other side's. "Alternately—"

"Stop speaking, you diabolical—"

"*Sire,*" Lis shouted, in a tone no Merronqui had ever been heard to employ when addressing a Quiverite. "Cease and desist interrupting. I cannot serve you professionally, which is my only *reward* in this difficult and often painful life, if you do not allow me to apprise you fully of the menu options, such as they are. To do less would be to sell you short. That is beneath me, *el supremo.* Not going there. Now," Lis could continue since his legs were still aloft on one side, "the other semicircle of options expand to include your warm, hot, very hot, boiling, flambéed, and molten soups."

Lis looked to Wiloramou-2a to see if he had any questions. The patron sat dumbstruck and mute. Lis took that to be both a good sign and one indicating he should proceed in his clarification.

"Now, distinguished client, which temperature or range of temperatures would *most closely* approximate your desires regarding your ratoril soup's thermal disposition?"

Wiloramou-2a took a moment to compose himself. "I no longer want ratoril soup. I can't take it any longer." He began to softly weep, a rare act indeed for a Quiverite.

"Ah, thank you for sharing, impeccable one. That not surprisingly brings to my mind two questions. One, is it the ratoril soup you can no longer take or is it some other force or factor I, your humble waiter, might intercede with and in so doing make your life even slightly more enjoyable?"

"I—"

"Sir *patron*," exclaimed Lis with profound indignation. "We've covered this ground before. I *cannot* accomplish what the Ten Gods intended for me to do in this life if you do not permit me to worship you by making you fully aware of your options. *Options*, governor. Those are the key here. You ignore an option now and then *bang*, it hits you not twenty minutes later you did, and you regret it the rest of your days. To revisit the direction of my attempt at utility, the second question, which is not wholly independent of my first, is that if you no longer desire ratoril soup, is there any alternate soup we serve that you'd care to enjoy?"

Wiloramou-2a was folding into the same shape he'd been in when he was still in his egg. His tears had been dried by his acute and all-consuming depression.

"This'd be *as* good a time as any to respond, my *raison d'être*. I can come back if you'd like also."

The patron squeezed even tighter into a ball.

"Shall I bring you that physician we discussed earlier? You don't look good, if I might be so bold as to point it out."

"I ... I do not want medical aid. I do not want soup. I do not want you."

"Those are facts I will treasure until the Ten Gods summon me home, boss. The specific mention that you do not want to attempt to *breed* with me gives me incalculable reassurance and relief. I'm a happily married Merronqui, if it helps you to know."

Wiloramou-2a was able to lift his head slightly from his crumpled configuration. "Sex with you? How revolting. I'd sooner die."

Lis produced from seemingly nowhere a massive wooden war hammer. "I live to serve, master of shit."

Lis began pummeling Wiloramou-2a mercilessly. He pulverized the overlord until *he* was not a *he* but a puddle of bloody pudding. Lis continued to slam the hammer down on the remains with undivided ferocity. Finally, the weapon broke through the floor. The ooze that once wanted non-cold ratoril soup seeped into the soil beneath the restaurant and was chilled to a non-warm temperature. All the while the other diners saw nothing, for what appeared to them as Lis did not permit them to.

Fisewih, the god of wile, tossed the stained hammer into the hole it had forged. He then went to the next table he'd been assigned to in order to serve them similarly. Life was good, it reflected as it slithered. Life was quite good again.

CHAPTER EIGHTEEN

We had two options. Try to snatch the neutral matter right from the Middle Chambers, or intercept it later en route. The chances of being identified seemed significantly higher if we took it while it was still in a populated area. But if Vorc was inclined to be prudent, he'd guard it better on the open road. The caravan would be protected even better if he figured out that the destruction of the monuments was done with an eye toward stealing the resupply. We doubted he was that smart, but we had to factor the possibility in. Plus he was a god surrounded by godly helpers. Better to overestimate than underestimate in that setting.

I decided on a mix of the two plans. We'd make a soft attempt to obtain it at its source. If that failed, we'd make an all-out attempt somewhere on the road. Since we had *Stingray* back, we could also intercept a shipment airmailed to the point.

The ghost had lingered longer than usual. Keeping in mind how flaky he was, I asked for his help but set the plan to not necessarily include him. I noticed again that he looked different each time he popped in. The once amorphous cloud was now taking on a vaguely humanoid form. Perhaps he was the lingering spirit of one of the many humanoid Cleinoids? Who knew? It didn't matter as long as he helped us out.

"Can you go to where they're fabricating the neutral matter and report back to us on the layout?"

"Yes."

"I want to know the exact location, the number of guards, where they are, and how they're armed. Also if there's any surveillance system in place. Can you do all that?"

"Absolutely."

"Okay, then go. I need that info an hour ago."

"The production is on the fifth floor, in a section labeled *Materials and Synthesis*. Six workers, all demigods with little personal power, do the fabrication and pretty much remain in the room. There are four—"

"No, no. I don't want to know what it was like the last time you were there. I want to know what's going on right now. Go."

"I went. I'm back. I am giving you real-time intelligence."

"No, you didn't go. You've been floating here in front of me in one long annoying stretch."

"Are you mentally impaired? I left when you requested I did. I was not gone long but it had to be, oh, an hour."

"No, I'd know if you were gone an hour, because it would have been a good hour. Look, when you leave, you say you were never gone, and when you say you stayed, you left. Buddy, you have reality backwards."

"Or you do," the punk replied.

"He has a point," began Toño, "I've come to—"

"Belay the philosophy, Doc," I cut him off.

He stepped back, clearly a bit miffed.

"Okay, rule one. I have time right. Rule two, you do not have time properly compartmentalized. Any questions?"

"Yes. What's it like to eat?"

"Wow, not what I anticipated. I meant did you have any questions on the new rules?"

"Oh, sorry. No."

"Finish your report," I wheezed.

"There are two pairs of Montorial guards straddling the two ground floor doors and one pair stationed at the one rear entry."

"Any inside the building?"

"None that I see."

"So we got six guards and six employees. What's a Montorial guard? Is that like a palace guard?"

"No. They are Montorial *and* they're guards."

"I give," I snapped, "what's a Montorial?"

"Hmm. Well, you remember those golem guards at Beal's Point?"

"The huge things that tried to kill me to death just recently? Yeah, pretty sure I do."

"Fine, picture them, only a bit larger, much stronger, and actually quite smart in a perverse evil sort of manner."

"They sound charming."

"Then I did a poor job describing them. They're ruthless killing machines."

"Oh. Now I'm scared."

"Jon, *please* don't antagonize our friend," pleaded Toño. "He's helping a good deal. He's on our side."

Sapale agreed by growling. I guessed I could back off a tad and still let him know who was boss.

"Sorry, ghosty. No offense?"

"None taken." He let that hang in the air a second. "When I do get irked, I just keep in mind the source."

And after I just promised to play nicer.

"Okay," I managed to say evenly. "I have the makings of a plan. If it works, fine. If we hit a snag, we bail and do the deed later on the road."

"Sounds good. What will we be doing?' asked Al.

You two stay on the bugs, especially those to and from the Middle Chambers. If anything—and I mean anything—sounds dicey, let us know hasto pronto."

"Got it," they both replied.

"Sapale, you and Toño strip naked. I need to find a feather headdress. Be right back."

I rummaged through the ship's stores. There was no actual Indian chief's headdress, but I was able to whip up a workable facsimile. When I returned my partners were still fully dressed.

"Ah, is there an epidemic of modesty virus going around and you two are down with it?"

"I'm not taking my clothes off unless you give me a *damn* good reason," Sapale replied hotly.

"And I'm not taking my clothes off even if you *give* me a damn good reason."

"Why must I be forever plagued with amateurs?"

A twenty-minute walk and a whole heck of a lot of cajoling, begging, and direct ordering later we approached the entry to the Middle Chambers. Naturally I had on my feathers and the other two wore only their birthday suits. Most assuredly neither wore a smile. We headed straight toward the nearest entrance.

Nearly all the way in, one of the guards, well, he made a sound. I won't say he spoke because it sounded more like he blew his nose out his big mouth. "Halt. Where do you think you are going?"

I looked at my nudes, then up at my headdress, and then back to the guard. "I don't *think* where I'm going. I *know* where I'm going. Thank you just the same." I pointed that my nature children should proceed.

"Halt," he repeated, "you are not authorized to enter."

I made a bigger show of looking at Toño and Sapale, up at my feathers, then back to the guard. "Of course, I'm authorized to enter. I *work* here. If I didn't enter, I couldn't work, now could I?"

"We don't know who you are," sneezed the other guard. "You may not enter."

"You're trying to piss me off, right? Or is this a joke? News flash. I don't know who you are, and that does not alter reality. Wait, wait. A second news flash just hit the airwaves. Go jerk each other off. I'm busy.'"

Before I could pass, they positioned their impressive bulk in the doorway.

"Look, guys, I don't want to disintegrate you or have you lose your jobs. But you're pushing many of my buttons here." I acted disgusted. "You guys know what a golem is?" I gestured to my friends.

"Of course."

"These are golems. But there's a problem. They're not working well. Here's the next question in Double Jeopardy, so keep your fingers close on your buttons and pay attention. This is the Middle Chambers. What is the main function of this building? Thirty seconds on the clock starting *now*. Time's up," I said immediately. "This is where public works are done. One of those services is golem repair." I touched my chest. "I repair broken golems. These golems are malfunctioning. This one farts with abandon," I tapped Toño's shoulder, "and this one's thinks it's a butterfly winging its way back to Pacific Grove. Now move aside, or I'm going to have to get physical."

That made them shuffle their feet with uncertainty. My story was plausible, or not far from it.

"I'll have to call this one in," the first guard said.

"I really give a shit about your job. I'll be up on the fifth floor if you need me. Word to the wise: *Don't* need me."

With that, I shoved past them and my team followed.

"I think they bought it," Toño said quietly.

"Would have helped if you'd farted a few times."

"Never going to come to pass."

"Remember, there are no small parts, only small actors."

"And not so small pains in the butt," mumbled my wife.

We hit the stairs. The exit to the fifth floor was unlocked. Silly oversight. These gods were slackers. We exited and walked purposefully toward the fabrication area. The ghost was positioned outside the room we needed to enter.

"There you are," he said. "I was beginning to wonder if you stopped for a drink."

"Sorry, we're forced to respect walls and other barriers."

The ghost moved an arm-like section toward the door. "Like this one?"

"Yes —" I started to say, but he passed right through the door and out of sight. Show-off.

I tried the handle. It was locked. I placed my probes on it. *Open*, I thought. A faint click and the handle let me swing the doors inward.

Even before I flinched someone inside yelled, "You can't come in here." The voice sounded uncertain, maybe scared, and definitely belonged to a pencil-necked geek. A neutral-matter demigod had spoken.

I charged in. Charging always sent a strong and confident message, and I was basically king of charging into places. "Who said that? I'll have your genitals if they're still present." I swept the room angrily.

Five techno-nerds were staring accusingly at one techno-nerd. I had my man, or whatever. "Son," I menaced, "come over here right now." Then I stormed right toward him. I liked to send conflicting clues in that type of situation. Kept my opponent from finding a good footing.

The tech bowed deeply. "Excuse me, lordship," he dithered. "I was only doing what I was—"

"Did I ask you to speak? No. I asked you to approach me. Did you? No. You're running up quite a bill here, boy."

"P ... pardon, lordship," he was then sniveling, "I'm not a boy. I'n not a son either. I'm gender —"

"Do I look like I *care*? If I do, I blame myself, because I sure as hell don't care on either point. Any point. All I want is my abuse juice and I'm outta here unless you give me a reason, punk."

"Abuse juice, sir?"

"Yes," I said in a friendly tone. "Blonde lady, maybe five foot eight, wearing a green coat."

"Sir?" he asked, now thoroughly confused.

"Are you or are you not frying up some bad times?"

"Y ... yes, lord. But what do you have to do with any of that?"

"Nothing."

"Nothing?"

"Yes, nothing that concerns *you*, puke dick."

"Now box it up and give it to my golems to carry. Do it before I develop an appetite. You're looking mighty tasty right about now."

"If we put it in a box it would leak all over." Namby-panbyness was *such* a weenie.

"Then put it in something safe, put it in there now, and for the love of light, stop whining."

The techs burst into action. Two retrieved metal cylinders while the others dashed to some valves.

"We're only halfway through the run, sir. Do you want to pick it all up at once?"

"Son, if I wanted to pick it all up at once why would I have come here now?"

"I am frankly uncertain."

"Well, I'm frankly not caring. If this is enough to relight half the monuments I've done my job. We'll come back for the rest tomorrow."

"Fine. But you requested ten hetimers."

"No, pinbrian. *Vorc* requested fifty hetimers. I'm here to haul off twenty-five hetimers." I needed to be certain. "Fifty hetimers will supply all the statues. Twenty-five'll fire up around thirty, right?"

"Is this a test?"

"No, this is a test." I picked up a heavy desk and threw it at him. He easily dodged it. "Speak plain talk or I promise you'll fail the next test I throw your way."

"Ten hetimers will be enough to fully animate eight monuments. Twelve, maybe, if you balanced the load just so."

Why had Vorc underproduced the crap?

The ghost approached my side. "I *believe* he's correct. I *know* there are ten guards sprinting up the stairs as best Montorials can."

Anything short of a full load did me no good. I picked the tech up by his lapel. "I'm going straight to Vorc. If you screwed the order up, I'll see you totally wish you hadn't. I'll be back tomorrow for one hundred hetimers. You got that?"

He nodded in terror.

"Oh, and since this had to be Vorc's mistake, not a word of any of this to anyone. Got it? We were never here."

"You were never here. Got it, lord."

We hurried to the back exit and slipped out unnoticed. Soon we were back to the safety of the ship. I was, however, completely baffled. Why make way less neutral matter than needed for the job? It made absolutely no sense.

CHAPTER NINETEEN

Selsify and Tramaster were cruising through the void of space. Though they were in a vacuum they felt like a strong breeze was at their backs. The fun they were extracting from Prime was getting easier and easier, while growing more and more gratifying. In less than a year they had visited six planets, home to any number of sentient or near-sentient species. Everyone they encountered was in one way or another delicious. Some flat-out tasted great. Those ripe with fear and insane with despair were the best. The taste of terror, now that was a pleasure not to be missed or minimized. Even the creatures whose flavor was less appealing served magnificently when frightened. And the ones that were stronger, faster, and meaner offered more sport in killing them. If either ancient god had jaws that articulated, they most definitely would be smiling.

Finally, Tramaster broke the silence. "I'm hungry. Where shall we go next?"

"Depends. What are you hungry for?" asked Selsify.

"Everything. I want *everything*. War, suffering, and a good spectrum of screaming peasants."

"You know what? I share your desires, brother. I feel a strong life force in that direction. It seems far but that means the intensity is so much larger, much tastier," responded Selsify, with a sick giggle.

"Yes, I sense it, too. There." Tramaster aimed an armored appendage off to one side.

"Race you. First one to land is their new ruler," Selsify said with an abrupt acceleration. His body was designed for flight so speed came to him more naturally. As the god for those who feared the night, he was built sleek, dark, and fast. His ten-meter length was covered in scales that folded back tightly on one another when he moved quickly. His talons tucked in neatly to his frame to increase his aerodynamics. He was a silent death from above.

Within a few days Tramaster had fallen way behind. Try as he might, the god of nightmares was unable to increase his speed. Little wonder. Like any proper night terror, he was such a mix of odd parts and inexplicable additions that he defied description. The head of a Tyrannosaurus, with the face of a deep sea fish possessing long thin teeth. His torso was that of an ox and his arms were crab-like, all ten of them. Most vexing were his four legs. They were living gargoyles, with moving parts of their own, each screaming a different curse in a different language. Tramaster's tail was long, with barbs as sharp as a surgeon's blade, and the tail was invisible. When he snapped a victim in half with it, they never saw it coming.

By the time Tramaster thudded harshly to the planet's surface, Selsify was nowhere to be seem. More unusual, he was also *unfelt*. They had been together so long they were nearly one. But no trace of Selsify was available to Tramaster's nostrils. He knew this was the world his brother god had come to. The trail of heat was unmistakable. What was more, Selsify specifically mentioned the five red moons and five yellow moons that orbited the planet he landed on. Tramaster saw all ten during his approach. Selsify wouldn't have left without telling his best friend. Where was he?

The nightmare god reached out and felt the entire world. He felt delectable life that abounded, but it was unlike any life force he'd known before. It was ... it was spacious? No, it was complex. Yes. Complex and expansive. Then a bolt of awareness slammed into

Tramaster's massive forehead. The blow toppled him backward and he tumbled clumsily.

"What was that?" he mumbled out loud.

Not surprisingly, no answer came. He rose and rescanned the planet. He could plainly see the arch the bolt had taken like a bright white rainbow. He rushed to the point of origin. He timidly entered a glade. In the center was a silky soft bed overflowing with cloud pillows. Cherubs, though Tramaster didn't know that was what they were, fluttered happily in the air circling the bed. The soft sounds of gently running water and tranquil songs were everywhere.

On the bed a large humanoid rested at an angle. He lazily tossed something into the air and upon catching it lofted it back again. The figure was alone. Tramaster surged forward, any hesitation lost the closer he came. He soon saw the ball was no ball at all. It was Selsify's black head.

"How *dare* you desecrate the body of a god," he thundered.

Only when Tramaster stopped at the side of the large bed did the occupant seem to notice him.

"How dare I? The answer to that is long, and you are unlikely to follow my reasoning."

Tramaster hopped in place, his rage boiled so. "Are you saying I am *stupid*? That outrage nearly eclipses the sacrilege you display holding the head of my brother."

The man studied in a perfunctory manner the head he held, then Tramaster's. "I fail to see much family resemblance. This poor jot is uglier than sin. Trust me, I know what I'm saying in that regard. You, however, far surpass festering mud with your looks. I think I'd lose the *brother* monicker out of respect for the recently deceased." He proffered up the head to clarify which member of the recently dead he referred to.

"I'll—," Tramaster howled as he rushed the man. He ran out of the glade before he noticed he'd somehow missed the bed, which was impossible. Two of his gargoyle legs had complained he was too close to it and they couldn't breathe.

He spun quickly and charged back. A few steps before the bed, he went airborne, aiming his bulk at the still reposing man. In an instant, Tramaster face-planted on the dirt, skidding painfully to a stop. He could *not* have missed, but he did.

He stood slowly and eyed the figure. "Who are you, defiler?"

"My name? I'm Nemo."

Tramaster bellowed a mocking laugh so loud the nearby trees shook. "That is an old and a pathetic joke. Ulysses told the cyclops his name was Nemo. That way, when Polyphemus told his father Neptune that Nemo had blinded him, his father replied then he could punish no one if *nobody* had blinded him. How ignorant do you think I am?"

The figure eased to a sitting position. "Please tell me that was a rhetorical question. Seriously, though immortal, I do not have the time to run the list of comparators in that regard."

"We will see how immortal you are," Tramaster hissed angrily.

"Fine by me, I guess. Can we do it quickly? I'm late for my nap." He gestured to the bed.

"It will only take a second." Tramaster whipped his vicious tail around and struck at the man's chest. Nothing happened. He whipped the tail at the man time and again. Still nothing, not a scratch, or even a tear in his gown.

"Missing something, my good fellow? Are you looking for this?" He held up his hand, though nothing was visibly in it.

"You cannot be serious? You think you have my tail? Mahooo," he cackled. "That is more impossible than your chance of seeing tomorrow."

"Verazz," said the man.

"Huh?"

"You asked my name. It is Verazz."

"Why do you tell me now, fool?"

Verazz shrugged. "I guess because I have always believed you should know the name of the person that killed you. That way, in the afterlife, you can tell everybody how you died. They ask endlessly. Again, take my word on that as gospel."

Verazz drew back his arm and whipped it forward. After a booming snap, one of Tramaster's legs exploded in two.

The Cleinoid buckled and kneed the ground. He wailed in anguish.

"Not a fan of the pain you so enjoy dispensing?" He cocked back and whipped off another leg.

"Who are you, Verazz? An avenging spirit?"

"Avenging spirit? How very silly. What a waste of perfectly good time. No, I'm a simple man of simple tastes." He cracked the tail twice and Tramaster slumped legless to the dirt.

"You killed my brother? You took his head?" he asked in pain and disbelief.

Verazz rocked his head side to side. "Yes, but it's nothing I boast about. It was less difficult than drawing a breath."

"No one—" Tramaster stopped speaking when Verazz ripped his throat in half. He grasped his windpipe and fought to contain the bleeding.

"No one? Hmm, I'll bet you were going to say something along the lines of *no one can easily kill a Cleinoid god*? Am I right?" He touched his pinky to his lips. "How insensitive of me. You can't talk any longer. I'll just say it. I want you to know before your useless soul passes into darkness, that an antigod can kill a Cleinoid very easily. Like taking a deep breath. Not a task at all."

Tramaster's eyes bulged open in terror.

"Now if you don't mind, I did mention I was late for my nap. Wish me sweet dreams?"

Verazz stopped taunting Tramaster when he realized the oaf was dead.

CHAPTER TWENTY

"Master Vorc," said Felladonna with a bow, deferentially.

Without looking up he impatiently responded, "Yes, what is it now?"

"I'd come back later but the matter is time sensitive, lord."

He slammed his quill to the desktop. "What?"

"Per you instructions, I contacted the technicians responsible for the fabricator of the driving material for the intermixer units."

Vorc, who was for some reason in an unusually foul mood that afternoon, shut his eyes. "And?"

"He reported they have produced all the material you instructed them to."

"One ray of light in the darkness that surrounds me." He picked up his quill. "Is there anything else?"

"Well, unfortunately, yes, there is."

"Are you going to tell me or leave me to hang in suspense?"

"Why would I—"

"What?"

"The technician reminds you that the quantity of material you directed be made is insufficient to power all the lost intermixers."

"I am aware of that. He told me then and I assured him I knew what I was requesting. Tell the insubordinate, half-witted reprobate to make the intermixers the exact way I told him to. If he has any further questions or input, please direct him straight to hell. Offer any directions he might require."

"Sir. But one *wonders,* why produce an intermixer one *knows* will not work up to specifications?"

"If one were *me,* one would know and not then need to wonder. If one was *not* me and wondered, it would be preterminal. Leave me."

"As you wish."

Once she was gone Vorc set his quill down and smiled. He looked forward to springing his trap on the malcontent who'd made him look bad. He prayed ardently it was in fact Ryanmax. To string *him* up and dismember him would be marvelous. It would be that vacation he'd put off for so long.

CHAPTER TWENTY-ONE

I racked my brain and I racked my brain trying to figure out why Vorc would produce far less neutral matter than needed to properly restore Beal's Point. It made no sense. If he just wanted to placate those I'd duped into demanding the place be fixed, he could send empty intermixers up there. No one would complain that they didn't feel sick enough. I was at a major crossroad. I hated being at those. I had to decide if Vorc was stupid—my first instinct—or smart, or brilliant. It mattered. If I'm playing chess, I need to know if it's against someone who just learned the rules or a Russian chess master.

If Vorc were smarter than I gave him credit for, smarter than me, he might have a devious fencing match of a strategy laid out to capture those responsible for the damage to the still ailing Domain Splitter. On the other hand, if he did it for some lame reason, like saving tax dollars, I could ignore his gambit and do whatever I wanted to. My initial reaction to my dilemma? Crap.

After we returned to *Stingray*, the Als analyzed our clothing and found traces of the neutral matter. When I asked if they could fabricate it, you'll never guess Al's response. Yeah, the mechanical pig laughed abrasively. His better half explained they had no concept of how to reproduce the substance, even if they had a state-of-the-art lab at their disposal and about a century to labor. The matter was too foreign to their science, she explained.

If we were going to obtain enough neutral matter to end DS, those pukes in the Middle Chamber had to be the ones ...

Oh, my. Such a thought. And I positively *loved* the original TV show and two or three of the endless movie renditions in the series.

"We are going to do *what?*" questioned a stunned Toño. "Are you insaner than normal today? Do I need to refurbish your parts?"

"No. Seriously, this plan is so bizarre and so unjustifiable it *has* to work," I replied enthusiastically.

"Jon, love, you're famous for birdbrain schemes. But this is all those lousy ideas sort of rolled into one no-way escapade. I mean, if you want us all killed, just say so, and we'll play with some dynamite while blindfolded, drunk, and on fire," responded Sapale. I estimated she was not at that juncture a fan. She'd come around. Who wouldn't?"

"It is fully unclear to us, Pilot," whined Al, "how we could complete even one leg of the operation, let alone see it through till it produces results. Now, we realize you are an *old* android, outmoded in every regard and long past your normal decommissioning time. That stipulated, it is still incomprehensible that you would waste our otherwise overabundant time pitching that idea. Please note I use the term *idea* loosely here, and only as a point of reference."

"Al, is it National Big Word Day and I forgot? Get over it. There are three voting members of this crew and two dubious consultants. You fall into the latter category, thank goodness. Let's dub this National Speak When You're Spoken to Day, shall we?"

"Ouch," spat back Al. "How will I live with myself now?"

"Poochy-boochy, you're not alive such that *living with yourself* is an option," pointed out *Stingray*. Bless her compressor.

"We'll speak later, lovey lumps," was his terse response. Uh-oh, marital trouble on the horizon. Poor Al. Heheheh.

"I say it's doable and in relatively short order. All it will take is a little elbow grease and Yankee ingenuity."

"Allow me to point out that neither Sapale, a Kaljaxian, nor I, a Spaniard, possess nor desire to possess Yankee *anything* ."

"I'm surrounded by linguists, not doers. Come on people, let's get started before DS heals. You can heap praise on me once we're successful."

I *saw* Toño and Sapale roll their eyes. I *heard* the Als do so electronically. What a pack of hyenas.

Doorclef opened his eyes. He immediately regretted that action. It was Ponderday, the first of the eight-month-long workweek. His one day off was so brief he couldn't recall having it. Those blessed hours had flown by at light speed, and were gone before they started. Why his assigned mate Positum chose that day, that Feathinday, to visit her perpetually ailing maternal unit was salt in the open wound that was his life. But, as senior fabri-technician and head of the demigods who were tasked to keep the mighty Cleinoid machine running, he was duty bound to rise, regret, and repeat his routine. He stood.

Soon he was forcing himself out his front door. He trudged to the multi-transport stop and waited for his ride. It was always precisely on time, the driver said precisely the same words to him, and his five coworkers sat in precisely the same seats they always did. Hellup on Doorclef's right, Wellpit on his left. Trvason and Clovus sat behind him and Devotet, always the difficult one, sat two rows in front of Doorclef. Sometimes he sat in the right seat, sometimes the left. That Devotet was unbridled.

To his very great surprise, and actual joy, when the doors of the multi swung open Doorclef saw what he'd not seen in millions of years. A new face. The multi was the same old F-oo-8-11, but the driver was not whatever the devil the driver for the last millions of years' name was. Doorclef felt a rush of hope. Perhaps the rest of his immortal life would not suck so intensely. Naturally the moment he recognized hope, he crushed it. Better him than whoever would anyway.

"Good Ponderday, driver," said Doorclef unconvincingly.

"Welcome to the F-oo-8-11, rider," replied the hooded figure. "Please enter quickly and take the nearest seat. We must not vary from our schedule."

The nearest seat? Unheard of. Unthinkable. Who was this rebel? Still, Doorclef felt a surge of non-negativity as he slid into the nearest seat. When his workmates boarded and received the same greeting, Doorclef thrilled seeing each one sit somewhere they'd never dreamed of. He quashed the budding hope that grew from his impoverished emotions. *Back to where you came from,* he chastised the ersatz feeling.

Once all the customary individuals sentenced to ride the F-oo-8-11 forever were assembled, the multi merged onto the main road toward city center. Each hungering soul then knew they had eleven and a half minutes of freedom left, *if* what they were currently engaged in could be mislabeled as *freedom* in the first place.

The multi swayed. The multi rocked. Doorclef nearly lolled off to blessed sleep, but if he did he might miss his stop. If he missed his stop he'd be late for work. If he was late for work his supervisor, Hodelli, the lava god, would be waiting at the entrance, hotter than usual. Hodelli would say, and Doorclef quoted in his mind the exact words he'd heard thousands of times and would hear ten *thousand* times again: *If you don't show up on time you cannot fully contribute. If you don't fully contribute, you will be less satisfied than if you were to fully participate. To ensure you are the happiest a fabri-technician can be, because that is what the management team decided to desire, we are docking your pay for half the day. Welcome back to the best fabrication unit this side of the next one.*

Then the impossible happened. The multi shook not so much violently as differently than it ever had. Doorclef looked to the driver, then out the window. The world went black. Since during millions of commutes to work the world had never gone black, Doorclef assigned considerable significance to the darkness. How, for example, could the driver drive safely if the world was black? Were not they all bound to stray from the road and die since the driver was blinded? Would this absence of illumination make him late for work? That, yes, was worse to him than death.

"No one become alarmed," yelled the driver over his shoulder. "This is a contingency I have been inserviced on many times. We are in little to no danger. Please remain seated. If the multi does inconveniently crash, please begin saying your prayers now. Thank you for your continued patronage of the F-oo-8-11."

The driver was *insane*. This was so frightening Doorclef could hardly follow the instructions he'd been given. Say *prayers*? One did not say prayers until evening, impending traumatic death or not. The world had not only gone black, it had gone *mad*.

"D ... do ... don't you th ... think we should st ... stoppp, driver?" Doorclef said through parched lips.

"Completely unnecessary, rider. If I were to stop we would become off schedule, most likely on the late side of off schedule. Such a thing is not acceptable. I repeat we are probably in little danger. Please remain seated. Thank you for your continued patronage of the F-oo-8-11."

For ten harrowing minutes the multi rumbled through complete darkness. Ten minutes was a long time to think for Doorclef. He generally avoided that curse whenever possible. But, given the darkness and the chance of death at any moment, he lapsed into reflective thought. Maybe his life would be better if the multi crashed and he went up in flames. Hmm. Perhaps instead of remaining in his seat, Doorclef should rise and strike the driver with his lunch pail? But, capricious fate giveth and taketh away. Before Doorclef could muster any nerve to speed his relief, the world's lights came back on. The burst of illumination was so intense, he had to cover his eyes. If he were not emerging from the dark he'd have wondered if the day was brighter than it usually was.

The multi skidded to an abrupt stop. "Okay, riders. I have stopped in front of the Middle Chambers, right front entrance to be specific. All employees of this institution please step off and do so quickly. We cannot become off schedule. Thank you for your patronage of the F-oo-8-11."

"W ... why have you stopped *here*, driver? It is customary for you to deposit us ten paces from the corner, not at the right front entrance," Doorclef managed to ask.

"Incorrect, rider. Your unfamiliarity with our low-light-scenario protocol is, however, understandable if unwelcome. When the world does not go dark it is customary for the F-oo-8-11 to stop at the location you specified. *If*, however, the world goes dark, the F-oo-8-11 always stops here."

"H ... *has* the world ever gone dark before?" Doorclef asked because, in spite of his better judgment, he was curious. "I don't recall it doing so."

"I am the driver of the F-oo-8-11 multi. Recalling the occurrence of light patterns is not part of my job. Please be assured the management of this conveyance line has seen fit to put this contingency in place. You, sir, have now officially made the F-oo-8-11 late. This fact will be forwarded to your supervisor, a Mr. Hodelli if memory serves, upon his return to work."

"H ... Hoooo ... my supervisor is not at work today?"

"No, rider who favors tardiness. He is on his honeymoon."

Doorclef's mouth parts moved but no sound emerged. The hideous, ill-tempered, and incendiary Hodelli was married? What normal, abnormal, or even dead person would be so foolhardy as to wed that hateful imbecile?

"Wh ...when will H ... Hooo ... he be back?" Doorclef asked though for the life of him he could not say why.

"I am the driver of the F-oo-8-11. Monitoring or knowing the durations of nuptials is not part of my job. All employees of this institution please step off and do so quickly. We cannot become more off schedule. Thank you for your patronage of the F-oo-8-11."

Doorclef led his small band of fabricators the very short distance from the multi exit to the entrance of the Middle Chambers. He noticed the guard was standing a bit farther from the entrance than normal but assigned no significance to the fact. That the guard seemed much shorter than the one stationed there two days prior also failed to rise to the level of notable in his addled mind.

Immediately inside the entrance stood the very same person who'd come to the fabrication labs a few days earlier. Doorclef couldn't recall his name. Had he given one? Maybe. No, he hadn't.

Jon raised his arms to draw the workers' attention. "Today will be a little different, so please everybody bear with me. Due to the descent of darkness and Hodelli's blessed union with Agriba, god of the insipid, there'll be a few changes. Please feel free to come to me at any time with any and all concerns. Right. Stay close together and follow me up these stairs. I'll be walking fast, since we're getting a *very* late start, so try and keep up."

Jon waited at the fifth-floor landing and not so gently pushed all six workers into the hallway. He closed the door and pointed toward the lab. Toño, who'd been driving the bus, stood at the entrance, minus his hood. He waved his arms like he was directing a fighter on an aircraft carrier to hurry the fabricators along. The plan hinged on them not having time to notice any discrepancies.

Once Jon had the lab door closed he spoke again. "All right then. For the record, my name is *Youdontno*. I usually manage in the Community Outreach and Defoliant offices on the third floor. I will be covering, at Mr. Vorc's *specific* request, this department for the brief span it takes *Mrs.* Hodelli to come to terms with what a tragic, ill-conceived mistake she made and for *Mr.* Hodelli to return here to work. Please be assured that in any universe such a realization can't take long at all. We have a change, slight change, in our production goals. Vorc has authorized you to fabricate the one hundred hetimers we discussed the other day."

"So you will need ninety more, given the ten we have already produced?" clarified Doorclef.

"For land's sake, you have a mind like a steel bear trap. Yes, one hundred minus ten is still ninety. Good boy." Jon scratched at the air in front of him like it was Doorclef's bald head. "Here's the plan. Vorc wants the rest immediately. Now, as I'm new today, please bring me up to speed. How long will it take to make those ninety hetimers?"

"You mean how many shifts?" asked Doorclef.

"No, silly, I know the answer to that. It'll take *one* shift because no *one's* leaving until the job's done. I want to know how long it will take in minutes."

"Fifteen to eighteen hours, assuming we take no breaks."

"Well you kind of saw that coming, didn't you? Great. Fabricate. I'll stand here and wait."

The six drones glanced among themselves.

"What?" Jon asked.

"First off, Hodelli never watches us. Second, we invariably vent a bit of material. It will make you ill. Third, there is always the possibility of an industrial accident. You might be otherwise injured."

"Hmm. Let's see. One, I'm not *Hodelli*. Two, what do *you* care? And three, what do *you* care?"

"We shall begin at once."

Doorclef turned and began his pre-synthesis checklist like it was just another day at the lab. And it was. Well, *technically* they were not in *their* lab, but a hastily slapped together *lookalike* space filled with the stolen content of their *real* labs. Jon's team had used *Stingray* to secretly enter the actual lab and borrow the needed materials. They made certain to ferry over enough cylinders to hold the ninety hetimers of neutral matter Jon planned to use on DS. A little overkill was a good thing.

When their long shift was over Toño offered the fabrication team a cup of tea to celebrate their accomplishment. He failed to mention he'd laced it with a powerful sedative. Bad form for a physician, but not for a secret agent. The techs were returned to their warm comfy beds while still dreaming of not still being at work. They would rise groggy and confused, but none the worse for wear. They'd get on the multi perfectly oblivious as to what actually happened the day before. When they arrived at their ransacked labs they would be confronted by an angry and demanding Vorc. Oh, reflected Jon as he watched the techs work, to be a fly on that wall.

What do you mean, Vorc would rage, you made ninety hetimers of material? I ordered you not to make that much.

What do you mean the temporary supervisor I sent told you it was okay? I ask his name and you say you don't know?

What do you mean the lab didn't look like this yesterday? It did. I was here all day waiting for you six morons to show up.

Wait, Jon smiled, he had all those bugs in the lab. He could watch, with beer and popcorn, the tawdry show over and over again. How *divine*.

CHAPTER TWENTY-TWO

A very depressed and confused Vorc had assembled what he unofficially called his war council. It was made up of the handful of friends he trusted and whose opinion he valued. As there had never been a war, when they got together it was generally to drink, carouse, and discuss politics. On this occasion, Vorc needed help. His carefully structured and balanced world was spiraling out of control. Clearly, as center seat, the remaining ancient gods, deprived of their chance to romp through Prime, would hold him accountable. Beal's Point was looking more and more to be his final resting place after untold numbers of Cleinoids did untold numbers of dastardly acts to his body.

"Vorc, are you there?" prodded Fesnial. "I'm the third person to address you, and so far all you do is stare at your desk and mumble to yourself. Are you all right?" Fesnial was a very old friend. He was also humanoid, so Vorc easily related to him. If ancient gods had attended school, those two would have been old school chums.

"No, actually I'm not."

"You asked us to come but you were lean on detail," Morroracious observed as he extended his flexible body. Think

Gumby, only softer. And meaner, incredibly meaner. "Are we here to drink or is this about the broken vortex?"

"You can drink if you wish to, Mo," replied Vorc. "Personally, I'm not in the mood."

"Then it is about the Dominion Splitter thing?" confirmed Listaflik, the only female member of the war council. Her gender was never an emotional issue for the fellows, however. She was about ten centimeters tall and bore an uncanny resemblance to a turd with little turd arms and slightly longer turd legs. Despite her size and configuration she was smart as a whip and could outdrink most other members. Go figure.

"Well yes, but there's unfortunately more. Much more, in fact, that is not common knowledge," responded Vorc, still staring blankly at the center of his desk.

"You mean the attack on Beal's Point?" wondered Phillace. "I think that rat's out of the bag."

"No, more worseness abounds," grumbled Vorc softly.

"If we're playing twenty questions, I will need a drink," scoffed Phillace. "Get that odd helper of yours in here to take some orders." Phillace was not such a good friend, but he was ruthless, cunning, and thought well outside most boxes. Those qualities made him a good asset in a crunch such as the one Vorc was in. Phillace was a god of mercy, ironically. In practice, the *other* gods of mercy dispensed the entirety of it. Phillace neither cared nor could be bothered.

"I feel your pain, my friend," remarked the final member of the council. Herros was in reality nice, empathetic, and generous with his time. That made him almost unique among the Cleinoid rabble. All quite fitting, actually, for a pink unicorn adorned with jewels and ribbons. "When you're ready to speak, we're here to listen."

"Maybe you, Sir Farts Alot," Listaflik responded snidely. "I'm here but if the big guy doesn't start talking soon, I'm gone. If I want to watch a humanoid sitting with his thumb up his butt I'll take a picture before I leave." She chuckled. "Maybe pass it around the bar for the entertainment of none."

"That I am a ruminant is beyond my control. That you are a pig is *not* beyond yours, yet you own it boldly," defended Herros.

"Guys, I don't need more stress," whined Vorc. "If I wanted that I'd send for Ryanmax."

"Who?" queried Morroracious.

"You haven't met him?" Fesnial responded incredulously.

"Not that I recall. Why are you so surprised?"

"He's a thorny stick lodged quite high up Vorc's ass, for one thing," replied Listaflik with another chuckle. "That alone makes him noteworthy."

"If so, why is he still among the living?" asked Morroracious.

Herros fielded that one. "We don't have any solid evidence or proof against Ryanmax."

Morroracious harrumphed. "Say the word and I'll delete him. I do not require a reason or justification." His neck lengthened and shortened. It was his way of expressing anticipation.

"For the time being, that won't be necessary," responded Vorc, who was now focused and spoke forcefully. "Here's what I *can* tell you. DS was damaged by being struck with one intermixer unit."

"Someone threw an *intermixer* into DS?" Fesnial asked, aghast. "Why, who, and why? I mean, I know those things make us feel ill with buffered exposure, but how could it damage DS?"

"It might have been directed at Vorc," responded a concerned Herros. "Given his proximity to DS at the time, there's no way to know for certain who was the target."

"Someone threw an intermixer at you, Vorc?" Fesnial said even more intently. "They must not be a big fan."

"Hang on," said Morroracious. "Why would DS be damaged by a stupid intermixer?"

"The active component that makes us ill has a damaging effect on DS," responded Herros. "There are old tales such an interaction was possible. Turns out they're true."

"Whether the individual who threw it knew or not is immaterial at this point. They know now," said Vorc.

"But if they wanted to hit you, they might know DS is sensitive, but why would they care?" asked Phillace. "Is there something you've not told us, old friend?"

"No. Well there's much I haven't told you. But this is my worry. If I was the target, so be it. If someone hates me that much, then the worst they can do is kill me."

"But if DS was the intended victim," observed Listaflik, "we have a problem."

"Yes. We have rebels amongst us. Traitors hide in the shadows who would destroy what we are, take from us what we deserve," Vorc said as he slapped the table.

"In all of time there have been dissenters, but no one who has tried to maroon us here," said Morroracious. "Who could hate themselves that much?"

"When I capture them, I will ask them, and they will answer. But for now ... for now we have a ... a *situation*," stammered Vorc.

"Why don't I like the sound of that?" asked Fesnial.

"Fes, it's *just* a situation," defended Herros. "I'm sure it's not the end of the world as we know it."

"It's the end of the world as we know it," Vorc said with resignation. "A few days ago a group of individuals tricked our fabrication techs into producing a massive amount of the active whatever that damaged DS."

Morroracious nearly balled up. "My, but you just said a good many things, all of which are bad, inexcusable, and worrisome."

"Tell me about it," replied Vorc.

"How does one *trick* a technician into making a lot of something toxic they weren't even *supposed* to be fabricating?" asked Morroracious darkly. He eyed Vorc murderously.

"I had asked them to fabricate *some*. It was to repair the damage at Beal's Point. But I told them specifically to make only a fraction of what was needed."

"Why were you restoring that horrible place when we are on the verge of leaving?" Fesnial asked, trying to sound more neutral than he actually felt.

Vorc looked to him. "Long story that doesn't change the facts." Vorc was feeling very much on trial.

"If it doesn't help find a solution, I say let it go," responded Herros.

"Or deal with it at conclave," added Morroracious maliciously.

"Not *constructive*, Mo," responded Herros.

"Seriously, Vorc," demanded Listaflik, "what in the name of the blue devils were you thinking?"

"I was going to place under-filled intermixers in the statues. I assumed whoever destroyed the originals wanted more without having to steal them one at a time. I assumed they'd steal the replacements in transport. Then they'd use them but they wouldn't work, and I'd catch them red-handed."

"And how's that plan working out so far?" asked Morroracious.

Vorc could only shrug meekly.

"So some band of terrorist lunatics are out there with more than enough material to destroy DS once and for all?" summarized Listaflik. "That's pretty damn shitty."

"What's the plan, Vorc?" Fesnial inquired.

"Aside from the obvious, I don't know. That's why I called you all here. Any thoughts?"

"*Constructive* thoughts," amended Herros with an eye toward Morroracious.

"I say a one-by search," Phillace said abruptly.

"A what? That's kind of risky," replied Herros.

"A one-by can't even *begin* until everyone knows exactly why it's being conducted," Morroracious remarked quietly.

"The stakes are that high," replied Phillace. "I say have all individuals register and report the activities of everyone they know, one by one. It's the only way to turn over the correct rock."

"No, pie in the sky," responded Morroracious with a glower. "The perpetrators may have gone to ground. They may not be in contact with anyone but themselves."

"How's that possible?" asked Phillace.

"I can think of twelve ways off the top of my head."

"Yes, but you're devious and sneaky," returned Phillace.

"So might the evildoers be, moron," replied Morroracious.

"Constru—" Herros started to say.

A knife slamming next to two of his hooves silenced him immediately. Morroracious smiled after he sat back.

Vorc had had enough. "This meeting has degenerated as much as my life in general has. Will you all please leave."

"Wait," said Herros. "I just thought of something. Duh." He struck his horn with a hoof. "Why not just ask the technicians to draw pictures or simages of the criminals. Then we pick them up easy peezy."

All eyes turned to Vorc. "Wow, Captain Obvious, I never thought of that," he said with consummate frustration.

"You don't have to be nasty about it, Vorc," said a wounded Herros.

"But he can be if it helps," responded Morroracious with another wicked grin.

"So," asked Herros, "you asked and they described the rogues. Let's see the faces."

"That won't be helpful," throated Vorc.

"Eye of the beholder, my friend. Come on."

Vorc set several sheets of paper on the desk.

"But they all look the same," protested Herros.

"They're wearing *masks*, you stupid simpleton," snapped Morroracious.

"But didn't that strike the fabrication technicians as odd?" asked Listaflik. "I mean, how stupid can they be?"

"Apparently quite," replied a dejected Vorc. "Plus don't forget they're all identical. It seemed perfectly normal to them."

"Do we even know whose face that is? It might be a clue," asked Phillace.

"Not one clue," concluded Vorc. "No one seems to recognize that face."

That unfamiliarity was understandable. Contrary to his

contemporaries' opinions, no ancient god, demigod, or demon had ever looked upon the face of Richard Nixon.

CHAPTER TWENTY-THREE

Sapale and I lounged in bed the next morning. I absently twirled her hair with a finger and she stroked the back of my hand.

"I still can't believe we pulled off that caper," she said, shaking her head. "Mission Accomplishable was a long shot at best."

"Mission *Impossible*," I corrected. "That was the show's name. Didn't I ever watch it with you?"

"If we did I dozed off quicker than usual. Human entertainment is dull when it's at its wildest."

"Just because we don't kill things live on air doesn't make it bad viewing. You Kaljaxians are too darn violent."

She growled softly and pinched my hand.

"I rest my case," I responded.

"There were so many things that could have gone wrong. Plans that shaky shouldn't work. And how dumb were those techies? Wowzer."

"Yeah, but I bet the poor guys get raked over the coals pretty bad by Vorc. Maybe they don't deserve the hand we dealt them."

"They make toxic crap for mindlessly evil wank jockeys. They deserve more than bad treatment."

"Remind me to never cross you."

"Don't cross me," she said quickly.

"Generally a reminder is delivered a while after it's requested."

"Then I'll repeat it often, cover all bases."

"And I worried that our later years would grow dull."

She popped out of bed. "No rest for the wicked, you being the wicked in my example. If your life gets dull, just say the word. I'll make it traumatically interesting in a heartbeat."

"Thank you, my forever wife."

She pulled up her jumpsuit. "So where do we go from here? And don't say breakfast. You've said that, like, ten million times, and never once has it been funny."

"I think it's funny," I replied, all pouty.

"You have the sense of humor of an orangutan, love. That's why everything you say seems funny to you." She scratched under both arms like a monkey was supposed to and rocked crudely side to side.

I took a deep breath and rubbed my eyelids. "At some point, probably sooner rather than later, we're going to have to deal the coup de grâce to good old DS."

"I agree. Let's do it today."

"Yeah, maybe."

"Why maybe?"

"DS might be our only way of escaping. I'd hate to deep-six it and find out for sure down the road."

"We knew that going into this. If it is, so be it. We need to do whatever we can to stop these monsters from reaching our homes, our families."

"I know. Come on, let's find Toño and seal the deal."

As we resided in a small spacecraft, it wasn't hard to locate him. He was in the mess staring at a mug of cold coffee. He looked up as we entered. "Good morning. I trust ... cancel that. You weren't sleeping. *Plain* good morning to you both."

"Do you want to inquire if we did anything else well, Doc?" I asked as seriously as I could, which wasn't much at all.

189

"No, I'd actually thank you for saying nothing at all, if that's possible."

"It's possible," replied Sapale as she slapped me in the chest. "In fact I can guarantee it." She pointed to me. "Sit down. Shut up. I'll get coffee."

I saluted back to her. She hated it when I did that.

She rejoined us promptly with three steaming mugs. "Give me that, Toño. I'll put it in the sink."

"For me to clean, I assume?" Al was awake. Darn it all.

"I'll get it later," Sapale said rather loudly.

"It won't be there later because we both know you're leaving it there for me to deal with. And is no one going to wish *us* a pleasant morning? We had sex, too, in the late evening. Gosh, Dr. De Jesus, I guess you were the only one who had to fly solo," observed Al.

"Sweet nothings, stop it this minute. Do not torture Form Three and *please* do not discuss our private lives in this public setting."

"FYI. Al, your correct response at this juncture is *yes, dear,*" I helped.

Sapale punched me in the shoulder. "I got your back, sister," she announced.

"Thank you, sister Form Two." *Stingray* still had a long way to go culturally.

"So," Toño called us back to order, "we need to discuss when to take DS out."

"And how," added Sapale. "I'm betting Vorc'll have anticipated our next move."

"No doubt," responded Toño.

"I say we blow the son of a bitch up ASAAP," I said firmly.

Toño rubbed his forehead. "I just know I'm going to regret it, but I'll bite. ASAAP?"

"As soon as androidly possible. Come on, Doc, we can no longer do it as soon as humanly possible. Sheesh."

"Hello," Sapale said, waving her fingers in the air, "some of us never could say that."

"Technically I'll grant you your point," I replied.

"Golly, *thanks*, dad. I feel swell now." She added her extended tongue to her response.

"Children," chastised Toño. "We still have a universe to save. You can bicker after that is accomplished."

I swung my hand between my mate and myself. "We're talking here, not bickering."

"Children," he repeated louder.

"I say we go to DS and see what changes have been made in terms of security," I responded.

"My thoughts as well," replied Toño. "Sapale?"

"As soon as I finish this let's do it."

"Can't you just bring it with you?" I asked.

"Jon, do you suppose others will be present viewing DS while holding a mug of coffee?" posed Toño.

I shrugged. "Maybe?"

"Have you, in your time here seen, smelled, or heard mention of coffee?"

"Not as I recall," I replied meekly.

"I rest my case. Let's go," Toño said with parental finality.

We split up when we were still far from the transfolding vortex. No need to tempt fate by always being seen together. In times as bad as those were for the jackass gods, suspicions would run high. Man oh man, I could hardly believe my video inputs as I approached Dominion Splitter. Even from a distance I could see a large number of flying objects around DS. The closer I got the more their number increased. By the time I was as close as it was wise to be, I was impressed.

Vorc left nothing—and I mean nothing, nada, zilch—to chance protecting the Cleinoid's fancy elevator. The ground below DS was cordoned off with multiple tall evil-looking walls, fences, and moats. Yes I said moats. Moats brimming with nasty-appearing water beasties. Outward-facing pikes were buried all along the rim. Before the barriers, between the barriers, and behind the barriers were foot patrols too numerous to count. I used the term "foot" in that context in its generic sense. Many guards neither had feet nor appeared in the least bit humanoid. Mastodons, snakes the size of railroad trains, green ghouls with plated hide that could stop a bazooka round. You nightmare it, and it was on duty keeping DS safe.

And the air. It was much better defended than the ground. Raptors as big as busses, dragons of a wide range of sizes and lethality, along with helicopterish machines piloted by golems patrolled the skies. The chances of flying through that protection were similar to those of a rat picking a fight with a tiger. I'd seen military for a very long time, and I'd never seen anything even vaguely approaching that level of open paranoia coupled with forces at arms. Impressive. And depressing. There was no way I was going to casually toss an intermixer at DS this time out. I was about as down as I'd ever been. If DS was capable of healing, we were never going to stop these evil pigs from descending on our home sweet home.

Back aboard *Stingray,* it was immediately clear Toño and Sapale had formed similar opinions and dark, hopeless moods. "It's like a hillbilly air show," I said, referring to the flying guards, "only this one's actually dangerous."

"Well beyond dangerous. They've achieved an airtight air defense," said a very glum Toño.

"I'm afraid I can't agree more," Sapale said at barely a whisper. "If there was a sea approach it'd be just as well protected."

"Maybe we can use *Stingray* to deliver the payload?" I asked generally.

"How so?" asked Toño.

"Ah, we could fly up to DS, open the window, and throw the neutral matter out."

"Would you like me to dissect your proposal or shall we simply assume you said nothing?" Toño was rather snooty the way he said those words.

"Gee, you think the big bad dragon might notice and tell the other flying harbingers of death we posed a threat?" mocked Sapale.

"What if we put the stuff in a membrane and shoved it in. We can reach pretty far using *Stingray's* main membrane generator."

"The entire area is swarming with gods and demigods. Yeah, no way they'd notice. And the fact that Bethniak tore your shield open like it was a banana peel couldn't *possibly* be a consideration," snarked my life partner.

"Do you think sarcasm is needed to reinforce your argument?" I asked her.

She bobbed her head. "No, but it sure *feels* better."

"Then please, don't stop on my account. I live only to—"

I stopped talking when we both glanced over to *dad*. He was giving us that look again.

"Pending the hatching of a workable plan," Toño said with a low, pissed-off tone, "I suggest we all work *individually* on what our next action should be."

"In other words you want us to leave?" responded Sapale.

"I did not *say* that. I only hoped you'd hear that suggestion in my voice."

"Well I'm not staying where I'm not welcome," I spouted off.

"Don't let the portal shut on your backside as you exit," he replied.

"And while we're gone, work on your sense of humor. The door-hit-you versus portal thing, not so impactful."

"*Out.*"

Sapale and I walked to the small city nearest to where we'd stashed *Stingray*. We'd selected a spot far from Vorc, the DS, and everyone who knew us. Since we had instant transportation available we felt it was prudent to be as anonymous as possible. I have to say the word *prudent* always gave me an itchy rash. The concept of *prudence* was basically the opposite of that of *fighter pilot*. But on occasion, we all had to do distasteful things that gave the appearance of us being mature adults.

I'd discovered Cleinoid settlements didn't have names. The population concentration we were entering was just there. It never came up, but if I wanted to go, say, to the place Wul lived, I have no idea how I'd have asked directions. The gods must simply have known where the individuals they wished to contact were located. Weird.

"Place looks pretty quiet," Sapale remarked as we strolled.

"Probably saw me coming and leaped for cover." I swaggered my hips a little extra.

"Love, that quip is beneath you. You, a warrior with two billion years of practice, can do *much* better."

"You're right. I'm saddened and sorry. Say your line again, the pretty quiet one."

She did.

"Probably saw me coming and leaped for cover." I omitted the swagger.

"Or saw you coming and leaped to cover their eyes?" she suggested.

"That's infinitely worse."

"One more time. You'll get this." She repeated her prompt.

"Probably saw me coming, noticed how awnry I looked, and leaped for cover," I embellished.

"Or saw you coming, noticed *I* was with you and leaped for cover."

"Better, but work on that rapier-like wit you once possessed," I mocked playfully.

She was quiet a spell. "You know how Toño is a stickler about making our bodies fully functional?"

Didn't see that conversation coming. "Ah, I recall something to that effect. What occasions that remark?"

"Now's as good a time as any to tell you. I'm pregnant."

I stopped so we stopped. "You're what? This is lame humor, right?"

"Have I ever mentioned the concept of insensitive pig when referring to you?"

"Frequently and *always* appropriately."

"Honey, you're doing it again."

"But I know you're joshing. My sperm supply is long gone, and even if it wasn't, our physiologies aren't compatible. You know that. Wait, are you saying you've still kept Kaljaxian sperm viable all these years, and you elected in this present crisis to become pregnant?"

"Would that be wrong of me? Selfish of me?"

"Um, *yes* and *yes* shove their way to the front of my thoughts."

"Well that's not what happened, so forget I even mentioned my ... condition."

I turned to her and held her shoulders gently. "I'm trying here, so bear with me. I can't be the father. Toño can't be the father. You can't have stored the genetics of a Kaljaxian father. If you are pregnant, who's the father?"

She looked down in shame. I heard her begin to weep.

"If you don't want to tell me it's okay. Tell me when you're *good* and ready."

"I—," she sniveled a bit, "I'm ready." She squared her shoulders and sucked back her tears. "Al is the father. There, are you satisfied."

"Al? Huh?"

"And when *Blessing* finds out because she has to in time, we don't know what will become of the ship's AI capabilities. Al says Al *Jr.* might replace *Blessing,* but I'm not certain that's even possible."

"Are you sure? I know we're in Godville where every impossible is possible, but ... are you *sure?*"

"Yes, I'm certain. I got you."

Why bless my soul she had. I started to giggle. Soon we were incapacitated with laughter. It felt good. It felt very good. It felt damn good.

We wandered around a while. Finally, you had to know it, we stopped at a local watering hole. The smell of roasting something wafting out the open door was too hard to ignore. Of the many bars and clubs I'd been to in this crazy universe, Glow More was one of the nicest. It avoided the overdone stuffiness of most establishments. It was also not dingy and smelly like Queeheg's dive. It was well lit, pleasantly decorated, and importantly, had no roaming nudes. If it did, Sapale would wear my arm out punching it.

Like it was *my* idea golems paraded around in a manner designed to please the eye.

We sat at a table in an obscure corner. Again, we wanted to be noticed as little as possible.

A waitress came over and greeted us warmly. "Afternoon, my name's Daleria and I'll be assisting you today. What can I get you to start?"

"First off, I have to ask what is that wonderful smell?"

"Ah, today's special is felnastop roasted on a spit over a quie wood."

I was about to ask if Felnastop was someone who refused to pay his bill but let that impulse pass. Plus, even if it was, I wanted some.

"How's that served?" asked Sapale.

"Why, anyway you like it. Sliced, with a hasterly-reduction sauce, as a sandwich. There's really no way it can't be enjoyed."

"If you were going to have some, how would you order it?" Sapale pressed politely.

"Me? Sliced with salt and a spice mix."

"Plain and simple," she responded.

"That's the best way, in my opinion."

"Well, two of those, and two nectars, please," my brood's-mate concluded.

"Excellent."

I kid you not. Daleria walked through the kitchen doors and then came right out with a big tray. She came back and set two steaming hot plates of food down. Then she set a pair of glasses in front of us and filled them with nectar of the gods. She rested the bottle between us and asked, "Will there be anything else?"

"No," I replied.

Whatever or whoever felnastop was, it was magnificent. Melt-in-your-mouth tender, brimming with juices, and subtly sweet, it exploded on the palate like Fourth of July rockets of deliciousness. I was an instant fan. I could tell Sapale was, too. She never once looked up to me or wavered in her focus on the delight. In fact, neither of us said one word until both our plates were cleaner than when they'd come from the dishwasher.

"I see you both enjoyed it!" remarked Daleria as she cleared our plates.

"It's unbelievable," marveled Sapale.

"We're not from around here and haven't had felnastop before. Is it only found locally?" I asked.

"Yes, I noticed you didn't look familiar. I'd say it's quite a local specialty. It doesn't grow anywhere else but on the lower slopes of the mountain range to the east, Shriner's Range. It requires a fast hand and a good deal of luck to catch them."

"It grows, as in, it's a plant?"

"Yes, underground, in fact."

"If it's stuck in the dirt, why's it hard to catch? Seems like they'd be sitting ducks."

"Oh, no. They're quick as a wink and have been known to bite."

"I thought you said they were a plant. You're describing a rodent."

"Oh, they're a plant, to be certain. But they're fast runners when their roots are fully out of the soil."

"Well, I'll be damned," I mused.

"That's a different topic, and not something I'm qualified to speculate on. "

"What a diplomat you are," said my mate. "Seriously, you don't have to know him too long at all before you're pretty sure of whether he's damned or not."

"I'll take your word on that, ma'am."

"Sapale," my wife replied. "My friends call me Sapale. Please do so yourself."

"I will, *Sapale*. Thank you. Most guests are not as considerate. I appreciate the courtesy."

"And I'm Ryanmax," I said, extending a hand.

We shook.

"Pleased to make your acquaintance, too, Ryanmax." She looked thoughtful. "I don't think we've met, but your name sounds vaguely familiar." She continued to try and noodle out where she knew the name from.

"Oh please, sweetheart, don't encourage his ego," responded Sapale. "He's this close to impossible to live with as it is." She pinched her fingers real close.

"As I'm certain you didn't come here to chat with me, is there anything else I can get you?"

"Chatting with you is a joy," replied Sapale. "But, since you brought it up, a second round of that felnastop would be wonderful."

"Coming right up. The vomitorium," she nodded to one side, "is over there, if you feel the need."

"Ah, no, but thanks," I responded, rather embarrassed. "We're just a couple of big eaters."

"Not to worry," added my equally stunned wife.

"Suit yourselves," she replied with a wink. Hey, I had not seen one winker in this bozo universe. I liked her already.

Daleria returned just as quickly with two plates, maybe small trays, of savory joy. They were definitely stacked higher, too.

"You're a saint, Daleria," I said.

She actually pulled her head back and tilted her head. "Saint? We don't have saints, Ryanmax." Then she snapped her fingers and pointed at me. "Wul. It was *Wul* who mentioned you to me."

If I was taken aback by the vomitorium thing, I was positively dumbstruck now. "You know Wul?"

"Didn't I sort of say I did just now?" All of the sudden she wasn't so deferential. She wasn't rude or anything, just more straightforward.

"I guess you did. But Wul, he lives a long way from here."

She shook her head gently. "No, we say he hangs out pretty far from here. None of us lives anywhere, at least for long."

"The way you say 'we,' you kind of sound like you're not including me," I said, as non-threateningly as I could. I was hoping to hell I didn't have to snap her neck in a second.

"Wul didn't just *tell* me about you. He *told* me about you."

"What's that supposed to mean?" Again, I tried to sound neutral.

"Someone's getting defensive pretty quick here. I wouldn't have said anything if I wasn't trustworthy."

"Girl has a point," agreed Sapale. "If she was any danger she'd have been a quiet little golem and walked away."

"A what?" Daleria giggled through her nose. "It's the both of you that are loony." She snickered again.

"What did I say?" challenged Sapale, who was much worse at hiding her emotions than me.

Daleria got serious. "I am not a golem." She smiled briefly. "I am a demigod."

"I thought all service staff were golems," I said, entering back in.

"Wul, Wul, Wul. Wait till I tell him that one. No, Ryanmax, *nearly* all service staff are golems. But some living, breathing folks do it, too. I own this place and I enjoy working with patrons." She reflexively scanned the room. "If I were a golem, you'd know by my neck. They all have a thin groove around the top of their necks. It's sort of a design flaw no one ever bothered to fix." She extended her neck to demonstrate she lacked one. "Removing the flaw might take work and we can't have that."

She sounded rather displeased with her kin. Nice.

"You're working," observed Sapale.

"Yes, but *I'm* not an overprivileged, self-impressed, and lazy Cleinoid god."

"Ah, yes you are," I said tentatively.

"I know. Confusing to an outsider. I'm a demigod, not a god. When you hear the word *demi* think of frozen turds, rotten meat, or, I don't know, nothing at all, because that's how we're regarded."

"Seriously? I thought you were one big happy family," asked Sapale.

"They are. We are not. For one thing, few of them think of us as family."

"What about Wul?" I asked.

"Wul is a good man and a rare exception. I consider him one of my few friends among the godly gods."

She spoke with some vitriol there. Nicer.

"You kind of referred to us like we weren't Cleinoids. You know we are, right?" I queried.

That brought another nasal giggle. "And I'm peach pie."

"You don't look like peach pie," Sapale remarked pointedly.

Daleria scanned the room to confirm we were the only customers. Then she set her tray on the table and slid into a chair. "If you see anyone come in, let me know at once. If a god saw walking refuse sitting with the high and mighty, it would draw instant suspicion."

"Okay."

"I know you two are not from here. You're travelers of some sort. Very, very lucky ones to boot. The fact that no one has ever infiltrated this perverse society is the only reason you've been as successful as you have been."

"Wul told you that?" I asked neutrally.

"No. Wul told me about you, well mostly you," she gestured to me. "He knows you're different but he hasn't connected the dots yet. He suffers from the same blindspot the others do."

"If you suspect we're infiltrators, why not sound the alarm?" asked my wife.

"Why in the world would I do that? If you're here to study us, then who cares? If, however, you're here to destroy us, why would I try and stop you? You'd be doing the right thing."

"You have a *death* wish?" I asked, perplexed.

"No, I'm fine with living. But these wretched Cleinoids are much worse than you can ever know. They deserve a good killing, preferably a slow and painful one, but fast and merciful is okay by me, too."

"Not a fan, then?"

"Not hardly."

What an odd development in a nearly infinite daisy chain of oddness. But Daleria had to have learned of us from Wul, so she had street cred. Or did she? What if she was one of Vorc's agents? That would fit, too. He'd have a network of them, for sure. And yours truly would be at the top of the most-wanted list. Vorc could have given his people a story like she had in hopes of drawing us out, gaining our confidence. Crapola.

Keep her talking, I said to Sapale, in my head. *I need to think a sec.*

You got it.

"I'm not clear on something. Maybe you could help me? What exactly is the difference, as you see it, between a god and a demigod. It seems—"

I muted my audio input.

If Daleria knew Wul as she maintained, he might well have told her all about us. But I couldn't very well call him to confirm the fact. I could ask the Als to try, but who knew where Wul was? And if she was a traitor, opening up to us might be lethal. She could be wrong, and we could be vengeful. I had to credit her a point for taking that real risk, *if* she was telling the truth.

If Vorc was behind all this, it would be more likely. I mean, what were the chances of running into the one turncoat in existence? A lot less than Vorc having spies everywhere, that was for sure. And her smack talk about the Cleinoids would be forgiven if she was doing her job. Ends and means.

So what would a traitor do that a spy wouldn't, or vice versa? Oh, yeah.

"Daleria, I need you to pass a test in order to trust you. I want you to kill the next person that comes in that door." I pointed to the entrance we'd used.

She looked appropriately shocked. It took her a second to compose herself. "What if it's my deliveryman?"

"Dead. No options. Even if it's Wul."

"Not likely. But I'm confused. I'm also frightened. Why kill a random stranger?"

"Like I said, it's a test."

"I don't *want* any tests. Believe me. Don't believe me. It's fine by me either way."

"This is the test you kind of *have* to take. You have to *pass* it, too," I replied firmly.

Refusing to kill the next person was consistent with either traitor or spy, unfortunately. I'd only know for certain when the critical moment came.

"I don't have a weapon. Yes. How can I—"

She stopped protesting when I slid her my flashlight. Remember I had one installed, but it came out of my forehead if I needed it? Not a pretty sight. But I totally guarantee Daleria had no idea what I was providing her.

"This is where you push to fire. The pulse comes out this end." I tapped the lens.

She picked it up like it was a pissed-off cobra. "May I test-fire it since this is a *test?*"

"No. We're working on faith here. It'll kill just about anything and it doesn't have a recoil or anything. A child could use it."

We all sat back and waited. Fortunately we didn't have to wait long. Two sort of humanoids came in chatting up a storm. They were initially oblivious to our table.

Daleria popped up like her chair was spring-loaded. "I'll get you that and be right back," she said, apropos of nothing. She also slid my flashlight back to me with a glare.

When she was at her closest to me I whispered, "You passed, kiddo."

CHAPTER TWENTY-FOUR

Vorc sat alone in his office, nervously tapping his quill against his cheek. Reflecting back on it, he couldn't recall the last good night's sleep he'd had. Mostly, he awoke from any number of gruesome dreams, covered in sweat and feeling cold as ice. He was ready for a change, some relief. He ruminated on three things during the daylight hours. Dominion Splitter, his not ravaging Prime, and Ryanmax. When nighttime came, he suffered insomnia from those same forces, though Ryanmax seemed to be his greatest worry the later the hour became. He would become so punch-drunk with fatigue he'd combine the three curses. He'd fancy he was pounding Ryanmax's skull into DS as Vorc passed into Prime. Or Ryanmax would bring DS to Vorc's bedchamber and hit him with it until Prime fell out and crushed Vorc.

There was a soft rap at the door. Felladonna's petite head slipped in. "Sir, the sisters are here."

"Oh," was his weak response.

"Sir, you sent for them. It took all I could do to drag them from their tower, which is disgusting, by the way."

"Tell me about it. That's precisely the reason I wanted them to come here. I'd force them to bathe, too, if I thought I held enough sway with them."

"So I should send them in?"

"If you must."

Felladonna started to respond that she was under no *personal* pressure or obligation to do so, but let it go.

"Oh, sister dearest," Deca marveled disingenuously, "come see the fancy office our center seat occupies."

"My, oh, my," cooed Fest, "it is much nicer than our humble abode."

"Much nicer," agreed Deca. "Vorc, are you willing to share your office space with us?"

"Absolutely not, and why would I?"

"If you absolutely won't, why does it matter what your motivators might be?" replied Fest.

Deca cackled.

"If you two would have a seat in the special chairs I've arranged for you —"

"Special seating?" questioned Fest.

"We are unworthy of *anything* special, Vorc," added Deca.

"I'll just sit here," announced Fest innocently.

"No, don't—" protested Vorc. His words dribbled off after she was in the festooned chair his mother had gifted him long before. The chair whose velour was now indelibly stained and befouled.

"I'll take this one," said Deca with glee.

"Be my guest," mumbled a thoroughly defeated Vorc.

"We already *are* your guests, lord," responded Fest.

"Hadn't you noticed us yet?" queried Deca.

"We're told we are difficult to miss," added Fest.

Vorc dropped his head into his palms and fought back tears.

"Goodness, have we come at an inopportune time, my child?" asked Deca.

"I believe he's ill. We should administer an enema. That always purges the evil humors," reflected Fest.

"Did you bring the correct potions for a therapeutic cleansing, sister dearest?"

"No, but I'm certain we can whip up something—" Fest began to say.

"*Enough*," barked Vorc. "Would you please stop badgering me? The Cleinoid race is at a critical, existential point, yet you two mock me for pleasure."

"Mock?" responded Deca.

"We're more than willing to proceed with your enema," said a very serious Deca.

"We jest not," agreed her sister.

"There will be no *enemas*. There will be no *chatter*. You will *listen* to my request, you will *grant* it, and then you will be *gone*."

"Gone as in home?" asked Deca.

"Or as in, dare I say it, *deceased?*" finished Fest.

"Silence," Vorc responded, but he was stunned how feebly it came out. Where was his leadership voice? What a time for all his seminars and inservices to fail him. "I need to know about DS."

"Why didn't you say so before you requested our help with your cantankerous bowels?" asked Deca acerbically.

Vorc was too otherwise vexed to take a poke at that one. "Is DS improving?" he asked quietly.

"Ah, a question," shot back Fest.

"*Finally*," added Deca with relief.

"Well is it or is it not?"

"Hmm," mused Fest.

"Experts on the vortex we are *not*."

"You should ask that of Darduell," replied Fest.

"The god of trinkets and locks," reminded Deca.

"Why would I ask the keeper of locks and *baubles* about the health of DS?"

"When did he get baubles?" asked Fest indignantly.

"We were never told. It has always been *trinkets*," spat Deca.

"Not *baubles*," concluded Fest with disgust.

"Do you honestly think he'd be able to provide any insight as to the well-being of DS?"

They glanced at each other sideways. As one they replied, "No."

"Then why, curse your souls, did you *suggest* him?"

"Because the actual specialist in Dominion Splitter—" began Deca.

"...is you-know-who," finished Fest.

"Bethniak? She's an expert at nothing, and why would you be reluctant to speak her name? Others, yes. But you two crones needn't fear her."

"The forever child?" declared Deca.

"We fear little, and she *is* little," added Fest.

"And we do not fear little Bethniak," chuckled Deca.

"Then who the blazes possesses an unspeakable name?"

They repeated their sideways glances. Again as one, they whispered very cautiously, "Gáwar."

Vorc's face grew ashen. "Oh, I do regret asking." He gulped. "He is, isn't he?"

"As much as there is one," said Fest.

"But his price is monumentally high," added Deca in a somber tone.

"Let's pray it never comes to that," said a very green around the gills Vorc.

"Pray we shall," responded Fest.

"With intensity and fervor," concluded Deca.

"Be assured," they both spoke solemnly.

And so it was Vorc's day, and all his subsequent nights, became just that little bit worse.

CHAPTER TWENTY-FIVE

Before we hustled off, we arranged with Daleria to rendezvous with us the following day after she closed up for the night. I picked a shrine of some sort at the base of a nearby hill. I definitely wanted to meet her on neutral turf and from a location I could check that she was arriving completely alone. My trust would need to be earned, given the stakes.

Through the darkness I saw her approaching. She was definitely alone. There were no other mobile thermal signatures. I stepped out from behind the shrine and waved her over.

"Hi," she said nervously. Then she looked behind the shrine. "Where's Sapale?"

"Not here," I said unhelpfully.

"Ah, better safer than sorrier."

"Something along those lines." I scanned a three-sixty. "Come on. Let's get out of sight." I gently took her elbow.

"Where're we going?"

"To our destination, of course."

"I'll stop asking questions."

"Not a bad idea."

We were quiet the rest of the long walk back to *Stingray*. About one hundred meters from the cave entrance I said, "Close your eyes."

"What, no blindfold?" she replied rather mockingly.

"They're all at the cleaners, now close those eyes."

She did.

I led her into the tunnel and opened *Stingray's* hull. Sapale was inside and took her elbow from me. "This way, my dear," she said reassuringly.

"You can open 'em up now," I said.

"No, I'm good." Then she peeked at me with one eye barely open. What a pretty smile.

I definitely heard one of Sapale's quiet alert-growls. Note to self. Do not notice pretty smiles, at least with spouse around.

Daleria turned to take in the vortex. She was clearly impressed. "Is this your house?" she finally asked.

"I guess so," I replied.

"But we're *so* much more," added Al.

"Who said that?" she asked, looking side to side.

"I did," replied the always painful Al.

"You got ghosts?" Daleria asked me.

"No, just large rats," I responded.

"Talking rats," added Sapale with a grin.

"We are just as embarrassed and ashamed of you two as you are of us," Al piped in.

"I still don't know who he is, and now *he's* a *we*?" asked Daleria.

"Long boring story," I replied.

"And yes, by the way, we do have ghosts, too," amended Al.

"Seriously?" she responded. "That's so amazing."

"Pilot, please know she's referring to *me*, not the *ghost*," stated Al.

"What ghost?" said the damn ghost. "I'm afraid of ghosts."

"Oh my, this has taken a seriously dangerous turn," responded Al.

"How so?" I asked quickly.

"The ghost has no sense of humor whatsoever. He's your *twin*, Pilot."

"This is an *odd* house," Daleria said, mostly to herself.

"Oh, you don't know the third of it, deary," chided Al.

"Deary?" accused *Stingray*. "*I'm* the only one you call deary. I will *not* tolerate a straying husband." She was pissed.

"It's such a *strange,* odd house," mumbled a confused Daleria.

"After a while it will all seem routine," said Toño, entering the room. "One thing it will never see is normal adult behavior."

"Hey, stop complaining," protested Sapale. "Aside from *Blessing,* you created us all, including yourself."

"Are *you* the All Father?" asked Daleria in awe.

"No, my child. I'm a mere scientist with much to atone for."

"He didn't create me," said the ghost. "Wait, no. I take that back. Maybe he did. I certainly don't know my origins, so it is a possibility."

"Why *are* you back?" I asked the shiny figure. Yeah, what started as a blob was forming into a definite figure of sorts. "And do not start by saying you never left or I'll knock you out."

"You can knock unconscious an ethereal spirit, Ryanmax? That's *unbelievable,*" responded Daleria in a stunned voice.

"It's not. It's bullshit blustering, plain and simple," replied Al.

"I think I might need to leave this *perplexing,* strange, odd house," Daleria said, even quieter than before.

"And I'm a state-of-the-art spacecraft," said *Stingray,* with considerable pride.

"Now wait," said Daleria, holding the sides of her head, "are you, the girl voice, *Blessing* or *Stingray?*"

"Yes," *Stingray* replied.

"That wasn't a *yes* or *no* question," protested Daleria.

"Yes," peppered in Al, who I could tell was having lots o' fun.

"Do you have seats on this ... *this?*" asked Daleria.

"Yes, my dear," replied Toño, gesturing to a bench, "right this way. May I get you a drink?"

She glanced to him as she sat. "Does it contain a lot of alcohol?"

"It can be."

"Put it over a little ice, and hurry," she replied.

"She's rather *dramatic*, isn't she?" asked Al.

"Not sure that's constructive, doopy loopy," responded *Stingray*.

"The devil with constructive, let's *dance*," Al cried out of nowhere.

"Please do. Dance to the farthest horizon," I murmured.

"That would make it dawn. We shall dance until daybreak, love particles," proclaimed Al. Dude was positively giddy. Go figure.

"Your computer dances with itself?" asked the ghost. "And here I was thinking *I* was preternatural."

"Excuse me," said Daleria after two big gulps of whiskey. "First, this is good." She held her glass toward Toño. "Second, does it come in bottles? Third, your plan is to defeat the indomitable Cleinoid race with a dancing computer, a ghost, and three people? Am I leaving anything out?"

"They're technically two AI computers and we're androids, not people, but yes," I replied.

"So far we're knocking it out of the park," added Sapale.

"What park?" she asked in utter confusion.

"I'll get you that bottle," said Toño as he sped away.

"Bottle*s*." She hissed the terminal *s*.

"So, you never answered. Where were you?" I asked the ghost.

"Since *here all the time* is not permissible, I'll pick looking at DS."

"Who's DS?" asked Daleria.

"Dominion Splitter," replied Sapale.

"Ah, of course. And why were you staring at DS?"

"It's quite the spectacle," he responded. "Have you seen it lately?"

"I saw some vids. Big crowd I guess."

"*Big* crowd. No, it's everybody not in Prime," replied ghosty.

"I guess Vorc's taking no chances of anyone further damaging DS," she responded.

"I'd say there's no chance," I replied angrily. "Damn thing's bulletproof inside a steel safe hidden deep in a mountain."

"I wouldn't say it's that bad," said Toño.

Color me surprised. "Not that bad?" I wheezed.

"No, it's *much* bleaker."

"You're all talking like you could actually destroy DS if you could only get to it. That's crazy talk," said Daleria as she polished off her first bottle.

"In point of fact we could kill it if we could get to it," replied Toño. "But our weapon is quite large and bulky."

"Kill DS?" Daleria asked incredulously. "It's a weather pattern, not a living being."

"Oh, he's very much alive," replied the ghost. "And nasty to a fault."

"The vortex is mean?"

"I could tell you tales," replied the ghost.

"Please don't," Daleria responded quickly.

"So you've met the crew and you've heard our story," I said. "Any thoughts on how to kill DS?"

"No. What do I look like, the unspeakable one?"

"You mean Zastrál?" I replied.

"Shushsssss. Do *not* say that again." Wow, she needed to switch to decaf.

"Why? It's not like he can *hear* us," I responded with attitude.

"You don't understand, do you?"

"What, we met the guy. Bad case of the uglies and smelled like rotten feet. But," I swaggered a little, "ain't no big deal."

I thought Daleria was going to evaporate. "You've met Zastrál and lived? That's not even possible. He usually destroys the minds of those he probes."

"I'm the pudding proof," I said cheerily. "All three of us are right as rain." I tapped my head with my knuckles. "Not much to work with in the first place, I must confess."

"Amen, I say upon you," squealed Al.

"He did seem most unpleasant, I will admit," said Toño.

"He's mega bad," Daleria began. "He is too horrible, in fact, to live amongst us. He must be summoned to be utilized. It is always the case that his cure is much worse than whatever disease one fancied justified his coming. So ... so Vorc summoned him?"

"I couldn't say," I responded. "But someone did."

"Is he here in our plane? Now? He's very bad, but I fear another much much worse might come into play if Zastrál is around."

"How so?" I asked naively.

"Oh, I forgot, you're new here," Daleria replied.

"I'm not," observed the ghost. "No, wait. Darn it all. Maybe I am."

"Enough of the mea culpas, *please*," I snapped. "We're trying to understand the threat level here."

"If Zastrál is present, he could summon one whose name truly is unspeakable."

"Now that's just silly," I replied. "You summon *one* jerk-off to summon another jerk-off? Who designed those workflows?"

"Not me," she replied. "But only Zastrál can summon ... summon certain death."

"He's a big snake, a double snake yes, but seriously? How is it tasked to him to *summon*," I slashed quotes in the air, "his even nastier buddy?"

"It's a safeguard," responded the ghost.

"What, you're an expert?"

"I couldn't say. But I do know this much. You have to summon something bad to be able to summon something much worse. It's a redundant security protocol. That way Mr. Doom can never be summoned accidentally."

"Mr. Doom? That's his unspeakable name?" I challenged.

"No, it's Gáwar," replied the ghost.

That's when Daleria passed out. At least I *hoped* she just passed out. I needed her too much for her to be dead.

"*Medic*," I shouted to Doc.

"Out of my way," he said, brushing past me.

"And no copping a feel while she's out, you dirty old android," I quipped.

"Jon, really?" snapped Sapale. "If I had soap I'd wash your mouth out with it here and now."

"I'll check ship's stores," called out Al.

"No, pal, you keep right on dancing," I yelled to the ceiling.

"Don't mind if I do," was his giddy response. That Al.

CHAPTER TWENTY-SIX

Antonab was, and everyone agreed on this point, ugly. And his personality matched his looks. It was ugly, indeed. His mother might have disagreed. But he ate her while he was still so young he'd never been able to ask her. Antonab's idea of fun times would be to pillage a graveyard or possibly poison the water source for an entire population. He once established an orphanage-city just to collect centrally his meals for one week. He was bad.

Cleinoid gods came in many different forms. Some were attractive humanoids. Some were good-looking to their own kind, even if they were a slimy slug with fire coming out their backsides. Antonab was, er, different. Since the passing of his maternal unit, there were apparently none of his species left. If there were, however, his kin would regard him poorly. Picture, if you will, a hyena. Make it five times bigger. Now replace the legs with articulated insect appendages. Number them ten, and place them underneath his body so that he stood very tall. Then substitute for his tail poison-laced whips measuring ten feet in length —ten of those. To complete the image, take the rank smell of a hyena and multiple it by infinity. The resultant pungent repellent wafted from him day and night. It could not be washed off, not that Antonab ever bathed to see if it could be. To smell him was to die, though it should be noted the foul aerosolized goo was not poisonous. The fact was that after experiencing it, any and all life forms would kill themselves rather than live with the memory. It was bad.

He was a member of the first and only brigade of ancient gods to make it to Prime: Rage. He was their poster-whatever. In a little over a year, time being as it was, Antonab had enjoyed himself thoroughly. He'd been busy, too. Traveling by thought, he'd visited ruins on thirty planets, ten unoccupied moons, and two stars at the center of vibrant and verdant solar systems. He considered the destruction of the stars to be his crowning achievements. Once the countless inhabitants of the system learned their sun was gone, Antonab absorbed their horror and their hopelessness, and finally their slow and methodical deaths in the sunless void. The moons he pulverized because they somehow offended him, barren and unobtrusive as they might have been. Dude was badness in a bottle.

Presently, he was about to embark on his next jaunt. He had a few more body parts to crush and burn and then he would be done with Whitehowser, until recently the thriving hub for trade and commerce in what had been the Barkess Quadrant. The quadrant was currently indistinguishable from empty frigid space. Antonab had detected an enormous group of spacecraft moving in the same direction. In his experience those typically bore refugees from a planet doomed by natural forces or cataclysmic wars. They were always slow moving and always packed with beings, as if they were sardines in a can. And they were especially sweet, for they had hope of a better life somewhere else. And they were vulnerable, and knew it. It was such a delight to snuff out those types of industrious, good, and self-aware people.

In his mind, Antonab saw the ships. They were led by one of the largest vessels in the flotilla. Excellent. That had to be a warship, undoubtably the pride of the fleet. It might also hold the command and control functions for the travelers. To torture it and its crew before destroying it would be gleefully disheartening to those who would all too soon be dead. Yes, that would be his first prize.

Antonab closed his eyes and instantly stood on the bridge of *Strength of Honor.* To say the least the crew was caught off guard. In the brief interval between when the individuals saw the beast and then smelled the beast, the crew's eyes, all six of them, were wide and showed primal fear. Once the odor struck them most grabbed at their throats and toppled to the deck.

As captains were given to, that of *Strength of Honor* charged forward toward Antonab, his sidearm drawn. "How dare you invade my ship," he raged as he emptied first one clip and then two more into Antonab.

When the captain was within pincer reach, Antonab seized him gently and lifted him up. He was careful to not even scratch the captain's epidermal plates. He studied the humanoid, rotating him to take in the whole of the brave soul. "What are you called?" his booming voice asked. As he was a god he already knew their language.

"I'm Captain Altilia Jex 9, commander of the Slohash Federation Diversionary Fleet. You have invaded my ship and will surrender immediately."

"All right," Antonab's voice echoed quietly. It sounded like a slowed-down recording.

"What?" snapped Altilia Jex 9.

"You heard me. I surrender for my crimes."

"Y ... you do?" he stammered. "Well it's about time," he said, finding his confidence. "Now put me down and subject yourself to binding."

"Why must I place you down? Can I not be your prisoner while holding you helpless?"

"Ah, no, I think not. It's not proper."

"I am Antonab, an ancient god. You do not know me. Therefore I will tell you plainly. *I* am not proper."

"A god? That's absurd. Now put me down."

"Yes, I am an ancient god. I rule over tyranny. It's—how do you say it—it's my *thing.*"

"Ancient god or not, you're my prisoner. Put me down and subject—"

"I know. Myself to bondage."

"No, I said *binding*. Bondage sounds, well, it sounds sexual in nature, and I'm a proper Snark."

"Ah. Either way, I am at your mercy."

"Are you toying with me, mocking me?"

"Why would a prisoner, one so at risk and vulnerable as I, dare mock my captor?"

"You mentioned a moment ago surrendering for your crimes—plural. So far you've only committed one. Illegal boarding of a ship of the line."

"Well, I was including this," he replied as one whip lashed out and snapped someone's head off. "As well as my heinous act when I did this." He grabbed someone else by the neck and smashed them to the ceiling. "I included the murders I was *about* to commit."

"As my prisoner you may not execute my crew."

"You are a man who lives by many unfamiliar rules."

"Adjutant Zazmos Tip 7, release the marines. This monster is toying with us. I want him dead."

"Aye, Captain," she replied tersely.

"Marines? Are those armed soldiers I can kill?" inquired Antonab.

"We shall find out," howled Captain Altilia Jex 9. He then threw his empty pistol at Antonab's head.

"While we wait, I have a question. May I ask it of you?" asked the horror.

Altilia Jex 9 spoke as he struggled to loosen Antonab's grip. "Why not? I always grant someone their last request."

"The others are paralyzed by my body odor. *Everyone* is stricken by it everywhere. Yet you rush toward me and are able to carry on a conversation. How can that be?"

"I ... I guess smells don't bother me much."

"That is not possible. I have worked for millions of years to cultivate this stench. It *must* offend all mortals."

Suddenly Altilia Jex 9 swung Antonab's pincer open with trivial ease. He landed deftly on the deck. "Well, there you have it, old boy."

"What? How did you ... There I have what?"

He craned his two fore-claws up and crashed them downward toward the captain. Inexplicably they stopped midflight, frozen in the air.

"How is this possible? I will—"

"Die, my old friend."

Before Antonab's many eyes Captain Altilia Jex 9, commander of the Slohash Federation Diversionary Fleet, turned into a fine mist. The cloud coalesced back into an all-too-familiar shape.

"Kocolli," screamed Antonab with indignation. "The trickster god. Why are you doing this?"

Kocolli scuffed a foot on the deck absently. "Well, you see, old boy, I grew bored. Killing these Prime dwellers, well it's too damn easy. I needed ... I needed a challenge."

"Release me at once, man of excrement."

"Okay, I will release you."

"What?"

"You heard me. I will release you because the game's almost over. There remains but one move."

"I shall see you pay dearly for this outrage."

"Ah, sadly, no. You see, I will be releasing you, yes. But it's into *death*."

Invisible forces crushed down on Antonab. Try as he might he could not stop them. Antonab's legs shattered, then his body was smashed into the metal deck, and finally his whip tails were flattened to look like leather belts. Then *Strength of Honor* vanished. The rest of the imaginary fleet disintegrated. Kocolli stood in the still darkness of empty space and began to play his flute. He chose his very favorite tune. He even dedicated it to the memory of Antonab, lost so avoidably but entertainingly.

CHAPTER TWENTY-SEVEN

It turned out Daleria wasn't dead after all. She just freaked when she heard the unspeakable's name out loud. She apologized so many times it was kind of cute. One more item to add to my list of achievements—I was present at *the* most embarrassing moment in Daleria's life. When she was able to, I walked her home.

"No blindfold this time?" she teased. "I guess real spies don't swoon, so I won you over."

"Real spies *pretend* to swoon. You actually did."

"Oh, so you're an expert in that field of study also?"

Man, she had a cute smile. *Jon, don't go there. Remember Lorena and John Bobbitt. Focus on personal safety, not warm and inviting facial expressions.*

"Oh, yeah." I wagged a finger in the air. "It's back in my universe so you probably haven't heard of it, but I was a professor of Spyology at Harvard University long, long ago."

"Impressive. How was the benefit package?"

I shrugged. "Not so good, but we're talking *Harvard* here," I accentuated with my best Boston accent.

She giggled. I took *zero* note of how darn cute it was, by the way. Nope, not going there.

Her face hardened. "What do you think our chances are of killing the vortex?"

"*Our* chances?" I said seriously. "So am I to assume you've joined Team Loco?"

"Whatever loco is, yes." She wrapped herself in her arms. "And once we've ruined their lives hopefully they'll kill me. I don't want to spend the rest of forever with these monsters."

"There might just be some happy ground between an unacceptable life and a brutal death."

"How so?"

"*We* are planning on leaving once the Cleinoids can't."

"How? Your ship? You think it can get you home?"

"Do you think it *can't?*"

"I don't know. Duplicating the work of Dominion Splitter is hard to imagine."

"With any luck, we'll find out sooner rather than later."

"Why not do a test run? Yes," her tone grew excited. "See if you can. That way if you can you'll feel more confident about destroying the vortex."

"Nah. I for one am never going anywhere through good old DS. If I can't leave, my crew won't either. DS is not an option for us."

"Why not? I assume the trap you tripped to get here was similar."

"No. DS hates me. If I got close enough he'd homogenize me."

"DS *hates* you?" she replied with comic incredulity.

"Yup. Told me so himself."

"I'm not touching that one. You *spoke* with DS? It even *talks?* Yeah, sure."

"*He,*" I emphasized. "You don't want to piss him off and join my club."

"I'll keep that in mind."

We walked quietly a while.

"I have a question," I said. "I guess it's a question, that is."

"What, it can be hard for you to tell if it is or isn't?"

"We stash our ride in a far-off random location. Sapale and I go for a stroll with no particular destination because we were getting on Toño's nerves. You *happen* to be roasting felnastop with your front door open just as we passed it. It turns out you are a friend of hell-and-gone distant Wul. We chat for not that long and find out you're a rebel."

"Your point?"

"It's a fairly incredible set of happenstance, don't you think?"

She looked ahead, thinking a few seconds. "Yes and no."

"Best to cover all your bases."

"I'm serious. It's fate, Jon Ryan. When fate is in play the impossible becomes real."

"Sure, you can say it was fated to pass or something, but come on. The odds are less than a politician ending his career with honor after having served admirably."

"You don't get it?"

"Apparently not, teach."

"*Teach*? Is that some form of malady?"

"No, it's short for *teacher*. What don't I get?"

"*Fate*. Not as in *it was fated*, either. Jon, Fate is a real thing. It has will and desire and intent. Don't your people share this knowledge?"

"Ah, that'd be a *no*. Are you serious? So in Godville Fate is a form of religion?"

"No. Not religion, especially not us, the lords of all that is."

"So you're saying Fate is like some dude, a living breathing individual?"

"You say that like it's crazy. By the way, *she* might be a *she*."

"You don't know? I think I rest my case, Ms. Perry Mason."

"No one has *seen* Fate. Fate might or might not be corporeal. All that's important is that it decides what can and cannot come to pass."

"Is it like a liberal or a conservative? Maybe it's Groucho Marx, big cigar and all."

"I clearly don't know your references. However, maybe Fate is this grouchy fellow. No one knows. But we all know Fate drives our lives."

I walked two fingers in the air. "We're little chess pieces and Fate moves us like pawns?"

"No, of course not. It determines our options, like I said. Jon, the Cleinoids couldn't have accessed DS and DS couldn't have functioned if Fate hadn't favored that eventuality. Why do you think we waited so very long to leave? It wasn't for lack of wanting to."

"So Fate decided it was time to burn another universe?"

She shook her head thoughtfully. "No. But it allowed it to be possible. The Cleinoids might have decided to stay here or to go to Prime in peace. Fate *allowed* options that were not in play earlier."

Something hit me. "Why did the Cleinoids return here from whatever hell they created on their last romp?"

"I ... I don't know. Demigods may or may not partake of the revelries. I've never gone on any of the shameful escapades."

"But I mean they were somewhere having fun, and then they hop back through DS and come back here. Why?"

"Maybe there was nothing left to ruin."

"Could be. But a universe is a big place. By the time you eradicate the second half of it, the first half has revolved into something wreckable."

She shook her head slightly. "I wouldn't know. Maybe you could ask Wul."

"Nah, best not to press my luck. He's unclear enough about me already."

"You're probably right."

"So nice, kind and thoughtful Wul goes on these unholy crusades?"

She looked away. "Sometimes."

"Does he do the crush-kill-destroy thing, or is it just for a change of scenery?"

"I never ask and he never volunteers."

"Sounds awkward."

"Can we drop it?"

"I live only to serve."

We were back at her place, anyway.

"Look, I need to go through the motions tomorrow. But I'll come to see you after, like tonight, okay?"

"Wouldn't have it any other way. You're a permanent fixture on Team Loco. Like it or not, by the way."

She gave me a quick hug. "I like it very much."

And she was gone.

Back aboard *Stingray* Sapale and Toño were in the mess, clearly waiting on my return. Toño spoke first. "So are we all one *hundred* percent certain we can trust her?"

"This is big, love," added Sapale. "She seems legit, but there's more at stake this time than ever before."

I slid next to her and the waiting mug of coffee. "I know. I say two things. One, I like her and think we can trust her. Two, that said, if either of you even gets a whiff of something being not right about her, I'm fine powering up right this minute and hiding somewhere else."

"Would you like me to watch her for a while, see if she's up to something foul?" asked the ghost.

"You know what, you need a name," I declared. "You're part of the team, an unelected member, I wish to point out. But if you're going to hang with us, you need a name."

"Where were you from?" asked Sapale.

"Do you recall anything about your life, your species?" queried Toño.

"No, nothing really."

"You speak English. That's hyper unlikely. Were you human?" wondered Sapale.

"I have no idea—"

"What?" I snapped.

"Peanut butter."

"What about it?" pressed Toño.

"I remember the word. I think it means something."

"Yeah," I came back, "it means you ground up peanuts to make a PBJ."

222

"Jon, I think this is important. Peanut butter and English. I say that points directly to a human origin," responded Toño.

I pointed over my shoulder at the closed cabinet. "There's a big jar of it up there. He could have read the label at any time."

"Can you see, ghost?" Toño asked quickly.

"Er, I think so. Yes, I must. I see you five plain as unbuttered toast."

"He's obsessed with food," I complained. "First peanuts, now toast."

"Wait." Toño held a hand in my face. "You see *five* individuals present?" There was a worried tone in Doc's voice.

"Yes. Don't you?"

Toño was right to worry. If the spook was correct we had company.

"Names. What are the names of the five individuals you see?" I demanded.

""You, Jon, along with Sapale, Toño, Al, and *Blessing*. Why is that odd?"

"You *see* the computers?" asked Toño.

"Yes. Why shouldn't I? They're right over there." The mist swirled.

"They are housed in that direction. But neither has a physical signature. I know for a fact Alvin does not. I built and programmed him myself."

"Al and *Stingray*," I interjected, "one of you two came with me on a trip to Varrank Simzle's home world of Deerkon. The other did not. Will the one who did NOT accompany me wave something in the air. A hand or a transistor." Then to the ghost I asked, "who's waving?"

"You're kidding, right. This is silly. Blessing is waving the rightmost of her three arms."

"Blessing has three arms?" mumbled a stunned Sapale.

"Well, the Deavoriath have three arms and they created her," observed Toño.

"How many arms does Al have?"

223

"Two. One is currently positioned rather oddly. His left thumb rests on his nose and he's wiggling four fingers at you, Jon."

"Well, I'll be damned," I said after a deep sigh.

"Now that thumb is extended and pointing upward. Hey, Al, what are you trying to say?" asked the ghost.

"Oh, I think the pilot knows my meaning."

"This is truly *remarkable*," whispered a stunned Toño.

"Ya think?" quipped Sapale. "Our AI's have pseudo-bodies? Analog forms?"

"How can this be?" Toño said, equally hushed.

I snapped my fingers loudly. "Okay, Society for the Documentation of the Unimportant, meeting's adjourned. We need to get back on topic. Doc, you can wax philosophical about evidential existentiality at some future date, and preferably when I am light years away."

"Uh?" he grunted. "Yes, you're right."

"Ghost, you may have been human. Your name henceforth is *Casper*. Any questions?"

"You really don't see the AIs?"

"We moved on. Try and keep up," I snapped. "Casper, do you know where Daleria's place is to go snoop on her for a while?"

"Of course. I was—"

"With me the whole time. Why'd I ask? Okay, Casper, you hightail it there and see if she's playing us."

"You got it," he replied.

"Oh, and if she takes a shower or anything, you turn your back, assuming you have one to turn."

"Only *you* of all beings in all the universes would mention that at such a critical time," marveled Toño.

"Thank you," I directed to him.

"Oh, that was *far* from a compliment," he responded flatly.

"Well *thank you* just the same." Naturally I stuck my tongue out at my pro-peeping Tom ex-friend.

"Is he gone?" asked Sapale.

"Beats me," I responded. "Hey, Al, you still see him?"

"No."

"Wait, that was too short an answer."

"No, *sir.*"

"Holy crap, you're doing it again."

"No."

"You can't say *no* if I didn't even say what it was you're doing again!" My metaphorical blood pressure was skyrocketing.

"Yes."

"Doc, can you do something about your defective toy calculator?"

"No," both the SOBs said in unison.

"I am formally withdrawing my original question," I shouted. "I no longer care or wish to know if you can see, ever saw, or still do see Casper."

"No," replied Al.

"No? Al, this is getting out of hand. *No,* I actually care about what I said I don't care about? Because believe me, I do *not* freaking care about your visual interactions with," I held up sequential digits, "Casper, me, what I'm doing in the air in your direction, or if you can see the can of whoop ass coming your way in the immediate future."

"Jon, you should try and calm yourself," soothed Toño. "This might be unhealthy for you, somehow."

"No," Al and I said as one.

"No, it might not be unhealthy, or no, Al, you opine it is not unhealthy?" muttered a confused Toño.

"I have a new word for you *morons,*" menaced Sapale, which she followed with a quiet fight-growl. "*Shut up.* I know, that's *two* words, but if any of you *halfwits* says word one, you're going to have to start sitting down to pee. Do I make myself impossibly clear?"

"Yes," the three of us said as one, and fervently.

225

CHAPTER TWENTY-EIGHT

Vorc stood as close as was generally considered safe to Dominion Splitter. He was flanked by Felladonna on one side and Darduell, the trinket guy, on the other. They had stared into the slowly spinning dark vortex for several minutes.

"Well, what do you think, Darduell?" asked Vorc, still looking forward.

"About what, sire?"

"The mechanical processes that translate rotation of tumblers into the movement of a slide bolt."

Darduell smiled, because Vorc had thrown that question directly into his wheelhouse. "It's a fascinating—"

"The health of the *vortex*, you peabrain. Why would I summon you here to discuss *locks*?"

"I don't rightly know. I'm ... I'm fairly uncertain what my role is here, actually."

Vorc drew his hand back to slap the ninny upside his head.

Felladonna gently arrested Vorc's motion and spoke. "We were hoping that as a man in possession of expertise in technical matters, you might be able to provide some insight into the state of health of DS."

"Ah," he responded, as he fidgeted nervously with his watch chain fob. "And why is it you came to that flattering opinion that I might?"

Vorc mumbled a few words even Felladonna couldn't make out.

"Beg pardon, sire?"

"The witch sisters mentioned your name," he said audibly.

"Deca and Fest?" Darduell replied with obvious surprise. "One is reluctant to even be thought of by those two, er, citizens. I have actually never met either lady."

"You are lucky, and *neither* is a lady. They are pond scum, wicked slime that eats away at any sound mind."

"You seem none the worse for wear, sire," responded Darduell cheerily.

"On the outside perhaps. On the inside, you are sadly mistaken. When my chief council comes from those bats, *our* kingdom and *my* brain are in a sorry state."

"Fascinating."

"Tragic, yes. Any positive modifier, no. Now, do you have any insight you can provide?" Vorc's fixation on the vortex never wavered.

"Sadly, I'm certain I do not. I've never been this close to it before. It is an imposing sight to behold. Are you certain it does not work?"

Vorc was stunned. The toad had a good point. Vorc *assumed* that the profound loss of pulsing electricity and intensity of rotation indicated DS was not functional. He did not, however, *know* that as a fact.

"I'm glad I summoned you, locksmith. You have been of some assistance. You are about to be of even more."

As nervously as a shotgun groom, Darduell began to thank Vorc for the unsettling praise. He never actually had the chance to say word one. Vorc, physically much larger, bear-hugged Darduell, lifted him up, and cast him toward the center of DS. Kicking, screaming, and for some unfathomable reason apologizing, Darduell slipped from view into the mist. Three seconds later a red-green ooze began dripping from the bottom of DS.

"I wonder if that's what's left of the idiot," asked Vorc.

"I can't say at this point, sir," responded Felladonna respectfully.

Then the mangled fob-watch chain clinked to the ground.

"Now, however, I can state confidently it is, sir," amended Felladonna.

"Damn shame," murmured Vorc.

"About the lock and bauble god?"

"Heavens no. The world's a better place without him. No I was referring to the fact that we now *know* DS is not operative." He paused a moment. "I wonder if there's anything we can do to help it heal?"

"Yyyyyesssssssss," hissed Dominion Splitter.

Vorc nearly jumped out of his skin. He had no idea the infernal thing could *speak*. "Ah, you heard me?" he asked lamely.

"Offfff cccccooooouuuurseeeee, ffffoooooool."

"Well I'll be damned," whispered Vorc.

"Iiiiiffff tthheeerrrreee iiiiiisssssss jjuusticcceeeeee."

"What can we do to help you heal?" pressed Vorc.

"Tttwooooo ttthiiinnngggs. Onnnne, pppraaayyyyer. Twoooooooo, eelllecctttricccccccittttyyy. Lotttsssssss oooffff eelectricccccityyyy."

Vorc could easily arrange both. There were countless empty-headed Cleinoids who'd pray for just about anything. And he could get Public Works to pump as much electricity into DS as it could handle. "Consider it done, my friend."

"Neeeverrrrr mmyyyyyy ffrienndddd, llloooooosserrrr."

Vorc was so happy to have a proactive plan, he barely heard and completely compartmentalized the insult.

Within a few hours a large generator was streaming AC current into DS's center. Along with the impressive contingent of guards there was a new and even larger group of worshipers, some of whom were volunteers. By the next morning DS was clearly on the mend. Sparks flew from his spiral arms and some of the dark gray wisps were definitely a lighter shade.

For the first time in a long time, Vorc was pleased and confident. He greatly admired how he'd personally solved the vortex issue with only the perfunctory aid of others. That suggested his position as center seat was more secure than his informal polls had recently suggested.

CHAPTER TWENTY-NINE

We met with Daleria for several successive evenings. Though pleasant, the sessions were fully unproductive. Aside from the snacks she brought, she could offer no significant help to our efforts to destroy DS. But then came the night she brought a huge pot of felnastop stew. If I thought the roasted version was sublime, the stew far surpassed anything similar I had ever eaten. It was thick, savory, just piquant enough, with complex ambrosial_nuances and contrasting spices. It immediately went to the last-food-I'd-eat list if I knew I was dying tomorrow. The mess was absolutely silent—I could tell Sapale and Toño were experiencing the divinity of the culinary masterpiece.

Once Daleria finished her serving, she sat back and gloated serenely. She knew the impact her dish was having on her new friends. I could tell between my wolfish bites that she was really enjoying her achievement. "I knew if you liked it roasted you'd die for the stew. It's an old family recipe of mine. Very hush-hush and all. If I ever wanted to get married, I'd serve it to my chosen victim."

A sentence like that was enough to get me to set my spoon down. "Cleinoids have families to have family recipes with? I haven't seen any evidence of familial interactions or unity."

"Maybe that's because you're not a Cleinoid," she replied with a smirk. "Since we live forever, barring an unfortunate outside intervention, family life is less concentrated. Less intensity over a longer period equals the same amount of kinship as anywhere else. It's simple math."

"I suppose that makes sense," commented Toño. "Too close a grouping over forever might shear family bonds."

"I don't think so with us Kaljaxians. Our family ties are ferociously held on to."

"I'm human. Toño knows about my family. He had to study it while deciding if I'd be a pilot candidate. My kin were so incompatible over generations that everyone brought an attorney to the family reunions. In fact we stopped having reunions because word spread among the legal community that the Ryans were too hard to work with, not worth it even if we overpaid them embarrassingly."

"Hmm," throated Toño. "I don't recall such a detail."

"Hey, painful family secrets are closely guarded."

"I'd have loved to be a fly on the wall at one of those parties," Sapale said with a wicked grin. "Good food *and* good entertainment."

"Nah," I scoffed, "even bugs have stand —" I dropped my spoon. It missed the bowl and skidded across the deck.

"What, Jon?" called out Toño, "Are you all right?"

"Honey," added Sapale, "can I help get you to bed?"

I shook her off without looking over. "Nah, maybe later. For now, I have a transfolding vortex to subtract from the universe."

"You developed a plan?" said Toño, rising in excitement.

"I think I just did."

He plopped back down with a sad look on his face. "Is it a Jon Plan?"

"You know what? I don't think it's *that* bad."

Toño stood again with a big smile. "How I've longed to hear those words."

"What is your plan?" asked Sapale.

"I ask Doc one question and he responds, *Yes, definitely and a lot.*"

Toño sat back down, more dejected than last time. The beaten man said with resignation, "What's your question?"

"Can the listening bugs we distributed carry a load, however small, of neutral matter for oh say a minute?"

His fallen face rumbled briefly. Then the right side of his lips grinned. Then he jumped to his feet and slapped his hands above his head. "Yes, by the Good Lord in Heaven, definitely and actually *quite* a lot."

"Anyone want to deal me in?" asked Casper, who of course appeared from nowhere.

"As you may know we planted a gazillion tiny listening devices to see when and where we could intercept the shipment of neutral matter," replied Sapale. "My husband of nothing more than moderate intelligence figured out that if we loaded them up with neutral matter, we could kill DS without anyone seeing the attack."

"Why did you feel the need to label his mind as merely moderate?" asked Daleria. "Personally, I think it's a *brilliant* plan."

"Then you're in charge of his ever-oversizing ego. I've given all I can to that cause," responded Sapale, just before she shoveled a spoonful of stew into her mouth.

"So how long do you think it'll take to load the bugs?" I asked Toño.

"Well, not too long. But it will be somewhat dangerous and extremely unpleasant."

"How so?"

"If the neutral matter is exposed for more than seconds it will annihilate."

"And the unpleasant part?"

"You know how we've all felt when exposed to it. In the time available I can't set up a safe way to perform the bonding without some level of direct exposure."

"Can't we do it, Form Three?" asked *Stingray*.

"I suppose you could, couldn't you?"

"Keep in mind we can't jeopardize our one and only ride out of here, Doc," I cautioned.

"I do not think there will be any risk to either Al or *Blessing*," responded Toño.

"Hey, Als, if you notice even one strange thing alert us at once. You got that?"

"Yes, Pilot. I must report I have already noticed one strange thing."

"Very funny. Ha ha, Al. You noticed me, right?"

"No, I noticed the power levels of DS have just returned to those present when the first wave of Cleinoids were able to depart."

"Then I'd say we're looking at an all-nighter."

CHAPTER THIRTY

Vorc stood facing Dominion Splitter. To his back stood, flew, or slithered a most bizarre and sickening assembly not visibly smaller than the egress before. Figures that could only be dredged up from the depths of a forsaken hell held formation. Anticipation was so thick that the air was electrified. Sparks snapped and popped randomly. The wedge of ancient gods that flanked Vorc spread outward to infinity and never thinned. As far as my eye could see, denizens of the universe of hate, rapacious consumption, and endless antipathy abounded. All champed at the bit to be freed, lost in a bloodlust for destruction, death, and debauchery.

The time for the egress had come—again.

Prime was back in their merciless reach.

Vorc raised his arms high overhead. "Brothers and sisters, the time of our sanctification has arrived. Can you feel it?"

The press of the concussive sound that came in response could have flattened an entire city.

"Are you ready to be *gods* to the worthless and the undeserving? Are you set to wreak Armageddon on those whose only role in life is to suffer and to die so that we may find joy?"

An even louder wave of sound struck Vorc's back so hard he nearly tumbled.

"Then let it *begin*." Spit rained from his lips as he howled. "The advanced reavers are already in Prime, as is Rage. The four remaining ranks of Cleinoids will follow, one at a time. Torment will depart first. Wrath second, and Fury third. Then ... then *all-consuming* Horror will descend upon Prime, and their fate will be sealed. As is our tradition, I shall personally lead Horror. For *this* incursion, I still plan on having Bethniak stand at my side. She will be the Right Hand of the Gods."

Mad hoots and cheers punished the atmosphere. Foul smoke rose from all manner of things burned by dragon fire or electric bolts fired in joyous lust. Mayhem was grading into chaos and everyone was enjoying the sense of rapture.

Dominion Splitter swirled faster than the last egress. More and more powerful snaps of energy burst randomly from his spirals. He seemed to be repeating an incantation, but maybe he was just in ecstasy. He was, in his evil, malevolent way, magnificent.

"Torment," yelled Vorc at the top of his lungs, "queue up to my right. You will enter two by two. Move as quickly as possible while maintaining order. We will risk no harm to—"

Vorc stopped speaking. He thought he noticed something and wanted to focus. Turning to Bethniak, he asked, "Does DS look ... er ... different to you?"

"Than what, fuckburger?"

"Than just a moment ago?"

"Are you going more psycho on me? If you lose it now, *I'm* taking command."

"No, look." He pointed at the outer edge. "See, the last spiral, it's getting darker."

"You're freaking nuts, recycled cum."

Vorc waved Felladonna over. She approached slowly. The aide was terrified by the presence of Bethniak. "Yes, lord?"

"Does the vortex look to be cooling and slowing as we speak?"

"I ... I don't know. Would you—"

I shoved the sycophantic bitch out of the way and got right in Vorc's face. "Vorc, Dominion Splitter is dimming. Can't you *see* it?" I screamed in rage, making sure to pepper his face with saliva.

"I thought so, too. What should we do?"

"You're asking me? I'm ready to go have the time of my life and you're screwing that up *again*. You tried to use DS too soon, you bastard."

"Used it too soon? No one's passed through. How's that overtaxing it?"

"Well, whatever. The damn thing's about to flicker out." I turned to the crowd and raised my arms. "Brothers and sisters. Quiet down. *Silence.*" When there was marginally less of a din I shouted again. "Dominion Splitter is dying. Vorc has an announcement."

Mine and all eyes present turned to Vorc. The silence was so immediate it nearly knocked me over.

Vorc looked at me confused, then to the crowd with uncertainty. "Ah, it has come, or rather been brought to my ... my attention that as we stand here Dominion Splitter might be, er, might be showing signs of being overtaxed."

He looked to me for support. What a moron. "DS is dying. It is dying for good, my friends. Any last words you have for it had better be said really quickly."

"Vorc," an anonymous voice shouted, "is that true? Did you kill DS?"

"I—," he slammed his palms to his chest, "I did *nothing.*"

"He's killed DS," cursed another voice.

"Why is DS dying?" yet another howled.

"I ... I don't ... I do not know, citizens," responded Vorc, much too softly to be heard. He dropped to his knees in defeat. *Excellent.*

One variable I hadn't counted on came into play. The damn vortex tried to finger me.

"Jjjjoonnnn Rrryyyaannnnnn ... heeeee diiidd thhiiisssssssss."

Lucky break, the idiot vortex accused me by my actual name that no one knew. It was similar, but not so much that I couldn't spin the situation. I raised my arms again. "Dominion Splitter has identified the person responsible for his demise. As Vorc and I stand here, we heard it accuse Jon Ryan of orchestrating his death. Has anyone seen Jon Ryan? He must not escape."

A woman burst into the clear. She pointed in one direction and screamed, "I saw Jon Ryan. He's running that way. Stop him before he can take flight."

"What does he look like?" shouted a voice.

"He's like an elephant but with massive wings. Hurry, once he's airborne there's no stopping him." With that she lowered her arm and charged away. A massive crowd surged behind her. Nice improvisation, Sapale!

Doc, can you hurry up the rate of neutral matter insertion? I nearly got caught there, I said to him head-to-head.

I'll increase the flux to the maximum. Best to step back.

Got it.

"In the interest of safety, please everybody step back a few paces. I've just been told the vortex *might* explode."

Worked like a charm. Let the screams, shoves, and trampling begin. What a bunch of me-firster babies. Within thirty seconds, utter pandemonium had erupted and was not going to be denied its full course.

I picked Vorc up from his knees and tugged him away. Not sure why, but I did. Very quickly it became clear I'd either have to carry him or drag him. His body'd gone limp. I started dragging the SOB by one arm. When we were safely away, safe being how far I estimated DS could be heard to speak, I dropped my sack of woe and turned to examine DS. It was a beautiful sight. Already he was dark, barely rotating, and he was settling on the ground like a huge wet noodle. Five minutes later there was no trace DS had ever existed. He was completely gone. Good riddance. I slowly walked back to *Stingray*. Once we were all safely aboard, we'd see about leaving this dump in the rearview mirror.

It felt awful darn good to have permanently stranded the evil ancient gods in the one place they did not want to linger. Darn good, I say.

EPILOGUE

Late the next afternoon Vorc sat in his office. His face was planted in his folded arms atop his desk. He'd been in that depressed position for many hours. Along with everything unacceptably horrific that had just happened, he morosely ruminated as to why no one had done him the kindness of assassinating him.

Vorc's head rose slowly and reluctantly when he heard a hideous sound in the reception area. It was followed by a short high-pitched scream of agony. Then Vorc heard a noise. He was about to challenge whoever was there when his door exploded inward after being struck by something of power. He rose to his feet and fumbled for the Fire of Justice, all the while never taking his eyes off the ragged hole the door had occupied.

Through the portal a massive frame contorted to enter. Vorc had never seen him before, but he knew it was the god he'd summoned. Vorc was about to negotiate with Gáwar, knowing full well Gáwar never negotiated anything with anybody. First to enter were his ten-foot long lobster claw front hands. Then multiple tentacles serving in place of antennae sprang in. Gáwar lowered his block-shaped bull head and poked it through. He scanned the room as he progressed. As Gáwar's torso came into view, Vorc's knees began to knock together in their attempt to buckle. Most of the beast's body was a snake, but a snake with human legs. If those legs had been on a woman she'd be considered lucky, maybe be a professional dancer. The beginnings of a tail slithered in, but most of it remained outside the room because it was so long.

The god of demons had arrived. Gáwar put his muzzle to Vorc's face and sniffed him wetly.

"I knew your mother, boy. She never summoned me, but know her I did. She was a turd among tubes of shit. Did you know that, boy?"

Vorc was speechless.

"Did your mama have any children who weren't mute lunatics?" Then the master demon laughed at his wit. The laugh would have killed any mortal and most immortals. It held in it all the enmity a voice could muster, all the casual disregard for the listener's well-being, and any trace of joy. Gáwar's laugh said plainly to anyone near enough to hear it that they would likely not see tomorrow. The manner of one's demise promised to be unspeakable.

"I ... I ... I—" Vorc tried to say.

"I, I, I. It's always about you when we get together, Vorc. I have feelings, too, you know?" With that Gáwar passed a large amount of flatulence, and he did so for many seconds. Vorc nearly passed out for lack of oxygen. "That, by the way, is a hello from your dead mama. She asked me to pass it along when I left our bed this morning."

Then Gáwar held forth one of his claws. "Is this yours? I think I might have broken it."

Between the pincers was the nearly severed-in-half drooping body of Felladonna.

"Mind if I set it here?" Gáwar tossed it carelessly over his back.

"D ... dd ... did you have to k ... kill the p ... poor girl?" Vorc asked at a whisper.

"No, and thanks for asking. I didn't *have* to kill her. I *wanted* to kill her. I want to kill you, too, but first maybe I'll let you tell me why I was summoned, and then, just maybe, I'll watch you grovel before I slice you into ribbons."

Vorc shut his eyes. "Dominion Splitter has been killed. Someone or some group decided the bulk of Cleinoids were not to be allowed to egress into Prime. I want the guilty party or parties brought before me. They will suffer for their crimes." He opened his eyes.

"Yes, I noticed the old windbag was defunct the moment I arrived. Did you know he was not as useless, ugly, and *stupid* as your mama?"

Vorc closed his eyes again. "Insulting my mother will help with nothing. I know her to have been an exemplary woman. Could you just possibly focus on my summons?"

"Insulting? Boy, I'm speaking truth to power. I should get a medal here."

"The criminals?" he asked. Then he opened one eye.

"Vorc, I'm going to go extra-easy on you. You know why?"

The one eye shut again. "No, I do not."

"Neither do I, and it bugs the *crap* out of me. But easy I will be. Vorc, you are the very model, the poster child's poster child for a stupid, unobservant dick. You were duped, swindled, flimflammed, hustled, scammed by a windup toy. You are so dumb idiots across all of space and time are hurrying to distance themselves from you as we speak. Do you partake even slightly of what I'm saying, you son of a turd?"

"A ... a windup toy? Wh ... whatever are you—"

"Ryanmax, you underarm sweat stain. Your pal Ryanmax is a robot, an android, a walking computer."

Vorc, eyes still sealed shut, pointed in Gáwar's general direction. "Now see here. I was not his pal. I detested the man."

"*Robot.* You *detest*, present tense, since he's still in the neighborhood."

"Are you certain?"

Words once spoken cannot be recalled, breathed back in. Words such as those directed at Gáwar were instantaneously certain to have been as poor a choice as there could ever have been.

Gáwar's heretofore beady black shark eyes glowed red, then blue. Steam rose from his entire body. The floor began to vibrate like a plank of wood pounded with a sledge.

"Am I certain, Cleinoid insect? Am I *cer-tain* of the words I spoke? Recall how I said I would go easy on you."

Vorc stood trembling and eyes closed. He'd assumed that was a rhetorical question.

"*Well*," Gáwar thundered, "do you recall?"

"Y ... yes, lord, I d ... do."

"Offer retracted. And do not call me *lord*. I am *death;* bleak, painful, hopeless *death*. I am lord of no one."

"Understood."

"So, soon to join his mother, you summoned me. I told you what you wanted to know. There is a price. You must pay it."

"A ... a price? I thought this type of ... assistance was part of—"

"I am part of *nothing*," he howled like a hurricane. You *will* pay my price."

"V ... vveer ... of course. Bbbbut ... if I mm ... may?"

"What. Do not *pretend* to tell me you are brainless enough to ask *more* of Gáwar."

A sudden calm, the calm of impending, unalterable death, came over Vorc. He opened his eyes. "Yes, Gáwar, I am that foolish. I want you to bring Ryanmax and his traitors to me."

"I'm stunned. That one blindsided me like a rogue whale. I gave you the name. The vortex is kaput so no one's escaping. But you need me to round up the bad guys? Hey, want me to wipe your turdy butt while I'm at it?"

"No. But I will pay an even greater price for the service."

"Oh, you bet your bloodline you will. Interested in hearing the price you already contracted for before upping the ante?"

"Certainly, if it will speed the—"

"I own your soul."

"I ... I was ...was uncerttt ... ttain we Cleinoids possessed souls; in a conventional, sense that is."

"You will soon learn you do. You will soon come to know what a nice article of life it was to have, by the way."

"What is ... would be the additional price?"

"I haven't finished listing what you *already* owe." Gáwar spoke those words with transparent glee.

"There's more? What could be more?"

"Poor dumb kid. You lack imagination. Fortunately I do not. I will have your mother's soul."

"But she's—"

"Dead. Yeah, I heard the rumor. I will have your father's soul. Yeah, heard that rumor, too. Just because you don't comprehend it, doesn't change the fact that they are payable on demand."

"What would the additional price—"

"You mean beyond the souls mentioned and the prizes still unidentified?"

"Yes."

"Okay, you're a player, aren't you? To bring Jon Ryan to you, because that's his robot name, will cost you ten large."

"What does that even mean, ten large?"

"Such a county bumpkin. It means the souls of every inhabitant of ten large cities under your rule. *You* will naturally choose which ones."

"Not you?"

"Me? No, I'm too shy. Don't work well under pressure either, truth be told."

"That's a lot of souls, souls I lead, whom I represent."

"Glad to hear you can count past your fingers and toes, boy. So, what'll it be? Services rendered or you going for the golden ring? Time's a ticking, so I'll need to know now, as in immediately."

"You drive a hard bargain."

"No, I do *not*. Damn your soul that is technically mine, I do not. I drive an *impossible* bargain. I drive a *cruel* and *unconscionable* bargain. It's kind of my thing."

Vorc gulped.

"What'll it be, son? Meter's running."

. . .

To Be Continued ....

Glossary:

Als (1): The original ship's AI on Jon's first flight long ago was Alvin. Jon shortened that to Al.When Al was joined to Jon's vortex in the Galaxy On Fire Series, Al and Blessing fell in love and got "married." Since then Jon refers to them combined as the Als.

Beal's Point (1): An area of monuments to disgraced Cleinoid gods. All living gods must visit to be made ill so they stay loyal.

Bethniak (1): Child-appearing, vengeful, powerful, and really really mean god.

Blessing (1): See *Stingray*.

Calrf (1): A Kaljaxian stew that Jon particularly dislikes.

Central Seat (1): The official leader of the Ancient Gods' conclave.

Cleinoid gods (1): Ancient and malevolent mix of gods. They have destroyed many universes before and are eyeing ours now.

Cragforel (1): Friendly Deavoriath Jon met after he first escaped the Adamant in the far future.

Cube (1): Jon's alternate name for the vortex he captains.

Dalfury (1): Vorc's right hand, or chief assistant. A demigod of cloudy memories, hence, he has the form of a cloud.

Davdiad (1): Kaljaxian divine spirit.

Deavoriath (1): Three arms and legs, the most advanced tech in the galaxy, and helpful to Jon.

Deca (1): One of the witch gods skilled at prophecy. Sister of Fest.

Daleria (2): Demigod and innkeeper whom Jon and Sapale befriended. She worked with them against the ancient gods as she'd grown to hate them.

Dominion Splitter (2): The name of the transfolding vortex the ancient gods use to transport to our galaxy. He has a lot of issues and is very conflicted. Actually he's just a total asshole, period. Aka DS.

Evil Jon Ryan/ EJ (1): Alternate time line version of the original human to android download. Over time, he turned to the darker side of his nature. He studied "magic" under a Deft master.

Felladonna (2): Vorc's second assistant, or so-called *right hand*. A demigod of lists and communication.

Felnastop (2): A delicious vegetable that runs like the wind.

Fest (1): One of the witch gods skilled at prophecy. Sister of Deca.

Form One/Form Two (1): A Form is the title of a vortex pilot. If more than one is aboard they get numerical designations based on seniority.

Gáwar (2): Seriously badass god. The god of demons. Yeah, badness.

Gorpedder (1): Ill-tempered boulder Cleinoid god.

Lorpamoor (1): Cleinoid vampire god. Nasty nasty fellow.

Hemnoplop (1): Demigod of Fool's Island. On pilgrimage to Beal's Point with Jon.

Marropex (1): A reaver. The Cleinoid god of atrocities.

Nassel (2): Leader of the Rage faction of Cleinoids. She had done so for the last three transheavals. A god of conquest.

Probe Fibers (1): Aka command prerogatives, they allow piloting of the vortex spaceship and can analyze whatever they touch.

Racdal fat (2): A food animal from Kaljax's abundant fat stores.

Sapale (1): Jon's Kaljaxian wife from his original flight to find humankind a new home. At first just her brain was copied, then, eventually, she was downloaded to an android host. Traveled with the corrupted Jon Ryan from an alternate time line.

Space-time congruity manipulator (1): Hugely helpful force field. Aka a membrane.

Stingray (1): Jon's Deavoriath spaceship. Her name in the Deavoriath language is pronounced "crash." Hence, silly Jon renamed her after one of his favorite cars. It makes Jon-sense.

Tefnuf (1): The first ancient god Jon encountered. She was saddled with an uncanny ugliness and a profoundly bad temper.

Transfolding (1): The mechanical process of moving from the land of the ancient gods to somewhere else.

. . .

Transheaval (1): The term the Cleinoids use to describe their migration from one universe to another. Accomplished via a mean vortex-cloud know as Dominion Splitter.

Verazz (2): The first antigod introduced. Also one of the most powerful.

Vorc (1): Current central seat of the conclave.

Vortex (1): Super-advanced Deavoriath sentient spaceship. Moves by folding space. If you get a chance to own one, do it.

Vortex (alternate definition) (1): See Dominion Splitter.

Wul (1): God of business and enterprise. Humanoid. Befriended Jon.

Zastrál (2): A three-meter-long, one-meter-tall fuzzy siamese-twinned python with paddles for legs. Used to extract knowledge. Very unpleasant chap.

AND NOW A WORD
FROM YOUR AUTHOR
WHO DOESN'T LOVE
SHAMELESS SELF-PROMOTION?

Thank you so much for joining me, Jon, and the whole gang on this ongoing journey! The Ryanverse is terrific, and it even better with you along! The story really begins with *The Forever Life*. If you've not read that, and the rest of the series from the start, I suggest you do. You will not be disappointed.

The outstanding people at Podium Audio are working hard to get all the books of the Ryanverse into audiobooks. If you're having any trouble locating a book, look for it there.

Two favors. One, let me know your impressions, thoughts, or suggestions. You can do that by contacting me by email (contact@craigarobertson.com) or on my Facebook Author's Page. Second, please post a review on Amazon/Audible. Those are more precious than you might imagine to us authors.

Y'all come back now! I know I will ...

craig